HOMELY IN THE CRADLE

AND OTHER BEDTIME STORIES

HOMELY IN THE CRADLE

AND OTHER BEDTIME STORIES

A.R. MORLAN

WILDSIDE PRESS

* * * *

"Professor Forbish's Hobby Horse" first appeared in *Eldritch Tales* *#27*, 1992

"Murder by Appointment" first appeared in *Pirate Writings*, Spring 1993

"At Funland by the Swings, with Big Chuck" first appeared in *RED EFT,* Vol. 2, Issue 1, Fall, 1997

"In the Great Milk-White Eye of God" first appeared in *Eldritch Tales #18*, 1989

"Size of a Silver Dollar" first appeared in *Women of the West*, edited by Kathryn Ptacek, for Doubleday, 1990

"Not a Haunted House at All" first appeared in *Talers' Tales #3*, 1996

"Just Another Bedtime Story" first appeared in *Night Cry*, Summer 1987

"The *Last* Bedtime Story" first appeared in *Grue #6*, 1987

"What the Janitor Found" first appeared in *Night Cry*, Spring 1987

"Mothrasaurus" first appeared in *Weird Tales #300*, Spring 1991

"Some May Wonder" first appeared in *Eldritch Tales #21*, 1989

"Just Herself" first appeared in *Eldritch Tales #20*, 1989

"Untitled 1/24/89" first appeared in *New Blood*, Winter 1989

"William Genesis Williams" first appeared in 1991.

"They Used to Put the Gold Star—" first appeared in *Scavenger's Newsletter*, ed. Janet Fox, No. 43, Sept. 1987

"Death of the Star-Fighter Gunner" first appeared in 1991

"Ruminations on the Photo…" first appeared in *Best Poems*, 1994

"War Cake" first appeared in *The Cutting* Edge, Issue 11, March, 1997

"The *Other* Easier Way" first appeared in *Eldritch Tales #29*, 1993

"The Mogul" first appeared in *Space & Time #100*, 2007

"With Cockles and Mussels, Alive, Alive-O" first appeared in 1992

"Pretty Birds" first appeared in *Challenging Destiny* (e-zine), 2006

"Cats in Fantasy…Cats in Fact" fist appeared in *Astromancer Quarterly*, May 1992

The Winter of the *Almost* Perfect Christmas Trees (first chapter of unpublished Ewerton novel, *Homely in the Cradle*; published here for the first time, 2015)

CONTENTS

THE WAR POEMS

HODGE PODGE

This collection is dedicated to

The memory of Robert Bloch (1917-1994),
"Master of the "last line...."

and to

Mary Wickizer Burgess

With thanks for all of her hard work and effort to bring this volume to life—couldn't do it without you, Mary!

Also in memory of:

Pretty Boy (?—January 23, 2014) and Winky (?—April 11, 2014)—both mature "last life" cats, who spent their final few years with me, and who will be missed beyond words. Love you both, sweet boy and girl....

FOREWORD

Those readers who have attended a rummage sale or even some garage sales have probably seen (maybe even bought) a grab-bag…one of those brown paper-bagged assortments of odds and ends and whatnots, usually marked with a vague teaser regarding the contents of said bag: "Men's Stuff," "Children," or some such notation. And once you open it, you're bound to find at least one thing you like (or at least can use), several others which may be useless but fun, or at least re-giftable, and at least one thing you just *don't* want or like.

Think of this collection as a literary grab-bag…chances are there's at least one story you'll like/love/enjoy, others which will amuse you, still others which might disturb, and perhaps one or so which you probably *won't* like. While the bulk of my fictional output over the years has been roughly divided between horror/dark fantasy, science fiction and erotica (of various types), a few pieces have either slipped through the genre cracks, or simply didn't make it into my other collections, either due to content, length, or availability at the time I was assembling those other collections. I've done a couple of western stories, and some undefined things which cover multiple genres, and some poetry which didn't fit in my other collections either—there's even a short non-fiction piece about my beloved, late cat Bruiser (the same cat featured in my novel *The Amulet*), as well as a chapter from an outlined but never written Ewerton novel.

To help you, the reader, out a bit, I've divided these pieces into some rough sub-groupings, by either genre or origin (aka how I came to write these stories), but bear in mind, there's some overlap when it comes to content—some of these stories were literary mash-ups of sorts, and come close to defying neat categorization.

So…dive in where you wish, and hope you find that one thing in here that you end up lovin!

—A.R. Morlan, 2015

THE MYSTERIES

PROFESSOR FORBISH'S
HOBBY HORSE

"'Ore '*ip*ment 'rrived thiss affer'*oon*," Verna told her husband when he stepped into the house thatf evening, shifting the mass of partly chewed candy to her left cheek as she spoke.

But Professor Montgomery P. Forbish, Lecturer in English, Clark College, Wisconsin, could tell that Verna was at it again. Cramming chocolate candy into her wide, ever-gaping mouth, until her speech was a slurping, gooey parody of the English tongue. Verna's breath could all but induce a diabetic coma, and her teeth were striated with thin lines of runny brown. The last-mentioned detail was the worst; for some obscure reason his wife's cocoa-butter smile reminded Professor Forbish of cheap Anglo-Italian horror movies—runny cheap sepia blood, and glaring too-white fangs among yellow-tinged incisors.

And Verna was *perfectly* aware that her husband was allergic to chocolate. It made him sneeze…said fact which she *also* took into consideration. She'd wait until he was engrossed in whatever hobby he was currently pursuing, be it ships-in-bottles, model trains, or recreations of Civil War battlegrounds (the latter was intended to be a visual aid for his lecture on *The Red Badge of Courage*), and *then*, just as he reached a critical point in his work, a most delicate and painstaking point—she'd strike.

And what made it all so insidious, so *brilliant*, was how she tried to make it seem as if she really wanted to *help* him:

"Oh, so *that's* how you do that—will it help if I hold the bottle?" she said, spraying him with fine chocolate mist; her words plosive enough to spray his face, his still-folded ship and the bottle itself with delicate brown drops. He quickly wiped away the offending sweet mist, but the damage was done—he began to sneeze violently, upsetting his knees-balanced work surface, the bottle and the in-progress ship model crashed to the lemon-oil polished floor.

"How sweet! Teensy tracks! And the trains, oh, tiny wheels!" she squealed, leaning in so close that her brown-dripping mouth was mere centimeters from his nose. Psychosomatic or not, the very *scent* of her cocoa-breath made the sneezing fit begin. And Professor Forbish was working on the machinery of the switching station, all open, vulnerable electric circuits…which shorted out when he tried to start up the train set.

"D'ya mean to say this was how the battle really looked? I'll *be*…" and she dropped one of her chocolate toffees in his bowl of fruit-flavored hard candies.

When he absentmindedly picked up the unwrapped toffee and popped it into his mouth, Verna was right there, big box of tissues in chocolate-scented hand, ready to help him during his cyclone-intensity sneezing fit. Spitting up the half-chewed toffee right on the cardboard and shoe-polish cannon only increased the damage Professor Forbish unintentionally inflicted on his hapless combatants. Since his lecture on Crane's novel was scheduled for the next morning, Forbish ended up using his splattered battlefield to tamp down the garbage in his huge rubber trash can.

If only Verna would *ask* for a divorce, separate bedrooms, the *moon*!

Professor Forbish was perfectly, *achingly* willing to do almost anything to please Verna enough to make her kick the cocoa-bean habit. Or leave him *alone*, whichever was easier for her. But Verna, the woman he once loved, the teacher's aide of his dreams (they read *Tristram Shandy* out loud to each other in the campus cafeteria), the living lamp which lit the darkness of his bachelor years—had grown away from him, in directions Professor Forbish could never bring himself to travel.

She abandoned *Tristram Shandy* and *Finnegan's Wake* in favor of *Love's Savage Fury* and *Passion's Sweet Revenge*; she kept her bodice-busters close at hand as she sat, feet up on the ottoman (*his* 18th Century ottoman, on which she rested her splintery Scholl-sandaled feet), the television tuned to soap opera after soap opera, which gave way to romance movies come afternoon. At night she watched four-hankie oldies, the ones which ran candy bar commercials every ten minutes. (Professor Forbish sneezed in his sleep upon the subliminal hearing of those abominable commercials!)

And what hurt most of all, more so than Verna's hot cocoa goodbye kisses when he left for the University, or her fudge-gooey goodnight smack on his cheek before she turned off the bedroom television set, was how she had *tricked* him. Pretending that she *cared* about poor Tristram Shandy's maimed Uncle Toby's curious love affair with the Widow Wadham.

Sharing Professor Forbish's delight over Uncle Toby's "hobby horses," as Laurence Sterne had so charmingly dubbed that character's pursuit of gentle hobbies.

All along Verna had played the part of the Widow Wadham, in order to snare herself a husband. Someone to buy her a remote control color television, or the latest romance novels.

Often, Montgomery Forbish wondered if Verna had set her sights on *him* simply because switching from pulp romances to real literature was the least painful path to Professor's Wifehood open to her. If she had decided to try for the *other* well-heeled old bachelor professor on the faculty, old man Swindham, Verna would have had to learn calculus—and there is no romance in numbers, aside from "1 + 1 = Just Married."

What most galled Forbish, however, was how Verna had used his precious books to poke fun at him. She'd rattle the carton containing his latest mail-order hobby supplies, and say through a mouthful of semi-chewed malted milk balls, "Think I hear a *hobby* horse in there."

Professor Forbish would smile at her, not wanting to further engage her curiosity, but knowing full well that he had to tell her *something*, or else she'd lean over his shoulder like a chocolate-breathing bird of carrion as he attempted to work.

Forbish was a fair man; he left her alone to her page-panters and her truffles, and he tried not to wince when the splintery soles of her sandals caught and ripped the delicate needle-point cover of his precious ottoman.

Montgomery Forbish could live with the thought of being duped by his former teaching assistant. He could tolerate the assembly-line romances on their bedside table. But he could *not* stomach his wife's continued inconsiderateness…especially when it came to his hobbies.

Ever since boyhood, he'd been a dabbler in this or that, depending on which book he had just read. *Toby Tyler*? Circus posters became his passion. *Moby Dick*? *He* carved scrimshaw "whale teeth" out of Ivory soap bars, and colored in the lines with shoe polish.

Later, when he became a professor, his "hobby horses" became unique visual aids, a sure way to perk up class interest in an "old" work of literature.

And that wretched Verna had feigned an intense fascination with his hobbies, his hand-crafted doodads (she loved his box of chocolate-covered cotton for *Catch-22*, although she pouted when she learned that the chocolate covering the cotton wasn't real), until Montgomery Forbish had come to the conclusion that he had found a *soul-mate*, a helper and confidante.

As it turned out, however, he wound up doing more sneezing than soul-mingling…which was the way Verna seemed to *like* it.

How did the *cliché* go? No fool like an old fool. Being a level-headed gentleman, not given to outward flights of fancy or irrational behavior,

Professor Forbish resigned himself to a bad choice. He was even willing to take the bitter with the milk-chocolate sweet…but Verna simply didn't know when to *let up*.

The chocoholic binges. The stuffing of her pliant cheeks with a sickly-sweet smelling mass of liquefying brown *glop*, those times were bad enough. (Embarrassing, too, at faculty mixers, when Verna positioned herself in front of the mint dish, like Mother Courage protecting her children.)

But—but to rob him of his pleasures…the satisfaction of working on his "hobby horsies," as she now so snidely dubbed them with a pucker of her brown-tinged lip—*that* verged on the inhuman!

So when Forbish heard that candy-filtered remark, "ore '*ip*ment 'rrived thiss affer'*oon*," he gritted his well-worn and oft-grinded teeth before saying:

"By UPS or regular mail, Verna dear?"

"Pony Express!" she chortled, before he realized what a mistake it'd been to try to deflect her inevitable quips with a neutral query. Too late, Forbish remembered how she'd pulled the same verbal trick on him when the toy railroad craft kit arrived.

He saw the latest carton sitting on the coffee table in the living room off the hall; the company had promised to send their *merchandise* in an unmarked box, with no…revealing designations to upset the possibly squeamish.

Professor Forbish smelled Verna before he heard or saw her coming; the combined odor of mint and chocolate wafted into the room seconds before Verna wheedled:

"What kind of a *hobby horsie* did you buy this time, Monty? A *brown* one? A *grey* one? A *palamino* one? A *black* one?"

When in a playful mood, Verna kept going until she mentioned every color of horsehide, plus paisley and polka-dots—until Forbish gave up and told her what was in his latest box of supplies.

His back still turned to her, Forbish opened the top of the box carefully with a nail file, slitting the fiber-impregnated strapping tape. He then opened up the flaps and pushed aside the soft, springy plastic "worms" which kept everything inside the carton from rattling around in transit from the factory.

The invoice rested under the first layer of "worms"; he scanned it quickly. Every item he had asked for was checked off; the bottom of the sheet was stamped PAID IN FULL—THANK YOU FOR YOUR ORDER.

In red…of *course*.

What he needed first was right on top, in a break-proof plastic bottle (the company did indeed know how to ship their…*merchandise* well).

As he worked to get the plastic shrink-wrap off the bottle cap, the minty-brown scent of Verna's wide, smacking mouth came nearer to him. Potentially sneeze-inducing spittle came dangerously close to his unprotected mouth and nose.

"Monty, that's the biggest box *yet*. Must be a real *big* horsie! You working on something to do with a Trojan horse, huh, Monty-wonty?"

Forbish felt the wet warmth of her breath on the exposed back of his neck, on the bare strip between his short-cropped hair and his shirt collar. Instinctively, he reached for the hankie he kept handy in his coat breast pocket. It would serve perfectly as a gag, once he poured the chloroform from the newly-opened bottle onto its white, initialed surface.

* * * *

The instructions which came with the things he had ordered weren't especially clear, but under the circumstances they suited Professor Forbish's purposes nicely.

Actually, it was all quite similar to the situation detailed in his reading. One thing he *hadn't* counted on: The bag of stuffing described in the catalog as "enough for a large project" wasn't *nearly* enough for his purposes.

But after rummaging about in the kitchen, he found a couple of boxes of tissues (no doubt Verna had planned an assault of epic proportions, perhaps hot cocoa spilled in his car, *à la* Hamlet's mother!), as well as a pile of crinkly-wrapped chocolate toffees. He found that they worked almost as well as the stuffing and those packing "worms" for the task at hand.

And they suited the *spirit* of his endeavors that evening, so much so that Professor Forbish found himself *grinning* as he worked, free of the worry that Verna would blast him with her atomizer breath, splattering his skin with chocolate.

He had finished the main body of his labors when the phone rang. One of his senior students from his class on "Themes in Modern Literature." The young man, whose voice and face Forbish could place, but the *name* eluded him, began:

"I've been sick for the past couple of days, Professor Forbish. My girlfriend took notes on the class for me, but she didn't know which book we're gonna discuss…."

"Going to discuss…."

Forbish cradled the receiver between his shoulder and head; his hands were busy inserting stuffing into his nearly-completed project.

"Yeah, 'going to discuss.' Well, she said it was either *The Scarf* or—"

"I believe that in this case 'or' would be the correct answer," the professor said with a smile in his voice.

He picked up another wrinkled wrapper and began to force it through the narrow opening under his fingers. The voice coming through the line drew an audible sigh of relief.

"Oh *great*. I saw the movie last night—I've got the book right at the top of my pile—"

"Mind you, there are certain differences between the novel and Sir Alfred's film...but if you've read the novel, you know that already."

Another wrinkled wrapper.

Another filled-up space within his project!

"Yeah, I read it. Hey, Prof—How's that wife of yours? She used to really liven up the classes, if you know what—"

"Yes, indeed, liven it up she did," Forbish replied without rancor, pushing in another delicately crinkling paper.

The nameless voice asked, "What's Verna up to now? Keeping up with Joyce, is she?"

As the student made his *double entendre*, Forbish stuck a couple of wrappers in through the eye cavity.

He liked the way the twisted plastic caught the lamp's light merrily, although he'd have to fashion *eyes* out of something later on.

Improvisation. *That* was the key! Norman Bates was such an *inventive* character. Surely Montgomery Forbish could do as well, under the circumstances!

Putting in the last of the crackling wrappers (the lingering scent of chocolate *almost* masked out the other odors in the room), Professor Forbish chuckled.

"Oh, she's not doing much...just stuffing her fat face."

AFTERWORD

Many years ago, back in the 1980s, I bought an anthology which contained a wonderfully nasty gem of a story entitled "The Night Before Christmas" by the late, literally great[1] writer Robert Bloch, a story which almost literally blew my mind.

---

1   Those writers who had the chance to even briefly contact Mr. Bloch will realize what a wonderful, kind and just plain good man he was; while many will think of him as the man who immortalized Ed Gein as "Norman Bates" in *Psycho*, the rest of us know that he was much, much more than that writer who ended up making Alfred Hitchcock even more famous....

For those of you who haven't yet had the pleasure of reading this tale for themselves, let me merely say it's worth seeking out. It was one of those the-last-line-is-a-zinger stories, in which a seemingly-unto-itself final line appears to be innocuous, but when placed within the context of the story as a whole, it is actually stunningly horrific.

As a writer, I realized that such a story has to be virtually written backwards, with one having that final last line in mind prior to creating the rest of the tale…it took me a few years to do it, but I finally thought up (what I thought) the perfect final line.

Once the story was actually written, however, I realized that my initial opinion of the perfection of that last line versus what came before it was a tad off kilter; the events leading up to my final line do seem a bit contrived/forced/what-have-you, but even though it isn't my best effort, I did enjoy the process of writing it.

When I was in college, initially majoring in English education with an emphasis on secondary school, then eventually majoring in English with a liberal arts emphasis (thanks to one of my English professors deciding that I didn't have "the personality" to be a teacher), even though I had straight A's in all my education classes up to what began as my junior year and finished as my senior year (I had taken so many classes in total that once the professor forced me out of the education track, I actually had enough total credits to be classified as a senior rather than a junior…which meant that I ended up getting my B.S. in three and a half years, and skipping my final semester, which in *turn* meant that said professor screwed his own employers out of one semester's worth of tuition!), I took a great many classes in English and American literature.

During one of them, we were assigned the novel *Tristram Shandy*, but as often happens in many college classes, the professor assigned more books than he actually intended to discuss in class, with poor old *Tristram Shandy* being one of the orphaned choices. I doubt many people in class even bothered to read it, but I did, and just adored it. It's a huge book, but incredibly fast-moving and relatively easy to read, even though it baffled some of my classmates who began it, only to cast it aside. I especially loved Uncle Toby's "hobby horses," hence their inclusion in the title of this story. I also threw in as many other literary references as I could; I suppose I did get carried away with them at times, but what else can one use a Liberal Arts English degree for these days?

I do realize that I fudged the entire section about the taxidermy kit; I seriously doubt that chemicals like chloroform come in a box like that… plus I realized (much later, after viewing the episode of the TV show *CSI: Crime Scene Investigation* entitled "Leapin' Lizards") that I totally messed up the process of curing and tanning a human head (again, watch that particular episode of *CSI* to see what I'm talking about).

But...I did work in my "killer" last line. Thankfully, the story is short, so the impact of my errors isn't *too* great.

When the story finally was published, I wanted to make sure that I sent Robert Bloch a copy, but the publisher misunderstood my desire (casually mentioned in a letter to him) to have a signed copy of the story come into Mr. Bloch's possession, and instead sent him a copy of the magazine directly, by-passing me (and my signature) completely.

Mr. Bloch did write me a generous thank you note, and I assume he did read the story, so I have that thought to comfort me...I don't know if he liked it or not, but considering that imitation is the sincerest form of flattery, I do hope he felt flattered at the least.

MURDER BY APPOINTMENT

"Good afternoon, this is Palladin Realty, may I help—"

"I'd like to speak with Gwendolyn Johnson, please," Gary Bowen said with a smoothness refined through many other similar requests, as he circled Gwendolyn Johnson's photograph in the Palladin Realty newspaper ad with a fine-tipped red marker.

While the receptionist put him on hold, Gary chuckled to himself, as he thought, This beats looking for girls in mall parking lots, or on crowded beaches…no witnesses.

And I get to pick exactly the girl *I* want.

"Hello? This is Gwen Johnson, how may I help you?"

The voice of Gary's soon-to-be-victim was just as he imagined it would be; soft, seductive, yet professional. The kind of girl Gary liked, right up until the moment he strangled her then left her body in whichever out-of-the-way empty house he'd pre-selected before calling her Realty office and making an appointment for a showing.

"Gwen, my name is Charles Stefano, and there's a property listed with your agency that I'm interested in seeing—"

"Could you please give me the address of the property, Mr. Stefano? Our listings are pre-assigned, and that one might not be mine to show—"

Gary was ready for this part, having gone through it six times in the last ten months.

Underlining the caption "Salesperson of the Month!" which appeared below her smiling image with his red pen, he said, "Now Gwen, is that how you became Salesperson of the Month? By refusing to show prospective clients one of your company's listings?"

A subtle threat, but one that never failed to work; every one of Gary's victims hadn't wanted to lose her status as a top-selling agent, even if it meant stealing a listing from a fellow Realtor.

"Oh, well, if you insist, Mr. Stefano, I'm sure we can work something out," Gwen soothed, before asking, "Now which property of ours do you wish to see?"

This time, Gary consulted a scrap of paper on which he'd written the address of the dilapidated house on the dead-end road—the Palladin Realty advertisement which accompanied the photo of Gwen didn't include the house he'd carefully chosen after two days of driving around this small mid-western town, searching for Palladin Realty signs.

As he recited "1118 West Elkton Drive" Gary thought about the run-down house partially hidden by overgrown hydrangea bushes. It was easily the worst-looking house he'd picked in any of the small towns he'd selected throughout the mid-west; the foundation was crumbling, and the clapboards were sun- and wind-warped; and the front screen door was almost off its hinges.

As he thanked Gwen for her help, and set up a six-thirty appointment (telling his soon-to-be-victim that he didn't get off work until then), Gary remembered the wind-torn scraps of some sort of notice which were still thumb-tacked by the corners on the bottom of that screen door.

Probably a "For Sale by Owner" sign, he told himself, as he began stuffing the short but lethal length of nylon rope into his jacket pocket, in anticipation of that afternoon's murder by appointment.

Gary had parked his car two blocks away from West Elkton Drive so that Gwen wouldn't have any reason to disbelieve his story about his car breaking down.

When the pretty ash-blonde Realtor showed up, she only smiled sweetly when she heard his excuse about the car, and said, "Oh, that's too bad. Perhaps I can give you a lift back to your home after the showing?"

"I'd appreciate that," he replied, while watching her fumble in her roomy purse for the keys to this house.

As she unlocked the inner door, he mentally went over what would happen next: He'd graciously let her take the first step into the silent, empty house, so that he could then loop the rope around her throat from behind, before choking her into semi-unconsciousness—

"Oh darn!"

Gwen's face twisted with disappointment as she looked down at her purse, which had fallen to the floor of the concrete porch, spilling most of its contents.

Still pretending to be the perfect gentleman, Gary knelt to help her pick up her scattered belongings—and received a face-full of pepper spray, just before he felt the sharp blow of Gwen's stiffened hand on the small of his neck....

"Mr. *'Stefano'*? You awake?"

Gwen's voice sounded thick, cottony, as Gary struggled to regain consciousness. When he did come to, he realized through a haze of thudding pain in his neck and his burning eyes, that his hands were bound behind his back with his own nylon killing rope, while his feet were tied tightly together with what seemed to be Gwen's own pantyhose—

But it was already so dark in the empty house that he could barely make out the pale oval of Gwen's face as she bent to stuff a cloth gag in his mouth.

"You're not the only one who reads the papers," she said with just a touch of sarcasm as she tied Gary's own handkerchief over his mouth. "I've been following the stories about those other murdered Realtors... and when you specifically requested to see *this* house, I knew you had to be a stranger here at best—or the Realtor Rapist at worst."

Through his gag, Gary asked a muffled, "How?"

Her smile barely visible through the tears which filled his burning eyes, Gwen replied, "Last week's storm blew the 'This Property is Condemned' sign off the door—but the real clincher was when you told me that you'd taken a cab here. This town has no taxi service."

On the floor, Gary strained against his bonds, making garbled, muffled pleas for mercy.

In reply, Gwen only walked away from him, saying over her shoulder as she reached the front door, "You should have noticed how old the Palladin sign out front was....this place has been condemned for ages. But then again, you won't have to wait in here too long...come six in the morning, this house will be bulldozed down—"

Writhing on the floor, Gary managed to mumble around his gag, "—eck...urst—"

"'Check first?' Oh yes, they always have a representative from the Realty firm on hand when a property like this one is demolished...but then again, this place *has* been locked up with no obvious break-ins. I doubt I'll even need to do much more than take a quick peek in here before I give the wrecking crew the all-clear.

"Good-bye, Mr. 'Stefano'...I'll be seeing you again in the morning...."

AFTERWORD

There's a fairly popular, if rather bland, women's magazine out there which once featured a very short mystery story in its relentlessly cheerful, mostly upbeat pages...while I didn't read the magazine myself, I did know some folks who did, and I'd get their last-week's-issue after they were done with it.

By this time, I was already publishing horror and sf stories, but I was trying to expand into mystery, and after reading a segment in the book, *What Cops Know*, concerning how some killers would pick a female victim based on her picture in the Realtor's office advertisements and/

or a photo on a "For Sale" sign in front of a house, I got the idea for this little tale.

I did submit it to the women's magazine, and you can bet your behind they not only didn't like it, but made it clear that I was not a good match for the magazine.

I suppose it was my fault—I'm just not a women's magazine type of writer.

I do want to pass along another story about a story of mine which was submitted to a women's magazine which shall remain nameless—it used to take fiction, but no longer does.

Back in the late 1980's when I had an agent who didn't really have a strong grasp of my target audience, she sent a copy of my short story "The Second Most Beautiful Woman in the World" (which deals in part with artist Georgia O'Keeffe) to this publication—and while they liked it, they ultimately rejected it because *they didn't think their readers would know who Georgia O'Keeffe was*…which is pretty damn sad.

That story has now been published in the collection, *The Second Most Beautiful Woman in the World, and Other Fantastic Ladies*, available from Wildside Press.

AT FUNLAND BY THE SWINGS, WITH BIG CHUCK

By the end of the first week in August, the kids who visited Funland confided in Big Chuck the Monitor, that the new girl who sat alone next to the swings—not on one of the rust-chained swings, but on the blunt grass next to the swings—was *really* weird.

"She don't know 'bout cooties, Big Chuck. We wiped them all on her and she went an' kept 'em."

"I asked her if she saw *The Monkees* last night and she didn't think the zoo was open then—what she mean?"

"Where's she come from? She never says 'cool' or 'guy' or anything right."

By noon, fifteen of the neighborhood regulars had come to Big Chuck, the college kid who helped watch over the tiny children's amusement park each summer, with their tales of how different that "funny-looking" girl was. How she didn't know about *The Dating Game*, or read Nancy Drew books, or remember what night *Star Trek* was on, or even play tetherball.

The first couple of days she'd wandered around Funland with its small assortment of scaled-down kiddie rides, snack booths and simple bottle toss and basketball throw games, no one had paid much attention to her. But by now the other kids had glommed to the fact that she wasn't just a stranger in their neighborhood…she was strange, period.

But Big Chuck—so dubbed by the elementary school age children he looked after during the day because he was over six feet tall—and called the same name by his college-age female contemporaries for a somewhat different reason—had noticed that the new little girl was odd long before the rest of the kids caught on.

It was the way she just sat, not running around spreading cooties, or giggling over by the ice cream stand, or just twisting her long dishwater blonde hair around her fingers, the way the other girls passed the time.

But she wasn't cowed-quiet, like some of the browbeaten kids who hung around Funland during the three months it was open each summer, after the real amusement parks and carnivals had long since passed through town, on their way to bigger venues to the south.

This quiet kid was content to simply sit there by the swings, taking things in. As if this was all new to her; the used-car-lot style flag-like banners stringing the booths together, the sweetish-sickly aroma of cotton candy and slushy cones, the needs-oiling squeal of the go-carts in their pen.

No parents ever brought her to Funland; Big Chuck had noticed that by the second day.

He liked that.

Parents who cut loose the apron strings got his vote. Best way; open the front door and let 'em go.

Not that the streets were a good place for kids to roam, but that was why the Town Council had set up Funland in one of the town parks, close to the year-round set up of swings and slides

The kids could vent their energies in Funland, and their parents didn't have to worry because Big Chuck, who came well-recommended by his alma mater, was there, ready in case of any emergency.

And he didn't breathe down their necks…let their teachers do that come fall.

In the park-like place, surrounded by and dotted with trees and bushes, as well as that set of swings, tire-jungle, monkey bars—funny, she didn't know about *The Monkees*—and tetherball poles, the kids were safe as long as Big Chuck was around.

Nice, clean-cut, gangly Big Chuck, with a supply of Band-Aids, Bactine, and Vicks Cough Drops in his slacks pockets. (No hippie bell bottoms on Big Chuck; come graduation he was headed for the Peace Corps.) Big Chuck had a supply of quarters in his back pocket, too.

But Big Chuck didn't dispense his quarters the same way he did the Band-Aids, Bactine, or cough drops, by giving them out for "owies" and coughs. The kids at Funland had to *earn* a quarter from Big Chuck. And even if a kid did get one, he or she could never tell where he or she had gotten it.

That was part of the Big Secret between Big Chuck and the kids.

A Funland secret.

Only some of the neighborhood kids received those shiny new quarters from Big Chuck. Not the ones whose parents brought them to Funland, and picked them up an hour later. And certainly never the gabby ones, whose teachers would pin long black construction paper "Tattle Tails" on their sweaters come fall.

Big Chuck wasn't just a nice guy, he was a very smart guy. He picked only the quiet, nice little boys and girls for his special quarters. And they didn't have to do a whole lot to earn those shiny silver coins.

And even if the kids who got the quarters from Big Chuck did wonder why their parents never paid them for taking off their underpants at home, none of them ever asked their Mommies and Daddies about it.

That would've been breaking the big Funland Secret, and then Big Chuck wouldn't give them any more coins for good stuff, like Orange Push-ups from the ice cream stand, or for an extra ride on the merry-go-round.

Sometimes Big Chuck did strange things to them that tickled, but they never giggled, just in case Big Chuck got mad and forgot to give them a quarter when he was done.

And now Big Chuck had begun to pay attention to the new little girl with the big head and the tiny, baby-like hands. As he watched her from his favorite spot close to the big tree near the go-cart pen, his fingers rubbed and rubbed the quarters in his left back pocket. For the past few weeks he'd paid out quarters, an awful lot of them, to most of the kids playing here today.

He knew them better than their folks did—better even than their doctors.

"Familiarity breeds contempt," …or so said one of his profs at the university. But Big Chuck had an even better saying.

"Familiarity breeds boredom," he told himself, as the coin between his forefinger and thumb grew greasy from being rotated so much.

He always liked the quiet kids, but this one was special. For one thing, she didn't wear shorts or pedal pushers or jeans, but had on one of those cute little short-skirted sundresses, the kind that rides up to the thighs and above when a little girl sits cross-legged in the ground.

Like this girl was doing now. The kind of dress which shows a small white rectangle of exposed panty, peeking from between small open legs.

Big Chuck's fingers stopped rubbing the coin. She was looking at him. The sun-warmed skin under his crew-cut began to tingle. She was smiling, a sunny little smile which showed off a full set of even tiny teeth.

Big Chuck wondered what tiny baby teeth like that would feel like.

Now she was patting the ground next to her, on the side away from the rust-mottled swings.

The side close to the tall bushes.

Opening a small plastic purse, she extracted a yellow pocket comb which she ran through her straight dirty-blonde hair, the kind of blonde

Big Chuck saw on the college girls all the time—blonde-growing-into-light-brown.

Big Chuck jerked as he heard the decisive click as she snapped her purse shut after replacing the comb.

Putting down the purse—in the past six days she'd been coming to Funland, she'd always had that cheap all-plastic purse close at hand—she picked up an empty eight-ounce 7-Up bottle and began to blow across the top of it, creating a low, moaning drone.

She didn't take her eyes off of him; wise eyes locked on his.

Rubbing the coin frantically between his slippery-hot fingers, Big Chuck ambled over to the little girl by the swings, a big smile creasing his tanned face.

The kids who saw him go up to the girl knew enough to go play somewhere else. They understood the unspoken rules of the Funland Big Secret Game. No peeking.

And no making any trouble while Big Chuck and his friend were busy elsewhere.

Just so none of the grown-ups would start asking why Big Chuck wasn't keeping order, like he was hired to do. Soon, the other children were on the rides, or standing by the candy booth.

"Hi."

Big Chuck hunkered down in front of the girl, knees spread out wide. She smiled shyly in return, before blowing across the top of the bottle again.

"That fun?"

A nod of her big head.

"Can I try?" A coy shake of the head, followed by a bigger smile.

Big Chuck liked that in a kid. Not big-mouthed, but fey all the same. Nice bare legs, with gently swelling calves which met white ankle socks.

And that tiny, short skirt. Like something out of that book he'd read in Modern Novels 355. *Lolita.*

"O.K. Can you talk?" Big Chuck crinkled his eyes against the descending sun behind the girl.

This time she laughed.

"Sure," she said in a surprisingly husky but small voice. "'bout what?"

She rested the bottle on the scruffy grass, but didn't let go of it.

Big Chuck sat down cross-legged in front of her. "Some of those kids been giving you a hard time?"

"I dunno." She shrugged, her eyes downcast, even as a smile played on her pale lips.

"Yeah, they can be mean, when they don't understand. Just because you're not in to passing cooties or watching *The Monkees*, they peg you for being weird...but I don't think you're weird at all."

"No?" An abrupt tilt of her head, as she looped her hand through the strap of her purse.

"Why should I think you are? Guy, I think you're a nice kid. And I like your dress."

He looked down at her skirt, and below.

Suddenly, the girl straightened one leg, to scratch an itch on her tanned knee (the golden sunlight made the fine hairs on her skin gleam), and her panties moved aside ever so slightly.

But enough.

She kept on smiling at him.

"What's your name?" Big Chuck asked, his eyes not focused on her face.

"'manda," she said coyly, not moving her leg.

"That's nice," Big Chuck mumbled, staring, before adding, "I know a rhyme..."

Big Chuck waited until she looked quizzically at him, before solemnly chanting, "I see France, I see...a little girl's underpants!"

Giggling she asked. "Know any more?" and didn't re-cross her legs.

"Nope...sorry. Hey, know what? All the time you've been coming to Funland, I've never seen you buy yourself an ice-cream bar or go on any of the rides."

Big Chuck paused, eyes downcast, before asking gently, "Haven't you got any money?"

"Uh-uh," she said, not seemingly perturbed, then picked up the bottle and began to tootle across the top, a mournful hoot.

"Wouldn't you like some? Wanna know where to earn some?"

Her pale eyes blank, she shrugged, then said, "Yeah," as if having the money to take in the attractions at Funland wasn't a very big deal.

"You don't have to spend the money here," Big Chuck added, placing his hand in his pocket full of quarters, filling the warm air with a delicate tinkling sound, one which the other kids knew very well.

She cocked her head at the sound.

"Know what this is, 'manda?"

"Change?"

Something about her *blasé* tone niggled the back of his mind, but Big Chuck was too excited to dwell on it.

"Yeah...change...quarters. Guess who for?"

"I dunno," but her eyes did know.

Big Chuck smiled down at her, and her soft brownish skin.

Standing up, he dusted off his pants bottoms then helped the girl to get up, taking one of her baby hands in his. Her strong grip was mildly surprising; he didn't notice how, but as she rose to her feet she broke her bottle against the nearest leg of the swing. Big Chuck expected her to drop it, but she held on to the neck of the bottle, plus the remaining three or four inches of shattered green glass.

As he dusted off her behind, whisking away the dead grass with his free hand, Big Chuck suggested. "Why don't we throw that in the Dumpster?"

"Uh-uh. I like blowing on the top."

Big Chuck had to laugh; some of these kids said the damnedest things, not even knowing what it sounded like.

"You really like uhm…blowing on it, huh?" he asked as he steered her to the nearby shrubs—after glancing back at the booths, to make sure none of the adults were watching—

—and she looked up at him, plastic purse on one arm, the bottle neck in her opposite hand, replying in an oddly flat voice, "Yeah, blowing bottles is fun," as she followed him into the surrounding dusty bushes.

Big Chuck thought he'd wear a hole clear through the quarter he was rubbing when she said that.

This one might be worth a couple of quarters, he thought, keeping that neat row of baby teeth in mind.

* * * *

Amanda had to spit on her tiny hands a few times, the saliva glistening golden-clear in the ever-lowering sunlight, before wiping them off—first on the leaves around her, and then on her underpants—before she closed her bulging purse with a click.

As she looped the strap over her wrist, she wished that she'd been able to find a bigger kiddie purse, one with a little more room inside, but this pink vinyl jobbie was the best she could find in the children's section. She would've liked to have used one of her own purses, but they all looked so adult—despite their scaled-down size—that they just wouldn't have been right.

Bad enough she'd had to buy herself a damned sun dress—like a six-year old.

And ankle socks—Amanda's mouth twisted into a bitter *moué*.

But Big Chuck had liked them, oh yes indeed. Liked the socks and the cotton picot panties enough to show her his first, after she told him she didn't think Funland was all that fun….

Amanda checked the seams of the pink purse; the thing was all one piece, a molded pouch of paisley-patterned plastic, like a thick sandwich bag molded into the purse, but she couldn't be too careful.

She knew from her observation of the rug rats who frequented the dump of an amusement park that they wouldn't come looking for their over-grown playmate, not while he was "busy"…and once the big kiddies noticed that Mr. Collegiate was missing, she'd be long gone…along with the rest of the carny.

Amanda knew that her suntan would prove just how easy she'd been taking things during her sick leave; hadn't they told her to take it easy, get lots of sun?

She'd meet up with one of the advance men tonight, catch a few connecting rides until she was back with the show..

But first she'd have to ditch the kiddie clothes and the cheapo plastic handbag—once she put its contents on ice, prior to curing it properly in a salt box.

Behind "Amanda the Amazing" ("Three Feet of Pure Woman!") Funland was winding down for the afternoon; the golden air rang with childish shouts and the tinny music of the nickel-a-throw rides.

The cloying smell of candy and popcorn masked the faint reek of what was stuffed in her purse (she'd actually had to *fold* it, with a wormy squish that more amused than sickened her) as Amanda casually left the bushes, oblivious to the buzzing drone of the flies already settling on Big Chuck.

There were ants, too, but at least they were quiet.

It was only a short walk to the motel room she'd rented; her real clothes were there, some in suitcases, others laid across the bed…close to the ice bucket she'd asked for that morning, the one waiting to be filled.

"You don't like Funland very much, do you?" he'd asked, before unzipping, and before she came forward, bottle in hand, points out.

"No, I don't," she said now, softly. She hadn't said anything before, in the bushes.

Big Chuck bored her, and she hadn't had much to say to him. Big Chuck, thinking he was so unique, thinking he was so special. Big man *off* campus, with his pocket full of quarters.

Quarters. Like it was some big deal. Earn a shiny quarter to spend at good old Funland.

"I could've bought and sold you ten times over, Big Chuck," she whispered to herself, as she crossed an intersection, the slightly warm plastic bag banging against her hip as she walked. "In hundred dollar bills, Big Boy."

Once it was properly cured—a trick she'd learned on the farm, before that summer years ago when she'd gone to see a carnival and joined it by nightfall, back when she was a mere teenager—Amanda thought she might hang it above her little bed in the trailer, as a reminder to the apple knockers who lingered to catch her show after the show—a warning not to get too rough.

If she felt like it, she might tell them she'd *bitten* it off, and not mention the soda bottle at all. The thought of seeing their shocked, not-wanting-to-believe-it faces was worth a week spent in a dive like Funland, wasting her vacation doing work, and low-level sideshow stuff at that.

But Amanda was smiling as she opened her motel room door. Mr. Collegiate wasn't lying. Big Chuck, *indeed*....

EDITOR'S NOTE

A time-travel version of this story appeared under the title "At the Playground by the Swings, with Big Chuck" in *Supernova* #1, 1990, and in the collection published by Wildside Press, *The Bone-God's Lair: And Other Tales of the Famous and the Infamous*. —M.E.B.

AFTERWORD

Whenever a pedophile is incarcerated, it is very likely that he (or occasionally she) will be placed in some sort of isolation, away from the other inmates—because if the other prisoners get an opportunity, they will use it to either beat the living crap out of these degenerates, or flat out kill them. Which is quite fine with me; since they're already in prison, I see nothing wrong with them doing a public service murder. At least it's a better form of justice for the victims of these sleazeballs than any sentence which falls short of being life in prison without the possibility of parole.

I know some readers might think I'm putting little people in a bad light with the character of Amanda, but she actually has nothing to do with little people in general—when I was younger, in many ways, I *was* Amanda. Starting at age seven-and-a-half I began to go into a very rapid form of premature puberty, so that when I was nine years old, I literally looked and sounded like an adult. My teachers and my classmates were freaked out by me, and I was severely bullied by both—some of the worst things said to me came out of the mouths of the teachers. One of them, in the fourth grade, was so grossed out by my appearance, and also frustrated by my lack of typical child-like behavior/speech (she was the one who was angry with me for not using the slang terms common back in mid-1960's California; I spent so little time with children when not in school, I never picked up on any of the slang terms they used, and since I didn't know what the slang *meant*, I refused to use it, which all but made that teacher crazy!), that she had the school bring in a doctor to see if I was really a teenager who was pretending to be an elementary school pupil. (My mother had been asked for my birth certificate to prove my real age, but since she didn't have it—when she and her mother kidnapped me after my mother lost custody of me to my father, she didn't have the time to get a duplicate certificate before fleeing Chicago!—I was forced to strip to the waist before this doctor, a school secretary, and the principal, and show them the inside of my mouth, just like a horse at an auction, in order to prove I was actually ten-years-old. And the only one of the witnesses that day who was female was the secretary.)

So, I was a complete freak…which led me to make my alter ego character a person who worked in a sideshow. I only made her a little person out of necessity….

THE WESTERNS

IN THE GREAT MILK
WHITE EYE OF GOD

"…she walked away like one in a dream of happiness; she did not know where she was going nor what she did. In the southern sky floated transparent little clouds; rainbow ribbons hung from them. She saw the rainbow's glow; her face was transfigured; she walked in ecstasy…"Are there signs for us in the sky?...That is the Glory of the Lord now….See!...the whole heavens are full of it!...There…and there again…everywhere!"

O. E. Rolvaag
Giants in the Earth (1927)

I.

The northeast wind whipped Ernest's coattails; the rough fabric *snicked* like twin flags, a sharp sound that provided counterpoint to the droning moan of the wind itself. Ernest looked around as he loaded the last of the supplies into the wagon, his eye passing safely before the mist-shrouded sun with nary a squint or blink.

Above him the sky was a dove-gray solid; no clouds or patches of blue broke up that horizon-wide sameness. Below his booted feet, the snow-blanketed soil was the color of cooled ash, and more ash-fine snow drifted down, down, onto his rough collar and sweat-banded hat. Only the soddie, the animal enclosure and the wagon broke the unending sameness which closed in on Ernest…and which would soon envelop his Pauline.

But when Ernest stared into the calm blue eyes of his wife, he saw none of his own fear reflected in those placid orbs. Pauline's eyes crinkled at the corners (fine lines plowed in the pale soft skin of her face) as she stood on tip-toe, pursed lips extended, and kissed his cheek.

Self-consciously Ernest rubbed his cheek, his gloved fingers moving slowly across the stubbled surface.

"You will be all right…here. Alone."

Ernest spoke slowly, his voice free of any question, as if his peace of mind depended on his statement being a *fact* without possibility of denial.

Pauline pulled her shawl around her shoulders as she replied, "Yes, Ernest, I will be fine. I have food, I have wood. I—You just go now. Waldemar will be wondering where you are, *Ernest*," she chided her unmoving husband, then added:

"The journey grows shorter with each forward step."

Ernest made a sound between a grunt and a cough, as he lowered his hat brim against the slanting snowflakes flying thick and fast in his direction.

He mounted the wagon, picking up the reins in his hands and giving the thin leather straps a weak shake before telling Pauline once more, "If you don't want me to go, Waldemar would understand…old Foss isn't an unreasonable man—"

Pauline playfully gave the horse closest to her a light whump on the flank, as she assured her husband that she'd be fine, simply fine in the hut, and warm besides. But even as the wagon rolled away, leaving a wake of twin twisting ruts in the packed snow, Ernest kept turning around in his seat, his mouth forming the same question over and over again, even as the sound of the words themselves was lost in the whistling, hooting moan of the wind.

"But will you be all *right*?"

The last time Ernest saw his Pauline, before he had to turn around and keep his eyes trained forward, she was standing, face up-turned, under the wide featureless grey sky, as if basking in the warmth of the summer sun itself.

II.

"6 November 187-
    A whole day with Mr. Douglas gone from our home, our hearth! But the wait is made more bearable when I hear the wind whistling past the door, for it carries the very breath he has exhaled, and the words he has uttered on his long journey."

Putting down her quill, Pauline studied the deep brown letters which gracefully looped across the creamy pages of her journal. Reading over her latest entry, Pauline blushed at the thought of her husband reading the shyly-worded declaration of her love for him. Such displays of emotion embarrassed Mr. Douglas; Ernest was so…literal-minded, so straightforward and *practical*.

Pauline burrowed deeper into the soft nest of quilts, animal-skin blankets and feather comforters she had made on top of the hut's only bed, breathing in the lingering scent of Ernest which clung to the bedding.

Ernest never understood how Pauline felt about him, nor did he understand how she could exist without him being near her.

Snuggling her cheek against the nearest quilt, Pauline let her journal fall to the cold black-brown floor of the sod hut. The cloth-covered book made a dull thumping sound as it hit the floor; Pauline smiled, remembering how it sounded like the pound of Ernest's feet on the ground.

Poor Ernest, she thought, *you can never know how close you are to me always.*

Her husband could only think of something in the *here and now* as being *with* him. For him, a memory was nothing more than a small dim thing in his mind, without life or *being*. And he could find something only in itself; for him, Pauline was Pauline only when she was in his sight, in his hearing, or was close enough to touch.

He did not realize that Pauline could be *everywhere*; she was the scent of her favorite flower, she was the warm touch of the sun on his skin, she was the moist gentle enveloping rain covering his body in summertime.

"We do not think alike, dear husband," Pauline said aloud to the time-whitened walls of the sod hut, but I still feel your warmth with me now, and hear your voice outside these four walls. My only wish…would be that you would see me with *my* eyes, hear me with *my* ears. For then you would realize *I* am with you always…."

* * * *

On the second full day her husband was away from her, Pauline felt a yen to read her Good Book, and not for the first time she bemoaned the flash flood of only four months before; the rains had come so hard, and so fast, that there had not been time for Pauline to empty out the wooden chest which sat upon the floor of the hut, and the rain had turned the black-brown floor to mud, mud which soaked through the bottom of the chest ruining all which lay within.

Including her Bible.

She had tried washing the book, but the pages were stuck fast in places, badly stained in others. The rich dark loam of the soil had leeched its darkness into her Bible, until the Word of God was overlaid with the Soil of the Dakotas. And God may have ruled the Heavens and the Earth, but the Soil got the best of even Him.

Pauline had kept her Bible, despite the fact that it was all but unreadable; both she and Ernest had been good, church-going Lutherans when they'd lived in Winnipeg, but once they'd journeyed south to the Dakota Territories, the Douglases had grown lax in their daily devotions, despite their continued belief in the Almighty.

Throwing away the ruined Bible would therefore have been the ultimate wrong-doing, worse by far than the fact that they no longer prayed aloud together at day's end, or tried to seek out more people of their faith in order to form a wilderness church. Their only neighbors were the Fosses, and Waldemar and Kjersti (*poor*, poor *Kjersti*, Pauline thought, huddling deeper into her den of coverlets) were Catholics, which was a somewhat rare faith among Norwegians (or so Waldemar explained in his broken English).

And being both Catholic and Norwegian, the Fosses' Bible had been of no use, despite Kersti's kind-hearted offer to translate it for Pauline. But Pauline had been touched by Kjersti's offer, for the very thought of the Norwegian woman, with her limited English vocabulary, trying to write out a rough translation of the *Bible* for someone of another faith *entirely* was an act of the purest Christian charity.

So Pauline had instead held onto both her stained Bible *and* the warmth of Kjersti's offer; now, huddled in her damply cold sod hut, watching the bright tongues of fire lick at the wood Ernest had chopped for her, Pauline could feel the very warmth of Kjersti with her...even though Kjersti herself was no longer warm at all anymore.

Pauline shook off her coverings, and padded across the clammy floor until she reached the flood-ruined wooden chest. Squatting down, Pauline felt around in the chest, past the folded linens and extra clothes, until she felt the leather cover of her Bible.

The Good Book in hand, she ran across the room, her feet barely making contact with the cold floor, then indecorously jumped on the bed like a schoolgirl and burrowed into the pile of still-warm quilts.

It was no matter that the light in the hut was dim, the white walls and flickering fire provided illumination enough for Pauline to read the lettering on the cover of her Bible.

Ernest couldn't understand it when she had explained it to him, but Kjersti *had* grasped Pauline's idea when Pauline explained to her why she didn't really *need* a new Bible:

"Just feeling the letters on the cover, the way they sink deep into the leather, and seeing the way the gold still shines in the light, that's all I really *need* for His Word to come through to me.

"The words I've heard and said hundreds of times, but they all boil down to those two words—'Holy Bible.' It's...it's like just smelling a rose brings the whole flower, soft petals and sharp thorns and all to a person.

"The words inside come *after* the words on the front of the Book; so it all comes back to those two words."

And Kjersti, dear sweet Kjersti with her coil of braid around her head, and her bright eyes, she had *understood*, even though she spoke only a score or so words of English.

Pressing the Book against her breast, Pauline sighed, and wondered, *Do you still understand me, Kjersti? Wrapped in those layers of old clothes, and wrapped further in those layers of cold snow, do you still understand me?*

Pauline could not bring herself to think of Kjersti in the past tense, as a "was" and not as "is," for weren't parts of Kjersti still all around Pauline?

The little crocheted cross woven through with an old bonnet ribbon which hung from a nail on the west wall of the hut. The very threads of that cross were still damp from the sweat of Kjersi's working fingers. Ernest couldn't feel that residual hand-warmth, but Pauline could. After Ernest stared oddly at her the first time, Pauline never mentioned Kjersti's warmth emanating from the cross again in his presence…at least not within his hearing.

Pauline had soon caught onto the fact that such declarations of Kjersti's continued *being*, despite that good woman's current residence in that huge snowbank outside the Foss hut, would cause Ernest to hover protectively around her, as if Pauline might actually harm *herself*.

Dear Mr. Douglas, you do worry too much *about me*, Pauline thought, as she lay on one side, cradling the Bible between her body and the mattress like a suckling child.

And, in a sense, the Bible itself *was* like a child; hadn't Kjersti been many years Pauline's junior, and hadn't Kjersti become one with this very Bible in Pauline's memory?

Pauline *did* pity her husband; poor man, thinking that she was all *alone* in the hut! If he only understood that the kettle he'd taken with him was her hot breath on the back of his neck during one of their long nights together, he'd have no reason at *all* to miss her companionship—and that was only the kettle!

The flour and milk he'd taken along were the white of her skin, the cinnamon in his dried squares of cooked porridge (waiting to be thawed and made smooth with the warm milk of herself) was the red of her hair…everything, all that he'd taken with him, was *her*, or *of* her.

Taking in a deep breath of Ernest, hugging Kjersti tight to her, Pauline decided that *she* was the lucky one, so surrounded by all she loved—not Ernest, with his *"real"* companion, Mr. Foss.

III.

"9 November, 187-

Sun today. The plains are the Cloth of His Robes, all aglow with diamonds and the fiery gems of Creation, as if a Rainbow froze and shattered against the very ground. Walking back to the hut from the animal stall, *I saw Kjersti...*"

Frowning, Pauline crossed out the last three words she had written and considered substituting, *"my footsteps were the stitches Kjersti made on that quilt of hers."*

But instead, she put away the book and quill. She could never be entirely sure if Ernest might read her journal, and if he saw any more references to Kjersti...well, Pauline doubted that he'd confine his reaction to an odd stare in her direction!

Lying on her back on the bed, Pauline crooked her arm around the back of her head and stared up at the rough willow ceiling, a slight frown on her face. Not that she was frowning because of the latest sign of Kjersti's continued presence in her life—Indeed, she welcomed new signs of Kjersti, of Ernest, of God Himself all around her. But this sign had been so...so...*odd*.

She'd only gone out to check on the cows and chickens because she couldn't remember for certain if Ernest had indeed left them enough feed in their rough enclosure, and she'd heard no answering pound of his footfalls across the floor when she'd asked about the feed when she awoke that morning. (Ernest sometimes turned a cold shoulder to her like that!)

Unlike the past few days, there was real sunlight outside; the sun was a cold-white ball high up in the sky of limitless blue, casting pure light on the sugar-gritty snow below. The colors alone had made her stop in her tracks, despite the cold which sucked at her body and pulled the last warmth from her lungs, her nostrils, her gaping mouth. Such colors she hadn't seen since she'd last attended church in Winnipeg, and raised her eyes in mid-prayer to stare at the stained glass windows.

But the glory of those windows couldn't compare with the endless plains of crushed jewels, the points of light scintillating and dancing in the distance. The dots of color formed pictures of every person in the Bible, just broken down into pure dots of living, moving color. In God's sight those fragments of color no doubt formed whole pictures, and vainly Pauline tried squeezing her eyes all-but-shut, trying to make the fragmented bits coalesce into the very picture of Glory.

The fresh, icy wind made her tearing eyes all but freeze shut, and with a shrug Pauline turned around and walked to the animal enclosure. The smell of the little barn was the presence of her father's farm in Manitoba; the freshly fertilized fields, the harvest, the new eggs for breakfast—it was all there in the little building.

After her short visit to her girlhood home, Pauline started back to the hut, feeling the faint warmth of the pale sun on her back.

Only when the warmth became concentrated in a spot no bigger than a woman-sized palm did Pauline whirl around—and caught the full glare of the rising sun in her eyes. Blinking for a few moments, Pauline wasn't *quite* sure what *else* she'd just seen (*a shape, a small shape against the sun, with light glinting off a rope-like coil*—) but when she looked down, all became clear.

The footprints followed her in a straight line, each toe slightly splayed outward, the imprint of each foot resembling thin lines of herringbone stitches.

The very same stitches Kjersti had used to join the pieces of fabric in the quilt she was working on only this past summer. Pauline had seen the quilt, and the stitches Kjersti made on it, when she and Ernest had last visited the Foss hut…at least it was the last time they'd visited there while Kjersti still filled the world with her live presence.

Pauline was so overcome by this new sign of Kjersti that she dropped to her knees in the snow, and touched the outline of each footprint with a wind-chapped hand.

Kjersti's stiches, *here*, on the snow of the farm!

Pauline thanked God that Kjersti's presence was not confined to that cold mound of packed snow outside the bigger mound of the Foss hut. She thanked God that He had allowed the sun to shine, so that she wouldn't miss this latest sign.

This new sign was so strong, in fact, that the line of snow-stitches followed Pauline all the way to the door of the sod hut—if she had come back to the house using the same path she'd used to *leave*, she'd have never seen the stitches at all! Putting another stick of wood in the fire, Pauline felt the warmth of Kjersti's work-worn hands against her cheeks, and Pauline muttered:

"For someone who has been marching outside, your hands are warm, Kjersti dear."

The fire fluttered an answer to her, and Pauline shook her head, adding, "Yes, I know how cold can almost burn the fingers, but warm hands *are* warm hands. Why, you've been hiding in *here* all along, haven't you?"

The ribbon woven in the crocheted cross blushed reddish in the fire, and Pauline smiled a most satisfied smile.

That Kjersti, always the one to try and make Pauline happy with her playful ways! Silly girl, dear girl, doing so much to brighten Pauline's day.

But a tiny cloud appeared on the bright sky of joy which surrounded Pauline; why had Kjersti been staying away before today? True, she had been in the hut, in the Bible and the cross, but Pauline had never encountered her *outside* like that before.

Yet now, with Ernest gone, Kjersti had chosen to dance, to make snow-stitches on the ground with her tiny feet, as she followed Pauline. If only Kjersti had done so earlier! *Then* let Ernest cast his odd looks in her direction!

Yes, it was an odd sign indeed, but not an unwelcome one.

As she pondered what she'd seen that day, Pauline got to thinking about her girlhood (that scamp Kjersti was little more than a girl), the days on the farm in Manitoba when she'd realized that new milk had a slightly bluish tinge in the big metal bucket. The color was like a pale morning sky before the blue gets going strong, the sort of vaguely-colored white like the whites of eyes.

More than once she'd thought during her girlhood that the very Eye of God must be that color; that delicate milky blue-white, but with a pupil of pure white-gold, like the sun itself.

And while she was praying in church, she'd imagined that Great Milk White Eye of God staring down on her, the vision in that Great Eye boring *through* the steepled roof of the church, right down to where she knelt in solemn prayer to the Almighty.

Suddenly, Pauline sat up on the bed, hugging her knees in her excitement. How silly she'd been; so close to the Truth and yet so far from it!

Yes, the sky was the Eye of the Lord, and the sun was the pupil, but He didn't have to look *out*—He was looking in!

Didn't she sometimes see tiny shapeless *things* floating in her line of vision, little wiggling semi-clear things that were trapped in her very eyes? Hadn't Papa explained it to her, telling her that eyes weren't hollow, but filled with wetness and veins and all sorts of tiny things that enabled people to see? Hadn't he sliced open the eye of the butchered cow (Papa had once dreamed of being a doctor, before his own Papa died and left him the farm), just to let her see how eyes worked?

Pauline almost chided herself for not thinking of this all sooner—*she* was one of the tiny things floating in the Eye of God!

She, the hut, Ernest, the distant willow trees by the distant creek, Kjersti, the cows, the chickens, the snow itself—simply everything was floating *in* God's sight!

And what better place to really *see* Kjersti than outside, in the unhampered and unimpeded Sight of God? Hadn't she glimpsed something against the sun? Against the very Pupil of God's Eye? The pupil was the most important part of the eye, or so her Papa had told her—

"Cover up the pupil and you cover up the sight," he'd told her, and hadn't that been true?

Being God, His Pupil couldn't *really* be covered by anything, because He was Almighty. But couldn't God's Eye sometimes get…foggy? Like Pauline's eyes sometimes became foggy when she'd read too much, or sewed in bad light?

There had been that terrible cloud-cover these past few weeks, including the time when poor, dear Kjersti took sick and Waldemar tried putting the poultices of cooked onions, linseed oil, milk and flour on her chest, and kept pouring bowls of hot milk and black pepper down her throat.

Waldemar hadn't dared to leave her side until it was too late…too late to do anything but comb out her golden hair and dress her in the good nightgown with the herringbone vines and little pink flowers across the breast.

He was kneeling by the bed when Pauline and Ernest had come to the hut, bearing frozen fish and bread and smoked duck (it was Waldemar's birthday, and they'd planned a secret surprise feast), and Pauline had dropped the loaves of bread she was carrying when she saw Kjersti… and the men had had to tie her to the bed with one of Kjersti's aprons while they carried Kjersti out the door and into the terrible cold and blowing snow, not heeding Pauline's cries that Kjersti wasn't dressed *warmly* enough to go out in the cold, why she was only in *stocking feet*—

But Kjersti was all right now.

That was the important thing to remember…*Kjersti was all right*. She couldn't be bothered by the cold, not if she was making herringbone stitches across the snowy ground. Pauline had done embroidery herself; she knew how much concentration a good herringbone stitch took to make.

The fire crackled out an invitation to Pauline; after a moment's consideration, she cast off her warm coverlets, and drew on her shoes and outside clothing, even though she doubted that Kjersti was wearing this much clothing outside.

Still, Kjersti came from Norway, and it was cold there….

The Pupil of the Great Milk White Eye was overhead, right above Pauline.

She had to stop and almost bend backwards to let her face meet that of the dazzling white-gold Pupil, and even with her eyes shut (brilliant red, like the Blood of Christ, washed across her field of vision) she could still *see*, oh yes, dear Lord, dear Kjersti, dear, dear Ernest (*you shouldn't have worried about me, husband dear*)—she could see *everything*, simply everything on earth, right before her closed, tearing eyes.

And the Warmth was touching her face a smooth caress like the one Kjersti gave Pauline when the older woman had taught the Norwegian girl how to do a chain-stitch (the poor girl's chains had been so *crooked!*), and then they'd hugged, and oh *God* how Pauline had wished that she'd had a daughter like Kjersti, and oh how she'd cursed herself for being barren for the twenty long years of marriage to Mr. Douglas.

For being forty and alone in the big wide plains was sometimes so *hard*, and so *lonely*, even if there were the signs of those she loved around her—

And Pauline reached up her arms and spread her fingers wide, feeling for the answering touch of a hand, any hand, be it of man or God—until she felt that touch, and finally, wholly, opened her eyes.

IV.

When Ernest and Waldemar Foss didn't find Pauline in the hut upon their return to the Douglas farm, they looked around outside the hut (no easy thing, considering the foot of snow dumped on the already snowy plain in the past twenty-four hours), calling her name as they tramped about.

The men looked until their fingers were stiff and numb, and their faces scraped raw by dull razors of wind, and only when Ernest heard the low mooing of the cows did he head in the direction of the animal pen—and stumble across a new bump in the ground.

Pauline was arrow straight, her body and arms forming a perfect line, and Waldemar got the blanket and wrapped her up while Ernest dug out the snow, forming a deeper crypt in the grainy whiteness.

And Waldemar didn't mention it to Ernest (knowing from experience that such things were best left unsaid), but when he touched his ungloved fingers against Pauline's blue ones, they were still warm, like the lowest part of a flame.

Wind whipped and slapped the men as they buried her in the bank, and up above them, the grey scud of cloud was broken in two places, in a pair of thin lines.

One a feathery herringbone, the other a perfect chain-stitch of pale gold-white.

AFTERWORD

I read O. E. Rolvaag's novel *Giants in the Earth* for some course in college (which one I'm not sure about; it was either a history course or some English one), and I was struck by how modern the book seemed in terms of describing-without-actually-naming the symptoms of cabin fever.

One passage has stuck with me for years, concerning the efforts of a pioneer husband to cheer up his wife by whitewashing the inside of their sod hut…so that when winter's snows came, she was stuck in the middle of a virtual white-out—white walls within, white land without. (I'm one of those people who cannot stand a bare wall of any color, and the thought of having to stare at white or…*white* is horrifying.)

This story is one of my personal favorites, even though I am not a religious person—the pioneers were, so my characters had to see their circumstances through a religious emotional filter.

A few years after its first publication, I sold it as a reprint to a now defunct magazine called *The Barrelhouse* (small press, nice editors), and when I received my contributors copies, the editor had jotted down a small note, wondering why a story like this had never been up for any awards.

Beats me—I've never been up for any awards in over 25 years of writing. But it was a nice thing for the person to write to me; at least someone thought it was deserving of some sort of award.…

SIZE OF A SILVER DOLLAR

The town councilmen exploded the gunpowder on the anvils shortly after sunrise, but it wasn't until near on ten o'clock in the morning that enough folks had gathered in the town proper to make starting the celebrations worthwhile.

And by that time, the sun was just high enough to shine painfully in Miz Myrtle Morgan's thin-lidded eyes as she sat on the high platform. The flimsy paper fan someone had gently pushed into her curled left hand was a poor shield against it. In fact, the red third of the fan made the filtered sunlight all the hotter, and after the Mayor gave her good morning greetings to the townsfolk assembled on Main Street, Miz Myrtle Morgan let the fan slide from her fingers, where it dropped unceremoniously to the planks below her feet.

No one came forward to pick it up and reposition it in her hand, for the time of the speeches had come, and all eyes were focused on the row of sixth-graders sitting on cane-bottom chairs behind the new microphone podium on the stage.

The little girl sitting nearest to Miz Myrtle (as the Widow Morgan was known to one and all present) wore her flax-colored hair in a long hangman's braid, which rested on her back, just touching the greyish stripe of sweat running down her spine.

Miz Myrtle eyed the braid with a dull mixture of dread and fascination—dread because dread of death was a fixture of her one hundred years, fascination because...just *because*.

Before her, the Mayor (the town's second woman mayor; Kansas had been in the forefront of the woman's suffrage movement for close to fifty or sixty years) had launched into a short Fourth of July speech, clear thin voice loudly and uncertainly amplified across the heads of the people assembled below the platform, hastily erected close by the hardware store and across from Hargrove's Dress Shop.

Miz Myrtle could see the shimmering reflection of all those on the platform in the shop window, a wavering blend of red, white, and blue, touched with washed-out pinks and the pale hemp yellow of the children's hair...with a blob of white-tipped black in the center of that pale mirror.

She, Miz Myrtle, was the shapeless black object: close on two hundred pounds, swathed in black, like an obscene parody of the Holy Infant, and wearing a ridiculous reproduction of a pioneer woman's bonnet in thin white netting, like the little hats the Mennonite women wore.

No help against the white glare of the sun, simply none at *all*.

Having reached the century mark, Miz Myrtle was not interested in looking down at the upturned, perspiring faces below her; she had seen those same faces from near infancy and had grown tired of them long ago. She had grown tired of the faces of the children, too, because they all began to look the same to her—or, in certain cases, *worse* than the same.

For she had never forgotten, despite the passing of sixty years, how the faces of her own children had looked…before the Indians came.

Before the Indians came….Those four words had become the line of demarcation in her life.

First had come the forty years of her life in which she was a wife, a mother, and a homesteader…and then, *after* the Indians, everything was changed.

For good and beyond.

Before the Indians came, she had been one part of eleven; eleven people in a soddy plowed from an acre of the Morgan claim, eleven lives lived in a place of dirt sifting down from the earthen walls, the cottonwood, willow, and sod roof. And muddy, soggy floors when it rained.

Horrible it had been, but she'd been a part of it, mother to nine, wife to Mr. Morgan…all before the Indians came.

Came to be that all she *could* think about anymore was that time before the coming of the Indians out of the flatness of the land and the hard blueness of the sky; curiously, what thoughts were old in her remained the clearest, while new thoughts came and went like pinpoints of hot twinkling light that fanned the ground in front of an oncoming prairie fire.

Miz Myrtle couldn't even remember exactly who it was who had half dragged, half hoisted her onto *this* platform, who had led her to this stout chair and placed the ridiculous little paper fan in her hand.

But she remembered *why* she was here; the reason was unmistakably clear. She was here to be tortured—oh, not officially; on the face of it she was the guest of honor, the woman of the day, as someone or other had told her over breakfast. Another voice, another face out of many at the home where she stayed, trapped for the most part by infirm limbs and immense weight.

And ironically, if memory served her (as it did, oh, how faithfully it did these days!) this just about *was* her day, as close as that to the day of the Indians. The day nothing, even old age and a capricious memory, would allow her to forget.

The Mayor's speech was coming to an emotional end, and as the sluggish breeze tugged at the woman's flimsy voile dress (making an almost imperceptible susurration that reminded Miz Myrtle of dried grass whispering under an endless horizon), Her Honor concluded:

"Women gave up their best years, their very strength, health, and material wealth, in order to tame and civilize the great western lands. And the cost of their sacrifices is one that cannot be totaled on any cash register or be figured in any ledger. That cost is known only to the Almighty. And yet…some of the sacrifices were not personal, but sacrifices which extended to the very *families* of these brave women.

"And it is the fact that these women, women such as our own Mrs. Morgan, not only survived such travails but persevered and prospered *despite* the cruel blows of Fate. *It is that fact*, citizens of Walnut Center, that made these simple farm women the true royalty of the West. And no greater honor can be bestowed to any mortal woman."

Amid the hearty clapping, hooting, and cheering that rose up from the heat-shimmering street full of people below them, the Mayor turned and applauded Miz Myrtle.

Miz Myrtle pretended to nod off.

Having suitably honored the dozing Miz Myrtle, the Mayor returned to the huge microphone.

"And now the sixth-grade students of the Walnut Center Elementary School will give their speeches. First up is"—the bob-haired woman consulted an index card—"Bessie Walters."

Miz Myrtle's strangely-bonneted head jerked up reflexively at the mention of the curly-headed girl's surname.

Walter—little Walter, the baby of the bunch—would have been sixty-one this year, come October. Only baby Walter hadn't made it to one year of age, let alone sixty-one.

With her "good" hand (her right arm was the only "good" limb left to her), Miz Myrtle groped for her drawstring handbag, sticking a fat finger into the puckered top and gently widening the opening until she could almost stick her whole hand into the bag.

While worming her way into the bag, she let her eyes drift down to her lap, where she stared at the absurdity of her bloated hands. The fingers were vaguely articulated sausages, with nails resembling nothing less than blobs of richly yellowed fat stuck in the bottom of the casings. And on the backs of them, countless misshapen brown dots seemed to hover above the dead white of her skin, each speck of dark pigmentation seemed to float in the strong sunlight.

Miz Myrtle was almost afraid the dots of color would peel off of her skin and drift away like ashes blown from an open fire. But most of all, she feared the shapes left behind on her hands after the departure of her age freckles, for how could she know what color the skin *underneath* them might be?

Little Bessie Walters was in place behind the microphone, standing on a footstool, wide-lined paper in hand. Her first few words were lost to the crowd, until a man came forward and adjusted the microphone head with an ear-stinging squeal. Only then did the child begin again.

"One—*one* hundred years ago a baby girl was born in Ohio, and her mother and father named her Myrtle. That year was eighteen and twenty-nine, and twenty-two years later, little Myrtle was a grown-up gir—*woman*, and she became a bride, and there was a big celebration, and…"

Fingers firmly around what lay in her bag, Miz Myrtle bit a fleshy lip and thought:

NO, little girl, it wasn't like that at all. Momma and Poppa hated Joshua. Thought him an ingrate and a good-for-nothing. And our union brought scant joy.

* * * *

The Myrtle Clarke of 1851 was a far cry from the Myrtle Clarke Morgan of 1852; in less than twelve months she made the sudden cocoon-less metamorphosis from graceful, flighty young miss to chastened, saggy-bellied, full-teated mother.

And when she wrote tearful letters to her dear mother, finally admitting her stupidity, her blindness in wedding Josh, it was too late. The letters were returned; her mother and father refused to pay the postage on them.

And baby Olive was always hungry, and the milk was slow in coming out of Myrtle's body. Joshua only laughed, berating her for her small breasts, laughing even as Olive squalled, red-faced and too thin in her mother's arms.

If only milk had flowed from Myrtle like liquor flowed from the present bottle in Joshua's hand!

Myrtle was careful in the next few years, not allowing Joshua's seed to stay within herself long enough for a child to flower inside her. And mostly he stayed too drunk to notice her swift departure from the bed, to her douches and washings-away of his maleness.

But before they left Ohio, when the government made cheap land in the Kansas Territory available to white men, Myrtle was unable to cleanse away all traces of Josh. Henry was born the year after they came to the western plains, born in the filth and near-darkness of the dugout Josh carved into the side of a low hillock that first year.

During all of 1856, the year of Henry's birth, Josh took bad with the ague, alternately sweating and freezing. So it was dose Josh with the quinine and sassafras tea, and nurse the baby, and tend to toddler Olive, and tend to their patchy garden and sickly livestock when she wasn't tending to her weak brood in the dank confines of the dugout.

Come the next year, when William was born, Josh was well enough (and sober, although that was no blessing, since the drink had at least kept him slightly jovial), to plow away blocks of prairie marble from an acre of their land and stack them with Myrtle's help into four walls a full two feet thick.

Myrtle also had helped to shape wood into window and door frames; the fine soft hands of her girlhood and youth were rough now, almost splintery to the touch. And the lifting and positioning of the sod made painful knots of muscle in her upper arms toughen and bulge slightly when she flexed her hands.

She ended up cutting the roof of cottonwood and willow brush herself, for as the work neared completion, Josh's ague came back, most conveniently, Myrtle thought at the time....

* * * *

Her head of bright curls all but hidden from the crowd by the microphone, Bessie Walters finished her speech, which ended with the lilting words:

"And that was how life was on the plains for Miz—Mrs. Morgan and her family. It was a hard life but a *pure* one," and with that Miss Walters stepped down from her stool and went back to her chair, where she did a little curtsy for the clapping crowd.

Miz Myrtle hoped the little girl wouldn't win the prize for Best Speech (said prize displayed on an easel-back stand near the podium, a gold medal the size of a silver dollar attached to a bright blue ribbon); she had made everything seem just too nice, too simple.

To quote Miss Walters, too *pure*.

Miz Myrtle's fingers slid over the leathery surface of the thing in the bag, caressing the well-worn roundness of it, but the vague movements of her fingers became jerky, tense, when the next child, a boy whose hair fluttered in the breeze like the silk of almost ripened corn, began his speech with the overemphasized phrase:

"On the *plains*, life was hard and many settlers' children *died*, so the families had *lots* and lots of *young*sters."

The boy paused dramatically then went on, "And our Widow Morgan was no exception."

The crowd below made a low murmur of disapproval. The subject of the speech was a touchy one, sure to displease.

But Miz Myrtle was too lost in thought to hear someone in the crowd grouse, "Don't the boy have any *consideration* for her?"

In the depths of her brain, names came forth, and years, and small wrinkled faces: In 1857, William, cross-eyed but quick to smile. Pearl, two years after, completely Josh's child. 1861 brought Carrie, she of the sad eyes and tiny mouth. Two summers later Josh was placated by Benjamin's arrival, and come 1865 Bernard brought the promise of more help on the farm, and perhaps a respite in later years for Myrtle. The next year was a setback, but Gertrude might be of use for housework, food gathering, and water hauling.

Before 1868, Myrtle had her hands full with three very young blond children to run around after—but Walter's arrival all but broke her, and even his cheerful gurgle and inquisitive little fingers and darting eyes couldn't bring much cheer to his mother.

For Josh was no help at child-rearing and little good as a farmer, not with his annual bouts of ague, and his almost on-the-dot announcement each summer:

"I dunno, Mother, feel mighty sickly, mighty peaked."

Myrtle wasn't such a fool that she didn't notice him wink at the older children in turn and, in turn, see them wink back and prepare their own tales of impending illness.

Miz Myrtle's fingers worked the worn leather circle feverishly, as she sat with hooded eyes lowered, the blackness of her lap her entire field of vision, not listening to the now-shamefaced boy hurriedly finish his speech, mumbling:

"The Morgan family was real lucky because not a one of their children succumbed to any sickness. That was a really rare thing to happen in those days. Mrs. Morgan nursed them through sicknesses very successfully. She was a very good wife and mother—and doctor."

The clapping sounded like fat drops of rain hitting a tin bucket—*splap, splap...splap.*

Then sun—and silence.

The next child was hurried onto the stepstool: the girl in the dotted dress (red specks of color against a creamy ground, and Miz Myrtle checked her own hands, seeing if the brown blotches had somehow turned, gone back to the way they'd been, once) wasted no time launching into her narration.

"How the Pioneers Dressed, by Etta Louise Oliver," she said precisely, capitalizing each important word aurally.

A safe topic, thought Miz Myrtle, no matter what sort of print the girl's dress was.

As if feeling Miz Myrtle's approval, Etta Louise singsonged pertly:

"When a plains wife wanted a new dress, she couldn't go down the street to the local dress shop—first of all, there weren't any *sidewalks*, only wooden boardwalks, and second, a dress shop was of little importance on the plains. When a plainswoman, like our very *own* Mrs. Morgan, wanted a new dress, she had to make and dye it her*self*, from a simple roll of unbleached muslin, or calico, if she had a roll of it. Denim had to suffice for the men of the family, and most people went barefoot come summer, to save their calfskin shoes. Sacks from flour became sturdy underwear, and some enterprising ladies constructed clothes from old blankets and even the very canvas of their wagons. The flowers and grasses they picked on the plains became colorful dyes that turned plain white cloth into butternut brown or Nankeen yellow—"

"Nankeen yellow," the red-dot girl said, and Miz Myrtle remembered the dress she'd been wearing the day of the Indians.

The shade of goldenrods, only the dress had faded irregularly, with dark patches of fabric under her arms and along the bottom of her skirt. She'd made and dyed the dress when Carrie was born and had yet to be lucky enough to rip or ruin it enough to suit Josh's dictum of no new dresses until the old ones were too indecent to wear.

Eight miserable, dirty, sweaty years, and still the dress looked unworn. The way it scratched at her armpits and rubbed at her neck was infernal. And the stiff skirt and long sleeves rubbed against her bug bites, making them itch.

Between her legs, the folded cloth had alternately tickled and rubbed, the moisture there hot and sticky. The only consolation *there* was that she was not with child again.

The children never seemed to mind the searing July heat; mostly they aped their father's mock chills, his exaggerated shivering. But they couldn't produce hot foreheads (oh, she'd seen William and Pearl rubbing their brows, trying to raise enough heat to fool their mother), and therefore they'd had to help her with the chores.

But somehow, even the oldest of them could turn a simple search for fire fuel into a chance to be lazy, to play when it was not time to do so.

Even Olive, with her long colt legs and skirt that needed lengthening. Olive couldn't even can fruit right; one batch she'd done in '67 had spoiled that winter in the warmth of the soddy. The girl had learned her father's secret, all right—do something so badly, so wrong, that Myrtle wouldn't want the thing done by that person again.

For foodstuffs could be scarce, and even though she knew the girls did it on purpose, Myrtle gave in and exempted them from helping with the food preparation. Wheat flour was hard to come by, and even corn was too precious to waste on rocklike bread and black pancakes.

And the boys; somehow they'd manage to get the corncobs wet and break the sunflower stalks into brittle, useless bits. She didn't trust any of them to collect what buffalo chips could be found.

She knew her children all too well—no, she knew *Joshua*'s children.

"And in the wintertime, what animals the father had shot and killed were used to keep the family warm, for their tanned hides and pelts became snug coats and comfy bedding—"

It was lucky Miz Myrtle had become a good shot, and it was even more fortunate that she naturally took to butchering, dressing out, and tanning the remains of what she killed.

Joshua was a poor marksman (oh, he could aim a fork at his mouth with stunning accuracy), and Henry showed promise of stepping gracefully into his father's footsteps. William was good at shooting the sod bricks of the chimney; once a chunk of sod clogged the chimney and everything in the house was dreadfully smoked and sooty.

Joshua had laughed like a coyote in heat over *that* one, as she cleaned what she could in the smoked house.

And there was no switching the bottom of William (or any other of Joshua's brood); Joshua claimed that his own father's constant use of the rod had "done spoiled me to the core." Myrtle chose to think of Joshua as one apple that was blighted as a blossom.

Miz Myrtle sat up with a start when a different childish voice intruded on her memories. A boy with hair so short she could see each bead of sweat pop out of his scalp was droning on about what people planted in their gardens; no gold medal for him, she thought petulantly.

Glancing at the row of seated children, she saw that she'd totally missed another girl, who sat between Etta Louise Oliver and an empty chair. Whatever her speech had been, Miz Myrtle supposed she wouldn't die just because she'd missed it.

After reaching one hundred years, things like that didn't bother her overmuch. As the shorn boy rambled on, Miz Myrtle took a slow look around her, at the bunting- and flag-decorated street, at the brick and wood buildings (wood buildings, now *there* was an extravagance!), at the new pale-grey sidewalks, installed only two summers ago.

Nothing like the town she'd crawled into, after the Indians came and went on the farm, leaving her alone, alive....

* * * *

The Morgan farmstead was situated midway between the Smoky Hill and Saline Rivers, just below the site of all the trouble in the valley between the settlers and the Indians. Fort Hays and Fort Wallace were only miles away, but that still had not stopped the massacre of two hundred settlers in the valley between the Solomon and Saline Rivers, the work of the vile Sioux and Cheyenne. The horse-mounted warriors, bearing lances and shields, as well as the ubiquitous ax-like tomahawk.

The scalp-takers and the women stealers.

Word of what had happened to poor Sarah White and Anna Brewster Morgan (the thought that the Morgan woman could have been *Myrtle Clarke* Morgan was not lost on Miz Myrtle), how they were kidnapped and worse by Indian braves, spread even to the Joshua Morgan farm, isolated and seldom-visited as it was.

It seemed that the coming of the Kansas Pacific Railroad, not to mention the many buffalo hunters who had preceded the trains, had infuriated the Indians beyond endurance.

Even what Miz Myrtle and her neighbors called the "good Indians"—the Pawnee, the Kansa, or so the other women called them—were looked upon with growing unease during those years, the time of the uprisings. And the years of Indian sightings still had not made it all that easy to tell one from another, and a warrior bent on vengeance could hide his tomahawk and pose as a merely curious Indian just to get into a soddy and do evil there.

But the women, Miz Myrtle included, still let them into their soddies and dugouts, let the braves taste their odd cooking, poke into their linens, peer inquisitively at their few Back East treasures, all in the hope that the Indians would be satisfied and leave peacefully.

As all the Indian braves Miz Myrtle had previously encountered had done…until the July day when the Indians came.

And when they were gone and her family lay dead, scalped and bloodied, and the livestock ran loose and frantic, Miz Myrtle had half crawled away, across fields of ripening corn, the rough stalks and heavy ears slapping and jabbing her. She hadn't cared that they pulled and yanked at her hair, pulling strands from her uncut and unbloodied scalp.

Across many acres of land, both cultivated and wild, she had dragged herself, and the acres turned into miles, and still she moved forward, clutching a small bloodied thing in one fist, hair flying across her face in moist strands, blood leaking slowly down her legs (the cloth tucked in her pantaloons gone, fallen out somewhere), and still she crawled on, northward at first, until she reached a point where her whirring mind slowed down long enough to ask if she should go northeast, to Fort Hays and the town recently settled there, or northwest, to Walnut Center.

A part of her mind that was still lucid whispered, *Josh said there's a thousand souls in Hays...too many eyes, too many people, too many*, and thus she went northwest, finally and literally crawling on her hands and knees, right hand fisted to protect what lay still warm and moist in her palm. And by the time she reached the collection of flimsy buildings, tents, and dugouts surrounding a buffalo sod street, she'd worn blood-ringed holes in the skirt of her hated Nankeen yellow dress.

The people of Walnut Center were kind and did not press her for details of what happened out at the farm. Men rode out, their horses' hooves kicking up choking clouds of brown, and then they rode back, many hours later, faces grim and rifles at the ready to shoot down the savages with the scalps on their rough clothing.

The nine scalps remained unaccounted for...the men knew where *one* of the scalps was, after some of the women gently pried it out of Myrtle's hand before letting her have it again.

It was the only way to quiet her, for her screams and hoarse shouts echoed in the hot still air, in the very spot where Main Street now stood in all its paved and brick-lined glory....

* * * *

In front of her, a girl with reddish bobbed hair and a pale blue pleated dress, solemnly told her captive audience that General Custer and his troops had been encamped in Hays only three months before the "Morgan Massacre" occurred and mused that:

"If only those brave troops had been handy, the fearsome Indians who murdered Mrs. Morgan's husband and children would have been caught and hung...."

From where she sat behind the strawberry-blond girl, Miz Myrtle snorted softly, thinking that the child needed to study her history better, especially the part about the Little Big Horn, until the girl added:

"For anyone evil enough to do such a horrid thing deserves to lie in the fires of Hades for all eternity!"

What do *you* know about it, Missy? Miz Myrtle found herself thinking, and then, try as she might, no matter how hard she rubbed the small soft leathery bit in her purse, the memories came at her again, jabbing and poking all the tender places like ears of corn banging into her fleeing body that July day sixty years ago....

* * * *

It was the first week of July, the time when the sun beat down like a live, sweating thing suspended in a sky of unflawed and painful blue; the time when water had to be drawn dozens of times a day from the well just to keep Joshua and the youngest boys from whimpering from the fevers they claimed to have "real bad" even if *she* couldn't detect any heat when she pressed dry lips to their cool foreheads; the time when the other children whooped and played at Indians, even though she kept telling them that such play was sure to bring bad luck, and the two eldest children were flinging chicken feed at each other instead of at the chickens; the time when her time of the month was the most bothersome, most uncomfortable in her lower belly.

And it was the time of the year when a baby's cries carry like thunder, booming and echoing in a mother's ears.

It was the time of summer when most of the harvesting would fall on her shoulders (Joshua's ague could last for weeks, even if she could hear Joshua and the children giggling and playing in the soddy while she worked until her hands were red and cracked with tiny diamond-shaped furrows deep in the flesh and her face grew burnt and freckled in the sun), for as sure as bread rises in the baking dish, when it came to real work needing to be done, Joshua would call on his memory of past illnesses and come up with a whole collection of "dangerous" symptoms.

July only meant thoughts of deep winter coming, the time when Joshua and whichever child happened to want to play sick with him would sit by the fire, sucking mullein plant candies to help ward off more winter colds, the time when Myrtle would have to venture out into winds that sliced across the land like a razor against a lathered cheek, scraping her bare and raw with the chill hardness of it, to gather chips or simply whatever she could find to lay on the fire.

Fourteen years had come and gone, and none had differed greatly for Myrtle, save for the number and supposed severity of the "illnesses" her family had affected.

Oh, true sicknesses did come and go, but true colds never seemed to last as long as the pretend variety. It was no fun to be really sick.

Fourteen springs of nearly single-handed planting. Fourteen summers of almost solitary labor in the garden. Fourteen falls of hunting and trapping by her lonesome. Fourteen winters of listening to feigned coughs—and cleaning up intentional messes in the beds.

"Fourteen *years*," she'd muttered to herself while she paused to push a sweaty hair out of her eyes as she used Joshua's ax to break up the buffalo chips—she liked them better in small pieces; they burned more efficiently come winter.

The younger children were whooping and playing the scamp, as usual; their voices set her teeth to grinding. She longed to take her broom to each child's behind, tanning the skin darker than a week's worth of exposure to sunlight. Off to her left, Olive and Henry had stopped throwing feed at each other and were now standing around, jabbering like magpies.

"Some wife you'll be, Ol," Henry scoffed, to which Olive—thin-legged, wide-faced, chipped-toothed Olive—replied reproachfully:

"Me, a *wife*? No man's good enough for *me*....Besides," she'd added, in what was supposed to be a whisper too low for their mother to hear, "why would I want to be a wife? I don't want to work like an old *nag*! Why, I'd get ugly muscles all *over* me!"

And they had giggled and whooped like ten-year-olds while Myrtle bit shaking lips and blinked watering eyes.

And then, when she'd looked up, she'd seen the Indians.

* * * *

The blue-dressed girl sat down, the end of her speech lost to Miz Myrtle, drowned out by the blood roaring in her large and fragile ears.

The girl with the hangman braid got up and took her place in front of the big shiny microphone (the glare of the rising sun turned it into a cold white thing, like sun shining through a fat icicle), and began a speech about the various Indian tribes who "roamed the land in the time of Widow Morgan," speaking in turn of the bad and the good Indians, of their habits, their quirks, their violence....

And this time, Miz Myrtle could not banish the memories, couldn't rub them away with fingers that were already sweaty and slick with repeated circular movements, for the girl's words brought back the day when the Indians came.

* * * *

There were five or six of them far out on the horizon, but not far enough out that they couldn't see her and recognize her.

Apparently, they were heading for Walnut Center and couldn't take the time to stop by the soddy, but they were polite enough to wave at her.

Myrtle put down the ax long enough to give them an enthusiastic two-armed wave in return; not so much because she was overly fond of the Indians but just because they treated her with something more than her family's scarcely concealed dislike and open ridicule.

Never had they laughed at her or refused to pay attention to her efforts to be hospitable. Their thanks had been said with their eyes, with simple gestures, but at least—at least they didn't make her want to chuck it all and run for Ohio. When they took food, they did it out of curiosity or hunger, not because they liked leeching off of her, *using* her day in and day out for fourteen years.

"Lookit, Henry, she's got herself some new *men* friends," Olive had drawled, not caring if Myrtle heard her or not.

Joshua and the boys had heard Olive's remark, for from within the soddy came the singsong chant, two piping voices and one deep one:

"Mama's got herself some Injins, Injins, Injins, got herself some Innnjiiins!"

And then *all* the children started in, Joshua's brood of wild animals, every last one of them, and Myrtle said nothing, did nothing to shut them up or show any emotion herself....for then the Indians came.

And the side of the ax shone first icy white, then dribbled silver-red in the hard blue glare of the sun and sky....

* * * *

"The Indians who scalped people did not do so just to be cruel. The warriors believed that the souls of their killed enemies would belong to the person who collected the scalp and kept it. The Indians believed that the scalp was like extra strength in *them*, and the Indians of the Plains tribes used to count the scalps as replacements for members of their tribe who had died."

Scanning the faces of the crowd before her, Miz Myrtle's eyes lingered on the weathered faces of the oldsters, the ones still young enough to have been her children.

How would Olive and Henry have looked with white hair and store-boughten teeth? Little Gertie and Walter with bifocals and big ears and noses? And the rest. Willie and Pearl, Carrie and Benjie, and Bernard, with C-curved spines and wattled chins?

And Mr. Morgan himself, an incredible one hundred and *six—imagine that*! Miz Myrtle tried to make light of the thought, but couldn't.

The riders from Walnut Center had buried them all on the spot and then rounded up what livestock they could, on the day the Indians came and went.

And from then on, she'd lived in town, seen it gain real buildings and boardwalks and a big general store, and then she'd seen the first jerking, smoking car come rolling down the street, and she'd heard the wireless and seen a flying machine glide across the unbroken hard blue of the sky.

After the massacre of her family, she'd done quite well for herself, working in the general store, then at the newspaper office. Finally she saved enough money to buy a boarding-house, and then, when she seemed at the pinnacle of success in a state of the union that welcomed and encouraged forward-looking women, she'd had her first stroke.

In July 1900, the first week of the month.

And almost every July or thereabouts, she'd suffer more little strokes, like tiny chops of an ax lopping off working bits of her, leaving dead useless flesh and bone in their place.

The last stroke, last year, had robbed her of her speech.

And now, in 1929, at this, her centennial, all Miz Myrtle could do was endlessly rub the scalp of her baby, the scalp which now looked for all the world like a scrap of chamois, worn thin from frequent fingering.

On that day, sixty years ago, the good men of Walnut Center had assumed that the Indians had taken the nine scalps with them, after dropping the tiniest, the cruelest one. Miz Myrtle had been too stunned to say different.

And the kind women had washed her blood-flecked hands, the dots of red covering the tops of both hands like premature old age spots. The ladies had burned her blood-streaked dress; the smell of the burning was a nose-curling thing, with raw scented smoke rising into the hot air.

And soon she was settled into a dugout with a nice family who let her help with household chores for her keep, and Miz Myrtle had never had it so easy in fourteen years.

Her only peculiarity was the little drawstring bag she kept tied to her apron. For a survivor of an Indian attack, Miz Myrtle was regarded as quite sane, quite brave.

A burst of applause brought Miz Myrtle back to the here and now; little Miss Etta Louise Oliver was standing up and pretending to be very, very surprised as the Mayor came forward and awarded her the bright medal, the gold disk glinting in the sun, a mote of color against fresh sun-lit snow.

Miz Myrtle nodded what looked like senile approval; the girl's speech had been innocuous, and well-delivered to boot. No one, in their approval of the winner of the speech contest, noticed Miz Myrtle rubbing the thing in her little bag with frantic intensity. The waiting brass band (sweating like plow horses in their red and gold-braid uniforms) struck up "My Country, 'Tis of Thee," and all the people joined in, save for Miz Myrtle.

Instead, she rubbed the tiny withered scalp, little Walter's scalp with a few downy hairs still embedded in it, in time to the music. The only scalp not thrown down the well by the Indians before they left.

Miz Myrtle had kept it with her always, because it had been the hardest, most heartbreaking scalp she had taken that morning that the Indians came, that tiny scalp the size of a silver dollar.

AFTERWORD

Recently, a reader sent me a letter asking me a question about this story, which I'd like to answer for all the readers out there who might not be clear on one aspect which puzzled the reader—this person wanted to know if Miz Myrtle actually killed her own baby along with the rest of her family, and if she herself scalped her children. Yes she did.

Back when I first heard of Kathy Ptacek's upcoming anthology of stories of the Old West written by women writers, I couldn't think of anything, and said so to my mother, who snapped, "Why not write about a woman who kills her entire family for being *rotten* and blames it on the Indians?" An ugly thought, and spoken with sufficient venom for me to realize that the emphasis on rotten was for my benefit, but…it eventually worked out as a story for me.

I think the work pretty much speaks for itself, so I'll say no more save than to pass on this rather ironic anecdote:

For years, one of my former college professor's wives has been harassing me about writing "that garbage science fiction" and *not* writing romance, or "stuff people *like* to read"; the woman is a bit…shall I say, unique, and mostly people have learned to ignore her nasty outbursts. But once she harangued me about not writing the type of material that they'd buy for the Ladysmith Public Library…a place where she spent a lot of time once the college closed; as usual, I let the nastiness slide, but a couple of years later, when the college was selling off books down in the basement (ones pulled from the shelves or donated by the public), I found a copy of *Women of the West* for sale. The Library had bought it, and then sold it. I was in it…but Mrs. "that garbage science fiction" never realized it was, indeed, part of the collection here. I had a reason for not knowing it was in there—due to not having a phone, I couldn't get a library card at the time, hence I seldom ventured in there, save to pick up tax forms each spring. I've even stopped buying books there—my own collection of books is far better than theirs, and in better shape.

Perhaps it is for the best that my nemesis didn't see the book, or read my story—I'm sure I never would have heard the end of it if she had! If she considers sf "garbage" I have no idea what she'd think of what Miz Myrtle did to her brood….

THE CHILDREN'S HOUR

NOT A HAUNTED HOUSE AT ALL

Deepening afternoon-into-twilight shadows transformed the cobbled street into a forest of sharp knives, pointed tips aimed at the shoes of the three boys who walked down the quiet residential avenue.

The tallest boy stepped ahead of his companions, turned around to face them, and, as he tilted his baseball cap at a defiant angle, said, "Am *not*."

"Are too...*paw-wukwukwuk*," came the reply from the shortest (and cockiest) of the trio of Little Leaguers, as he flapped bent arms up and down, making the *Bannerton Braves* insignia on the back of his baseball shirt dance over his shoulder blades.

"Aw, Gene, why doncha let ole Chicken Lady Gavin alone?" the third boy, the one with the bat clutched in a grimy left hand, taunted. "He can't help it if he's too...*chicken* to go knock on some old door on some old haunted house—"

"Am *not* 'chicken,' Chad," Gavin shot back.

Gene quit his arm-flapping and cluck-clucking long enough to ask, "If you ain't, how come you won't do it then? You scared of a big *empty* house? Huh? Think Ole Man Dooley is gonna come out and bite ya' on the bum?"

"F' cryin' out loud, he's dead," Gavin replied in a how-can-you-be-so-*dumb* tone of voice. He flexed his hand inside his mitt, as if testing its strength.

"That's what they *say*, but 'who knows what evil lurks—'"

"Aw quit havin' us on," Gavin snapped.

Scarping a bit of grass clinging to his baseball shoes onto the cobbled surface below—Bannerton was one of the few towns in Ontario which still had cobbled streets—Gavin stared past Gene, toward the Dooley house up on the hill.

As far as "haunted houses" went, the Dooley house really didn't have *much* of a reputation yet; no headless ghouls slinking around the widow's walk, or hounds from Hades chasing after the postman, but... considering that Old Man Dooley had been dead a couple of years, it was just haunted enough for the three ten-year-olds who were now approaching it on this listless late August afternoon.

Didn't a lot of pets in town tend to get lost in *this* neighborhood? And didn't Gavin's sister hear something strange near the house while collecting paper for her Sparks troop paper drive this spring?

Oh, after a *while* she'd calmed down and claimed it was only a dog yapping, but all three boys remembered her white lips, and her cry of, "It sounded like it was *screaming*...."

Far off, the painted metal sign which still hung on the big maple on Dooley's lawn thunked against the snaggy greyish trunk. The boys knew its inscription by heart: "Dooley's Fine House Plants, Exotics and Annuals—Inquire at Back Door."

When the old man was alive their mothers used to buy aloe, African violets, and mother-in-law-tongues from him, and they'd read the sign over and over again while waiting in the car (either that, or Mom's latest issue of *Chatelaine* out of the grocery sack).

Now the sign hung by only two chains; the left one had broken last fall. That break explained why the sign hung slightly crooked—*and* the fact that it was now hanging slightly off kilter lent some credence to the boys' notion that the place was, indeed, haunted....

Pulling his cap over one eye, Gene handed down the ultimate ultimatum even as he kept his free eye on the swaying sign.

"Either you go up on the porch, and touch the door, or we'll start calling you 'Ginny' from now on...at *every* game—"

"Maybe his folks got him and his sister mixed up," Chad added, bouncing the thick end of his bat on the cobbles, until the sultry air rang with a muted *ponging* sound.

"You guys wouldn't do *that*," Gavin pleaded anxiously.

All of a sudden, he remembered the last time any of them had seen Old Man Dooley alive, the Halloween before last. The light under the pulled-down cloth shades had looked almost greenish, but all the plants in the house probably accounted for that. Still, it made the flickering pumpkins along the edge of the porch look...weird.

And it seemed like they'd been knocking for most of eternity before the door shuddered open with a rattle of the knob, and a *whoosh* of displaced cold air, and there before them was a huge Plant Monster, all deep rotted green and slimy and trailing limp leafy tentacles, and smelling so *bad*, like the goop in the sink after Mom let the dishwater out once she'd finished scraping the pots and pans.

It hovered over them for what seemed like forever, before it let out a phlegmy laugh, and shook off some of the dead leaves...and it was only Old Man Dooley, with his mottled pink bald spot, and store-bought orange-gummed choppers.

He gave them full-sized Crispy Crunch bars before they ran off…but Gavin had been glad that he'd worn that Darth Vader costume and not a clinging ghost sheet—otherwise, the guys might've seen how he'd wet himself. As it was, Gene kept reminding him how he'd screamed "just like a girl."

"Oh yeah…Ginny?" Gene now crossed his freckled arms, as a nasty smile slid into home plate on his face. Chad seconded the gesture—and smirk.

"If you guys are so brave, why don't you don't *you* go up there your-selves?"

"But *you're* team captain, and captains always go before their mates," Gene sneered.

"Yeah, *you're* the one who *wanted* to be captain," Chad added.

Gavin took another look up at the house, looming green like the sage in his mother's spice rack; it was sort of lonely-looking, up there on the hill, the large green-house jutting from the second story roof shone dully in the fading light, like the folded wings of a great, dead insect… but no matter how hard he tried to shake the image from his mind, Gavin couldn't forget that Plant Monster—

Yet, when he thought about the coming Little League games (and never mind the coming school year!), and being called "Ginny" by all the *guys*, maybe even the girls, too.…

Handing his mitt to Chad, Gavin stalked off without another word, up the hill. The house seemed to grow even bigger as he approached, hovering like Old Man Dooley did on that long-ago Hallow's Eve.…

Silly, he chided himself. *It's not a haunted house at all.* Still, it cer-tainly did *look* haunted.

The unkempt grass was littered with torn candy wrappers, old curled leaves, and fragments of sun-yellowed newspaper. Purposefully, Gavin waded through the debris, marched onto the porch, over the warped boards, and up to the rusted screen door which hung askew in front of the carved inner door.

The screen was snagged in spots, like when a cat gets its claws stuck and tries to drag and pull its way loose. And the brass knob felt cool and slightly greasy under his fingertips, reminding Gavin of the time Mom and Dad took them all on a holiday to Philadelphia in the States, and he'd reached over the cloth-rope barrier to touch the Liberty Bell's protruding lip.

Historical to the Americans or not, it felt *slimy*, even if the tour guide chided him for saying so at the time.

"Betcha won't go *in*," Gene continued taunting from his safe posi-tion on the edge of the lawn.

Angry at his team-mates for tricking him, and madder at himself for allowing them to up the ante, Gavin turned the knob, opened the screen, then tried the inner, more elaborately molded brass knob and—finding to his dismay that it was, indeed, unlocked—went in without a backwards glance.

He'd show them a *Ginny*....

Inside, it was warm and dry. Thick dust-kitties clung to his spikes, no matter how hard he tried to kick them off, and his shoes soon resembled fuzzy house-slippers, the kind Mom and Julie got for Christmas.

Beyond, the empty rooms echoed the least bit of noise, and the sagging-papered walls looked as if they'd been crying brown tears. To Gavin's left was a staircase, the kind with the heavily-carved banisters like the ones on the *This Old House* do-it-yourself shows, and flowered carpeting secured with greenish brass bars in the middle of the treads.

The wallpaper along the stairway was vine-covered and beginning to mold along the bottom. The hallway above wasn't much better; with each step Gavin glanced behind him to see if the Plant Monster was slinking along, ready to smear oozing green palms on his back.

That's dumb, he reassured himself. *The old guy's been dead for two years almost. Just an old coot who sold plants for a living, and gussied himself up in cotton clippings for a laugh. Even his plants must be dead by now.*

Comforting himself with that thought, Gavin almost missed seeing the tiny door tucked under the staircase leading to the third floor; unlike the other doors which openly revealed the empty rooms beyond, *this* door was open only a crack...enough to let a slice of green show.

Deep, cool, minty, *live* green—

Gavin hesitated, thinking, *It's only the wallpaper, just sun on the wallpaper*, but he still couldn't resist taking a peek inside. Just because it *was* such a bright, fresh green—

"It's not a haunted house at all, it's not a *haunted*—he kept chanting under his breath, as he pushed the door open slowly....

* * * *

A few minutes later, the old-fashioned street lamps—the kind that had been in Bannerton since the days when the Golden Horseshoe area of Ontario was freshly struck, so to speak—flickered on, casting wan golden light on the two boys who sat on the curb near the Dooley House.

Chad bounced his bat up and down on the cobbles until Gene reached out with one foot and knocked the bat out of his friend's hand.

The bat was resting across Chad's lap now, covered with Gavin's mitt. Chad didn't want to put his hand in there, not after he and Gene heard that fine, shrill sound that *must've* been a cat, but didn't quite sound like one. That had been about a quarter of an hour after Gavin actually walked into that...*place*.

The rust-flaking sign thunked against the tree, a dull, hollow *bong*, as Chad re-read the words for about the hundredth time that evening.

"Gene, what sort of plants did the old man sell?"

"You know." Those were the first syllables Gene had uttered in nearly two hours.

"No I don't. Mom only went there for plant food, and even that was only once or twice."

More silence from Gene, then, reluctantly:

"Plants, y'know. *Plants*."

"But what *kind*? Like, what were the...'Exotics'?"

"Uhm...aloe, orchids, Venus flytraps, ornamental fruit trees...*just* plants, stupid."

Gene went back to hugging his knees, chin balanced on his knee-caps.

A pause, then Chad's voice came softly, "Don't that flytrap thing eat...meat?"

Ignoring Chad, Gene interjected, "He had some hybrids, did some cross-breeding and stuff. But *none* of it could live without the heat in the house bein' on.....'cause they're 'Exotics.' Now shut your—"

"Don't it eat flies, and hamburger, and stuff like—"

"You know what? I'll bet Gavin snuck out the back way and ran home...that's what he did, went off and left us here like *saps*. Probably laughing his guts out for having us on while we sit and—"

"That *is* the plant that eats meat, *raw* meat...*isn't it Gene*—"

Moving stiffly on cramped legs, Gene got up and took off across the shadow-submerged cobbles.

"Last one home's a Chicken Lady," he shouted over his shoulder, as Chad staggered to his feet and followed, hampered by the weight of his bat and the mitt he didn't even want to touch anymore, as he shouted back in a thin, echoing voice:

"What *sort* of 'cross-breeding' did he—" but the sound was soon masked by the sharp *pings* of Gene's spiked soles hitting the cobbles.

And as his aching legs warmed to their task, Gene let fly, easily outdistancing his question-yelling friend.

For if he continued to run fast enough, maybe Chad—and his endless, unanswerable questions—might never catch up with him...for Gene didn't want to give Chad, or anyone else, reason to call him "Geena"....

And it didn't seem too likely now that Gavin would be around to hear anybody call *him* "Ginny."

AFTERWORD

About the same time as I had that hideous nightmare about the little girl whose mother as about to kill her, which eventually generated the radically diverse stories "Garbage Day in Ewerton" (which in itself helped to spawn the tangentially related stories "Trick or Treat!" and "Street Coffins" [co-written with John S. Postovit], both of which can be found in *Ewerton Death Trip*, also available from Wildside Press), "The Last Bedtime Story" and "Just Another Bedtime Story," I had another, somewhat less horrific dream about a group of young boys who were daring another boy to go into an empty old Victorian-style house—pretty standard fare, but once the boy actually went *in*, and climbed the steep staircase, he found a slightly opened door on the landing, behind which was this intense, deep-but-bright *green*, like sunlight shining through a new spring elm leaf.

I woke up before the boy opened the door all the way, so I don't know what was so green behind that door, but the whole thing was so vivid and intense I just started wondering what *was* lending the upstairs room that verdant hue.

I came up with this story first (giving it the most obvious explanation for the green), then abandoned the whole color thing and went in a couple of diverse directions, in "Double Dare Ya" and "The Holiday House." Each story had roughly the same basic plotline, albeit with a few changes in specific details, and the same general type of characters, but all three stories had radically different "haunts" behind that door.

I like all three versions, although "Double Dare Ya" (in another collection from Wildside) has perhaps the most unique "haunt" of the trio. I eventually utilized elements of "The Holiday House" into *Dark Journey* (one early draft of the novel had a revamped version of this particular tale woven into it, but I later cut it, which in some ways was a mistake, but that bridge has already burned into ashes in the river, so....)—in case you haven't read either the story or the book, I won't elaborate further here.

I suppose coming up with the "thing behind the door" is far more difficult than the tantalizing creeping horror of contemplating the door *prior* to opening it, but I do think that I did ok here, and with the other two stories.

At least this particular nightmare hasn't haunted me like the mother/daughter one has—once I wrote the three stories, it stopped bothering me, and it has pretty much faded from my memory....

JUST ANOTHER BEDTIME STORY

"…adults are only obsolete children…"

—Dr. Seuss (Theodor Geisel)

Once upon a time…

"Skeletor!"

"She-Ra!"

"Go-Bots!"

"My Little Pony!"

"*Spydor*!"

"*Shaddup! Both* of you! Melissa, Mikey, it is late, and I do not *care* whose toys are better…they all cost an arm and a leg anyway—"

"*Whose* arm? Yours or Daddy's—"

"*Melissa—can—it*!"

Helpful, Mikey held up his free can of Masters of the Universe—The Evil Horde Slime (some freebie; Victor had had to buy Mike two of those junky plastic figures to get a small can of snotty yellow-green *glop*) and asked with the innocent candor of a four-year-old:

"Can I put the can over Melissa?" as he made a lunge for his sister's summer night-gowned back.

Visions of Slime-covered Cabbage Patch Kids sheets, comforter, and bed filled Lynda's head.

"*No*! You give me that can this min—"

"*Mom*—my, my doll! Ohhh, Megan Violet!"

Lynda plucked up the Slime-coated Cabbage Patch doll between two fingers, shook off the excess goo onto the bare floor (a few chartreuse drops landed on the latch-hook Smurfette rug Vic's mom had made for them, but that could be cleaned later—she hoped), then sprinted across the hall to the bathroom, screaming over her shoulder—

"Either of you monsters get out of bed and it's no more Disney Channel for a month, you *hear*?"

As she ran cold water over the lumpy doll's yellow yarn braids, watching the Slime drop off in clumps into the sink, Lynda said to herself, "Victor, you bring Mike home any more of this crap and I'll make you *eat* it," while Melissa sing-songed from the bedroom:

"Mom-*my*, there's a fun-*ny* lit-*tle* ma-*an* lookin' in the win*der*—"

Damned kids. Too much imagination.

And at the worst times, too. It seemed like they instinctively *knew* that she wanted to do nothing more than go downstairs and curl up in front of the tube and watch *Masterpiece Theatre* on PBS.

When Vic was home they were perfect little *dah*-lings, *Yes Daddy, we brushed our teeth* and *Sure, Daddy, let's watch Mousercize* together. What a team, Daddo-and-the-kidlets, all yucking it up over *cartoons*.

But just let Vic work the evening shift, and watch out, Mommy, here come Hell's Littlest Angels.

Having washed off the overpriced and overhyped rag and plastic doll, Lynda draped it—sorry, Melissa, *Megan Violet*—over the tub faucets.

While she soaped up her hands and rinsed the last of the Slime down the drain, Mike babbled, "Mommy, the widdle man wants *in*, now."

Shaking her head, Lynda told herself, *At least Mom had enough sense to keep me from all those stupid kiddie shows and fairy-tale books when I was a kid…children come up with enough silly ideas on their own without stuffing their noggins full of "Fraggle Rock" and Nickelodeon, let alone Strawberry Shortcake and—*

"Hurry *up*, Mommy, he doesn't *like* bein' on the winder ledge—"

—the rest of that slop Victor buys for them, and watches with them… he's a prime example of a fantasy-fed child who won't grow up—

"*He's He-re*," came Melissa's parody of the little girl in those *Poltergeist* commercials.

As she crossed the hallway, pausing to take out and light up a Virginia Slims, Lynda made up her mind to call the cable company first thing in the morning and have them put a lock on all the channels except for CNN and PBS—and she was cancelling that juvenile Disney Channel and Nickelodeon, no matter how much Victor protested—

A chitter of what sounded like long nails being drawn across the window screen made Lynda run into the children's room, where she arrived just in time to see the gnarled troglodyte, who was crouching on the outside window ledge, finish pushing out the screen with his horny fingertips. It thunked lightly on the floor, bounced, and landed next to the closet door.

That accomplished he plopped down on the Snoopy rug under the window.

This isn't happening, thought Lynda, blowing the smoke out through her nose, and gagging because she hadn't done that since she was in high school, trying to look cool. *This just can't be!*

The hump-backed dwarf (he stood no higher than the two-shelf Mickey-Mouse book case) took off his grungy white stocking cap, wiped off his sweaty forehead with it, then quickly jammed it over his mottled bald head, down to the hairy tips of his pointed ears.

"Spock-ears, Spock-ears," chimed Melissa as she bounced up and down on her bed in glee.

Mikey bounced too, and chattered, "Murf, Murf! Papa Smurf!"

"Damned hod out dere," the little man wheezed, scratching at the mosquito bites (Lynda prayed that they *were* mosquito bites—but considering how filthy he looked, and how he *smelled*, she couldn't completely rule out fleas) under his burlap tunic.

Pointing a knobby forefinger at the children, he asked, "Dey twins?"

"I'm five…*he's* only *four*," piped Melissa, while Mikey cried, "Four! Four!"

"Hokay," the wizened being replied, then faced Lynda.

"Yew come up wid my nambe already, or yew jus' gonna hand her ober? C'*mon*, Lady, I yain't god all—"

"*What?*"

Unobtrusively holding her fingers over her nose—didn't Mom and Dad say to be polite to strangers, no matter how smelly they were?— Lynda shot back:

"Who *are* you? What's this bit about 'come up with your name'? And why do you want my Melissa?" (Only a minute before, Lynda would have gladly traded 'my Melissa' in for a raging case of chickenpox.)

The gremlin's wattled, warty face twisted into a *moué*; in a patient, yet clearly exasperated tone he replied, "I can't tell yew my *nambe*, 'hit's against da *rules*, Lady, don'chew rec'amember dat pardy where yew tole me whad yew'd do ta gedda dade wid dat hair-ball in da funny fur suit? Uhmm…"

From the folds of his ratty tunic, the…being pulled out a little spiral notebook with "Accounts Due" written in crabbed letters cross the front cover. Thumbing the dirty pages, the gnome quickly found what he was looking for, and squinting, he read:

"'Six years ago, da Mu Chi Phi frat pardy, one wish granded, wid paymend to be made upon—' aw Lady, don'chew rec'amember yer *promise?*"

Suddenly, Lynda *did* remember, and dropped her cigarette on the floor then pressed her hands over her face.

"Litter bug! Mommy's a litterbug!" the kids chanted.

The goblin ambled over, stomped out the butt with his thickly-callused feet—he'd only come for her kid, not to burn down her house—then walked back to the window and waited for Lynda to get over her crying jag.

Melissa and Mikey kept on bouncing up and down, giggling. This was fun!

Six years ago, she ruefully remembered, Victor's fraternity had held a Halloween party in the campus gym.

Frosh Lynda—dressed as some fairy-tale chick with a long, *long* wig (the woman at the costume shop had told her the name of the character, but it was unfamiliar and she promptly forgot it)—had had an unrequited crush on the frat president, a hirsute business major named Vic. He was the only reason she came to the party—solo—but he hadn't said "Boo!" or "Get Lost!" or *any*thing to her all evening.

As Lynda—her long yellow wig trailing mashed cigarette butts and party confetti—watched her secret love boogie with a sorority sister named Heidi who was dressed as Minnie Mouse (Vic was a rather hairy Tarzan), while she cryied into her Diet Tab, she had actually said out loud—to herself only, she had thought—

"I'd give up my first-born child just for a chance at him," and suddenly, standing next to her, was this really short person with a grimy sheet thrown over his or her head

She'd assumed it was a frat pledge walking on his knees—Vic was known to make pledges do weird stunts like that—but after she had spoken her wish, the ghost cut in to dance with Heidi-*cum*-Minnie, and Vic strolled up to her, the only girl in the gym who wasn't dancing at the time…

…and later there was Melissa, then Mikey, and Vic's promotion to manager at MacDonald's and their new house in the suburbs—

—*and now there's a stinky, grungy* creature *standing on the Snoopy rug, waiting for me to tell him his* 'nambe'!

"*Oh—my—God*!" (*Great going, Lynda,* now *you sound like that Higgins character on* Magnum PI.)

Lynda peeled her fingers away from her face, wiped her wet palms on her shorts (Mikey squealed, "Fy'in', 'fy'in', Mommy's been 'fy'in'"), and stammered:

"Wh-what d-do y-you *m-mean*, t-t-tell you y-your *name*?"

His crossed eyes widened in disbelief.

"Y'mean yew don'nd *know*? C'mon, I hadda hard nuff time *findin'* yew afta grad-e-ation, an' weddin' an ole fuzz-ball's promotions, so don'nd gimme no hard timbe, hokay? Here's da derms of da condrac'; Yew've thwee chances da guess my nambe, an' iffen yew don'nd ged id, I getcha old'es kid—"

"My name's Melissa!"

"Hokey-dokey. I getcha *Melissa*."

Now Lynda dimly remembered hearing some of the other kids in grade school discussing some fairy tale about a little man who had a funny sounding name, and did some favors and expected something in return. But little Lynda hadn't been *into* things like that, and anyway, didn't her mom tell her not to fill up on "junk reading"—the same way she told Lynda not to eat "junk food"?

—so now the little man's funny name was as much of a blank to her as the name of the woman with the long, long yellow hair…*oh why oh why didn't I keep my yap shut at that frat party? Too bad I didn't know then what an overgrown* kidlet *Victor really is….*

The tiny…being didn't look like he'd be likely to leave without his *payment*, and Lynda knew that a bargain was a bargain and that a contract was a contract…and it wasn't as if the gnome had reneged on *his* half of the deal….

Lighting a fresh cigarette, and blowing out a quick puff in a futile effort to cover up the creature's really *bad* aroma, Lynda decided that he reminded her of someone…*seven* little someone's to be exact.

While Lynda had never seen any of the Disney films her best friend Janet in the fourth grade had known all the dwarf's names by heart; there was Doc, and Happy, Bashful and Sleepy, and the little one with the jug ears, Dopey, and—*and*—

The creature "humphed" and crossed his arms, waiting for her to get on with it—*there* she had it!

"Grumpy?"

"Lady! I'm a Troll, nodda sebbenth dwarf!"

Lynda puffed deeply. Only two more guesses.

The…*troll* put his left elbow on the empty windowsill, and rested his tufted chin in his dirty cupped palm, just killing time.

Mike and Melissa shouted suggestions at her:

"Maybe he's a Fraggle, Mommy!"

"Nah, *Mikey's* a Fraggle, *that's* the Lucky Charms Lep-re-kahn!"

The troll gave Lynda a withering glare and sniffed, "*Mikey*? Aw Lady, yew didden nambe him fer dat *cereal* commershal, didchew?"

Desperate for inspiration, Lynda scanned the toys which were scattered all over the floor, the dresser tops, and in and around the bookcase—Barbie dolls with day-glo bright hair, stuffed Smurfs, a battered GloWorm, Big Bird, bristle-blocks, Mike's Master of the Universe figures, including that ugly Skeletor, He-Man, and that skunk-headed thing that smelled like a carton of rotten eggs—

"Stinkior!"

"When id's hod, I sweats, Lady, so don'nd rub id in!"

"Oh…sorry."

How do I get out of this mess? Lynda exhaled, shaking her head. *I can just hear Vic…*

"See what happens when you don't share things with the children? You've got to acknowledge the child within you, to free that child inside!"

Pearls of wisdom from a man whose company had Ronald MacDonald and a walking hamburger on the payroll.

"Lady? Yew deef? I yain't god all nide…..I god quotas ta meed, places ta visit, an' I yain't lookin' forward ta jumpin' down oudda dad winder, so…look, Lady, don'nd say nuttin' 'bout dis to nobuddy, bud I'll gibe ya a *hint*—jus' ta speed dis up, of course—my nambe stards wid an R—"

Mikey yelled, "Teddy Ruxpin the talking bear!" and Melisa took a swipe at him with her pillow.

Taking a long drag, Lynda told herself:

Typical male behavior, if you think of it…barge in, throw his weight around, then assume that I won't be able to guess his stupid name…so he's magnanimous, giving me a hint, like I needed one…Macho pig Troll, thinks he's gonna show me how invincible he is—suddenly, she *had* it.

Pointing a triumphant finger at her unwelcome creditor, she said, "*Rambo!*"

Pointing a *more* triumphant (and more crooked) finger at her, the troll said, "Wrongbo!"

Then, seeing her deflated look, added as he walked over to Melissa's bed, "Sorry, Lady, we made a deal…aw, now, don'nd *cry*, yer young, yew kin habe annuder kid—"

Mikey gleefully shouted, "Wanta baby brudder, baby brudder!" while Melissa crossed her eyes, stuck out her tongue and wiggled her fingers in her ears.

Lynda thought, *She will make a great Troll!*.

"—or gedda divorce, whadhabeyew. I kin't help id iffen yew didden know my nambe…. I thod *every* liddle kid had heard o' me."

As he spoke, he bundled Melissa up in her Cabbage Patch Kids comforter (she didn't even ask for her damned *doll*), threw her over his knobby shoulder, and carried her to the open window.

Mikey began to sniffle, "Wanna go toom, go wiff the little man, Mommy!"

Before jumping out the Troll waggled a forefinger at Lynda, saying, "See whad happened 'cuz yew didden read fairy dales an' bedtime stories an' nice Grimm's books?" in a voice uncomfortably like Victor's.

Lynda reached the window in time to see him scurry down the gravel driveway, and hear Melissa's awed: "Are you a Gnome or a Smurf?"

Lynda made a quivering noise of indignation.

They *deserved* each other. Behind her, Mikey kept saying, "Wanna go wiff the Murf!"

Mikey not only looked like Vic, Lynda realized, he even *sounded* like his father...

Suddenly, Lynda was back at the window, yelling, "Yo, Troll! Want to make it a matched set of kids?"

As the troll made tracks back to the house, Lynda quickly scribbled an address and a message on the back of her torn cigarette box, using one of the children's crayons. Carefully she safety-pinned the note to Mikey's PJs:

> Dear Troll with the R name—this is where Melissa and Mikey's Daddy works. I think he'd love to go with you too. Does this let me out of our bargain?

After getting Megan Violet out of the bathroom, she led Mikey downstairs and out the door, and waved as the Troll led the children away down the lamp-lit sidewalk, off to where Victor worked.

Now free of her over-imaginative brood, Lynda sat down and caught the last part of *Masterpiece Theatre*.

...and lived happily ever after.

AFTERWORD

While it may not read like it, this is the third story which I created after having the mother of all nightmares, about a woman sitting smoking in a rocker, while contemplating killing her little girl, as the child lay pretending to sleep in her bed nearby.

The first two, "Garbage Day in Ewerton" and "The Last Bedtime Story," were taken virtually verbatim from various parts of the dream, but this one...is something of a mental decompression.

I kept the mother, the bedroom, and the little girl, but added in a brother, *and* Rumplestiltskin.

I had a very specific reason for choosing that particular fairy tale figure; back in the late 1970's, when I was in college majoring in English, one of my professors (whom I also used as the basis for a character in *The Amulet*) was into bowdlerizing classic Grimm's and Hans Christian Andersen fairy tales (I don't know what he made of the dark, tragic fairy tales of Oscar Wilde; that author never came up in class discussions), taking out virtually all the danger, menace and lesson-learning, and substituting nicey-nice, peachy-keen drivel in their place.

When it came to Rumplestiltskin, *his* version ended with the nasty ogre being turned into a cookie, which the poor girl then ate.

A few of us in the class tried to argue that Professor Happy-Happy-Joy-Joy's ending was rather disgusting in itself, but he insisted that it was the only sort of "nice" ending children should be exposed to...

This paragon of all things sugar-coated and passive brought up the example of how he "punished" his eldest daughter (then a rather bratty preschooler)—by telling her she'd have to stay in her room "until she can smile again."

In this particular class there were a few older female students, all of them mothers, and when he uttered that last bit about "until she can smile again" his words were greeted with snorts and hoots of derisive laughter.

For the first time since I'd had that nightmare, *I* was able to smile after finishing this final version of the dream scenario—after all, to a small kid, a guy like Rumplestiltskin probably would seem like a cool playmate/caretaker....

THE LAST BEDTIME STORY

"Wants pawn term dare worsted ladle gull…"
—H. L. Chace, *Anguish Languish*

Spirals of cigarette smoke did a languid death-dance over the top of the Strawberry Shortcake lamp before dissipating in the stale air which filled Jennifer's bedroom.

Whenever Monica happened to glance her daughter's way, between paragraphs of *The Adventures of Strawberry Shortcake and Her Friends*, Jennifer would roll her pale blue eyes up toward her reddish bangs and part her lips in a noiseless sigh.

This time, Monica ignored her.

Other nights, during other story hours, they would do that old "I don't like it, Mommy"—"Did I ask you if you liked it?" two-step, but tonight….She hadn't *told* Jennifer, that would have been against the rules that Jennifer didn't know about, either; but on this night, this last bedtime story night, it just would have seemed wrong to fight with Jennifer.

Not that she wasn't tempted, no matter if this was the night that was chosen for it to happen, but giving in to her temper, especially under the circumstance, would be an act sure to haunt her more than she knew she'd be haunted….

The next time she looked up from the page she was reading—and dropping stray ashes on—Monica avoided Jennifer's white Sears canopy bed.

Instead, her eyes were drawn to the window where, on this hot July night, the combination storm/screen panel was opened a crack. The lowest automatic setting on the window was notched for a four-inch opening, but tonight only a one-inch slit was to be allowed, so Dave had propped up the window with a couple of Miller High-Life matchbooks. And he had to bend them to fit. He'd finally had to use Jennifer's new Garfield ruler, the one Monica had bought at the K-Mart for her daughter's first-grade pencil case, to make sure the opening was just right.

Not that a fraction more or less would have made any difference, but they weren't sure if they'd be checking—afterwards—to make sure that all orders had been complied with to the letter. Staring at the window, she tried to remember if she had kept the sales slip from the K-Mart. The Garfield ruler hadn't been used otherwise.

Her eyes darted back to the bed when Jennifer turned over. The suddenness of her move, coupled with the fullness of her yellow-checked nightie (wryly, Monica remembered that she had bought it in the next largest size so that Jennifer would get a couple of years wear out of it) left Jennifer tangled tightly between her Care Bears sheet and the gingham gown.

Dimly, Monica knew that she should crawl out of the white child-sized Bentwood rocker into which she was jammed, and walk the short distance to Jennifer's bed to untangle the mess of loose fabric, but she just sat there, mindlessly sticking her cigarette into her face at regular intervals, just watching the little girl struggle.

It was so hard to believe that a body so small could move independently; Jennifer resembled one of those dolls that flails its arms and legs when you pop in the Duracells and flip the hidden switch. Strange to think of such a being as a thinking, feeling, hurting person...try as she might, Monica could not remember ever being so tiny, yet so alive, when she was only six.

Not that she didn't remember her childhood. Why, she could rattle off the names of all her dolls—both store-bought and homemade—Moonbeam from the Dick Tracy comics, her favorite Chatty Cathy, Samantha from *Bewitched*, Betsy Wetsy, who wet for a week after taking a bath with her, Molly made from men's "monkey-socks," and the Alice in Wonderland doll Mom made from a mail-order kit.

And moments from first grade were also there, embedded in the soft matter of her mind like dried-up flies; how she cried when the little Chinese boy told her she looked like a pig in her new glasses, her first crush—his hair was dark brown and his name was Mike, and the Valentine's Day party when she kicked up a stink because one boy gave Valentines to only a few kids in class, and skipped her among others.

All that really important shit. But she couldn't remember how it felt, how it *was*. To be little and alive and taking life in huge, unfamiliar doses, while she got bigger and bigger until the world was old and familiar and she was starting all over again with Jennifer.

Jennifer, who seldom said more than ten words at a time to her.

True, her own childhood was still there, shriveled inside her like a forgotten seed, but the state of her adulthood impinged upon the purity of those days, those memories. She wished she could ask Jennifer, "What's it like, huh? Is it scary, or neat, or just...what? I can't get it back anymore, the way it was, the way you are, now. Can you clue me in?"

Perhaps, if things had been different between them, she could have actually done just that; not that a six-year-old would understand a semi-philosophical query, but it would have been something to say, something to share....

Not even bothering to ask Monica for help, Jennifer pulled herself out of the tight wrappings then settled down on her belly under the gaily-printed perma-press sheets.

By now, it was a given between them that Jennifer regarded Monica as someone useful under limited circumstances—opening and heating cans of Cosmic Kids in chicken sauce, breaking up the dry lumps in her glass of Quik—but otherwise, daughter thought of Mommy as part of the Daddy package deal, sort of akin to the thorns and rose deal.

It was partly her fault, Monica reminded herself, letting Dave spoil Jennifer to the point of rottenness, but Dave was the one who had hoped for a girl. At least he'd had his wish...for a while.

Unfortunately, he couldn't take the night off; it had taken him four years to become night manager, so he couldn't use up a sick day—even on this night.

Touching the end of her spent cigarette to a fresh one, she mused that maybe having to work at the 7-11 tonight was getting off easy for him. All he had had to do was weather-strip the frame around Jennifer's door, and haul up a bundle of newspapers to fold into tight strips, just in case the weather-stripping wasn't airtight enough.

A neat pile of folded paper rested outside Jennifer's room.

Dave didn't have to sit in here, choking from the smoke build-up, but unable to stop adding to the miasma, reading drivel by the hour to a child that didn't give a damn about him, waiting.

If it wasn't for the sheer numbing anticipation and helplessness of it all—it was coming, but so *slowly*—perhaps she wouldn't be so nervous.

Granted, she could have done what she usually did when Jennifer raised a stink—like she did during supper when she found out that Daddy was working tonight, pounding her plastic Mickey Mouse cup on the table, splattering the walls and part of the ceiling with gooey Strawberry Quik—which was march the offender up to bed; no goodnight kiss, no story, and no Snoopy night-light in the hallway.

But tonight—tonight should be as good as possible. Or at least as bearable as Monica could make it for Jennifer—and for herself.

"Mommy, can I ask you something'"?

This in the "I'm-buttering-her-up-for-the-kill" voice.

By accident, Monica ground out her new cigarette, swore, then lit a fresh one.

"What?" She had given up on "What, Jenny?" Or "What sorta some-thin', puddin'?"

Winding a wisp of fine red-blonde hair around a pudgy forefinger, Jennifer went on in her best nonchalant tone, "I'm not sleepy yet, but I will be if we play anudder—"

"Forget it,"

Monida had given in to Jennifer earlier that evening, but all Jennifer wanted to play was that Strawberry Shortcake video game; a morbid little musical-body-parts romp that showed the Purple Pieman hacking up Strawberry and her pastry-named cohorts into a random field of wiggling arms and legs and heads, in total defiance of human mortality or physiology. They didn't even bleed strawberry blood, for Chrissakes.

It didn't bother Jennifer. Snip, snip, hack, hack, come together and play another day.

Jennifer gave her mother a hard, cold stare; the kind of look that only a dimpled and gap-toothed little girl *can* give her mother without getting paddled with a book—hardbound, preferably—and whispered:

"You're just jealous 'cause I was winnin'," before turning over to stare at the latch-hook Smurfette rug and Paddington Bear poster on the opposite wall. Only yesterday, such a move would have left her facing another direction. The pale pink carpeting still bore four deep indentations near the window.

Reflexively, Monica raised her arm, heavy book in hand, in a wide arc that stopped short over Jennifer's hind end when reason, and an incipient guilty conscience, took over.

Dropping the book in her lap, Monica settled for a muttered "Brat-tinksi," before taking another deep puff. The moment she exhaled, Jennifer began a series of muffled, very pointed coughs. Needless to say, Her Daddy didn't smoke.

Monica ground out her Merit menthol (happy, kiddo?), threw the book down on the messy pile next to her sandaled feet then picked up the thick pamphlet from the government.

She didn't need to look at it, really; she and Dave knew its contents much too well by now. Jennifer didn't, but of course that was part of the plan, the great "humane" design. For "units of minor status age" ignorance was the name of the game, folks.

Monica could grudgingly see the wisdom in such a directive; it did make a humane, if slightly deceptive, sort of sense. Not that it making sense made it fair. Making it fair didn't include allowing the Williams' next door to substitute their black Scottie for their regulation "single unit per household" tonight.

Sure, they got permission, and sure, Dave reasoned that an old couple like Palmer and Vera Williams couldn't very well make a choice like that; after tonight the other one wouldn't be able to *cope*, and *sure*, a dog, even a little Scottie, can consume an awful lot of food in a year, maybe as much as a kid—but damn, damn, *damn*, it was *not fair*.

Angry as she was, Monica was beyond putting blame for the...situation on any one person's head, let alone any government; tonight was the fastest and fairest (?) way to correct a bad situation, but for Monica, knowing the *what*, and the *why*, and the *thus we have to*...didn't help tonight.

Even the knowledge that she wasn't alone in her waiting, that every house held someone doing more or less what she was doing right now—trying not to let on what was to happen tonight; that useless knowledge didn't make the gnaw in her guts or the shake in her fingers go away. The cigarettes helped the latter only.

Briefly, she wondered if everyone was complying. Like they had been ordered to. Probably they were; the thought of that line—"Non-participants will be severely and swiftly punished to the full extent of the law"—with its promise of utterly unknown and most likely awful justice (to the full extent of *what* law?) was somehow even more frightening than what was coming tonight.

Monica wondered if the pamphlets in other countries said the same thing.

Across from Monica, next to the slightly-opened door (an oval china plaque embellished with daisies read "jennifer's room" in a child-like script) was Jennifer's toy-box, currently covered with her dolls. My Friend Mandy, the "feather-leather" E. T., a Miss Piggy beanbag with snarled hair, plush Smurfs and Grumpy Bear stared at Monica with flat, uncomprehending plastic and paint eyes.

She was reminded of the highly-gilded and jeweled animal and human figures the Egyptians used to seal in their pyramids. The kind they found in the Boy King's tomb; the same one she and Dave drove down to Chicago to see a few years ago. She wondered then, did they do the same, all the fuss and gewgaws, for female royalty who died? Now she wished she had taken the time to look up the answer. Maybe E.T. and Grumpy Bear would do in a pinch.

They'd have to, now.

"Whatchew lookin' at, Mommy?" Jennifer was as possessive of her toys as she was of her Daddy.

"Nothing. How about if you get some shut-eye, Miss?"

Jennifer rolled over on her back, arms crossed behind her head. "Not tired."

"Who's not tired?" Monica reached for a new cigarette.

"*I'm* not tired, Mommy."

Monica ignored the petulant undertone in her answer. Jennifer, not taking her eyes off the ceiling, with its dense cover of glow-in-the-dark stars, asked "Whatchew readin', Mommy?"

"A pamphlet." Why lie about it? No harm done.

"The one that came in the mail? The 'portant one from Uncle Sam?"

Damn Dave and fucking euphemisms. Jennifer didn't even *have* any Uncle Sam, never did, never would.

"Yeah, Jennifer. The same one."

C'mon, kid, fall asleep already.

Turning over to face Monica, Jennifer wheedled, "Read it to me, please, Mommy, pretty please?"

It usually worked with Dave, that "pretty please" shit; a phrase enclosed in a pink glass box, next to the BREAK GLASS IN EMERGENCY sign....

Monica' eyes flittered across the thick black words on heavy rag paper; seeing the letters as something apart from what they spelled, gimme an E, gimme a U, a T, an H, gimme an A, an N, and an "asia"...not that Jennifer would even know what the word meant, but what with TV and all you couldn't be sure anymore.

"*Mommy...*"

Years ago, when she was still an education major at the University, the Education 421 instructor had handed the class a mimeographed story that began, "Wants pawn term dare worsted ladle gull hoe..." which turned out, after they had taken turns reading out loud, "Little Red Riding Hood," in Anguish Languish.

Monica had kept the sheet along with all her college papers; she had been saving it for Jennifer to read when she reached the fifth or sixth grade. But the story was down in the basement, in the big cardboard box from toilet paper that contained Monica's college education neatly stacked in labeled manila envelopes.

And it was nearly Time anyway.

Besides, Jennifer didn't want to hear about "Ladle Rat Rotten Hut," she was whining for the pamphlet.

Monica stared at the stiff paper in her hands. She hadn't been that good at decoding that fairy tale, but she had grasped the general idea... haltingly, she began to read the last bedtime story, a mixed-up tale about a couple of guys named Vol and Terry and a youth in Asia. It didn't make a lot of sense.

Soon, Jennifer was nodding off for real.

Monica stopped mouthing the nonsense words, leaving the fate of the youth in Asia in serious doubt, when she heard a low rumble, not unlike a street cleaner without the whooshing of the water brushes.

Gingerly, she wormed her way out of the tiny rocker and went quietly to the window.

Pushing aside the limp pink curtains, she watched the huge blocky truck with the long ridged rubber arms—nearly two dozen of them blindly waving in the warm night air—make its way down the center line of the street.

Moth-like, it shuddered slightly, then stopped, still and quiet.

Each of the arms, enough for every house on both sides of the block, was shaped something like the extension arm on a vacuum cleaner. The long, narrowly rectangular "mouths" were equipped with sharp silvery gripper teeth, and again she was reminded of the cleaner head that came with the Hoover, only hers had rows of stiff black bristles around the opening.

She knew for certain that the "mouths" would precisely fit an opening an inch wide by twenty inches long. The pamphlet had said so, but it didn't show any pictures.

And it didn't mention the teeth, either. (The better to grip you with, my dear, said the Big Bad…)

Suddenly she was glad that Dave had insisted on moving Jennifer's bed away from the window. She had argued at the time that once it came to the window, nothing would matter anymore, but he was right; knowing that it's coming is one thing, but having to see it come for you is yet another.

The rubbery arms had picked up the signal emitted by the small round metal disks that were hung on the outside sills of the designated windows. The disks were free at Hardware Hank's and the TruValue stores. Having to pay for them would have been adding insult to…something a bit more than injury.

The Williamses had hung theirs by the Scottie's doghouse door, which wasn't there last week, but which did bear a one inch wide slit along one side.

Not much time left.

Now that the wait was almost over, Monica wished that it was five o'clock again, and that she and Dave and Jennifer were back at the dinner table, eating Jennifer's chosen menu of Chef Boy-ar-Dee Ravioli, dry Cap'n Crunch and Strawberry Quik.

And Jennifer could splash the whole house with Quik if she wanted to.

Monica pulled the curtains closed, not that it mattered, or made any difference. Gas could permeate even the heaviest cloth, and Jennifer's curtains were pink dotted Swiss, so sheer you could almost see through them.

Perfunctorily, she bent over Jennifer and made a smacking noise near her left ear. Monica was never much good at goodbyes. She looked at Jennifer, then at the guard toys who watched the scene impartially.

Take good care of her, she mouthed silently. Monica could hear the sharp, chitinous *click!* of metal touching metal not far off, and she knew that she had only seconds to get out, shut the door, and start stuffing newspapers into the places the weather-stripping didn't block off.

Monica took a last look at Jennifer, who abruptly opened her eyes and asked in a matter of fact, oddly neutral tone:

"Will I be dead for a long time, Mommy?"

"Just a while, Jenny," then Monica was on the other side of the door.

When she felt her heartbeats slow down to a semi-normal rate, Monica noticed the hardness in her left palm. Opening her clenched hand, she saw the sticky-backed china plaque.

She didn't remember grabbing it.

Not even noticing the close-by metallic *click*, Monica rummaged in her smock pocket for the fine-line marker she usually carried there. Changing the lower-case R to a T with two strokes of the pen, she considered crossing out the extra O and adding a B, but she left it alone.

Sticking the plaque squarely in the center of the upper panel, she thought, *that's how Jennifer might have spelled it*.

Then she began stuffing the folded strips of paper into the cracks around the door.

AFTERWORD

This story (as well as "Just Another Bedtime Story") was inspired by the same nightmare as the one which produced "Garbage Day in Ewerton" which appeared in *Ewerton Death Trip* (and originally, *Night Cry* magazine)—the images of that nightmare were (and still are) so vivid, I could not get them out of my head for months afterward, not until I originally wrote this version, then wrote "Garbage Day..." and finally, as the horribleness of the dream scenario began to ease up somewhat, the much more benign "Just Another...", which was also published in *NC*. This version appeared in *Grue Magazine*, and Peggy Nadramia liked it better than "Garbage Day..."—so do I, even though I pretty much like all three versions of the general plotline.

Back when I was in college, and still on the Education track (I had to drop out of a degree in Secondary Education due to my advisor deciding I wouldn't be a good teacher), one of my classes had a section on "Anguish Languish" which I eventually worked into this piece.

This time around, I tried to come up with an outside reason why the couple was killing their own child—having the State make one do it somewhat spreads the guilt around, but either way, be it a couple killing their child for economic reasons ("Garbage Day...") or for political reasons (this version), a life *is* lost.

By the time I wrote "Just Another..." I was starting to work my way through the shock and horror of that dream, and was able to go from death to mere physical loss of the child, albeit a still living child. But it was still a terrible, terrible thing to see in a nightmare....

POEMS

WHAT THE JANITOR FOUND

Blue flutters of skirt

> (pleated roundness against
> bare thighs, pushing outward)

at the swinging Women
door, a chitter of laughter,

> (a buzzing shrill, too high, and much
> too forced the janitor thinks, politely
> backing away, soggy grey-haired mop
> in hand)

down echoing halls the rumble of cheerleader feet

> (five pairs of blue and white, special-
> order-from-the-athletic-uniform-catalog
> saddle shoes, ten calves surrounded in
> woolen blue scissoring away from him)

grows softer, dimmer

> (they didn't look my way…where
> was the chirp "Hiyah, Slim!" what hap-
> pened to "See ya later?")
> cut off with the pneumatic swish of
> blonde oak door behind him.

(Ten white basins surmounted with ten oblong
mirrors, faced with ten stalls, enameled cherry
tomato red tampon and napkin dispensers facing the
swinging door. Skin-textured, tile floor, broken
into tiny rectangles and squares in pink, cream,
scarlet, and sand.)

His metal bucket on the wheeled platform, rags, toilet brush
and plunger, bottles of gritty cleaner and sharp-smelling
spray are alien,

> (harsh IUDs thrust into
> this womb of feminine
> pinkness)

unnatural, but an indignity to be only briefly endured.
Down the row, a toilet continues to fill, a burbling rush of water
(Janitor Muzak, he thinks,
uncapping the cleaner)

masking out the footfalls outside the closed door.
(no one will be entering;
the huge wheeled
Dumpster outside the
door is a mute indicator
of his intrusion.)

Splatter each bowl with a spray of blue-green cleanser, wipe,
move on, squirt, wipe, step over, splatter, gone, go on
(the water keeps bubbling,
like some damned
tourist-trap coin fountain,
endlessly—)

down the row, pause, check the white wall-hung
(sounds like something's
stuck, she probably tried
to flush a used napkin—)

machines, make sure they're reasonably full
(would the blood drip down their legs if it was empty, red
twisting ribbons like that biology chart upstairs, the...the
DNA spiral. Would it do that if the machine was empty...)
then enter the

last stall by the wall, prop the door open with the wooden
wedge taken from his overall pocket
(still running, gonna have
to plunge 'er out—)

then begin the second ritual: lift the seat, clean the bowl,
wash and rinse the seat, flush down the murky tendrils of
cleanser, remove the wedge, to the next stall,
(hasn't stopped yet, sounds
like a few stalls away—)

lift, swab, wash, rinse, flush, remove...begin and end over
again and—
(no wonder they didn't stop to talk—)

—encounter a little interruption in the routine.

> (Wedged down there, under a feathery
> caul of white biodegradable paper, in
> the place where the throat of the
> hole recedes from one's line of
> vision; packed tight, legs and body
> and one arm stuck, head and other
> arm waving out at him, moving
> languidly in a silent hello.)

Hands wrapped around the splintery handle of the scrub brush,
he stands, unable to return the small one's mute gesture

> (did the blood run down
> her legs, did she catch it
> with a wad of toilet
> paper before it stained
> those high stockings, did
> it have a chance to cry
> out before taking that
> short dive?)

no longer hearing the watery song of the tank,

> (did she look in there
> after getting off the seat,
> did her friends buy her
> a napkin or tampon to
> stop the flow, did she
> press it up *there*, and
> walk tight-legged out of
> the stall, even as it
> floated there?)

enraptured with that miniature ballet of water bubbles and
baby, watching its miniscule hand (nails, it has nails on the
fingers) slowly gesticulate down there, brushing delicately
against the rounded whiteness of the bowl.

> (did she think it would
> slip down, did she flush
> and flush until most of it
> was gone, and cover up
> the rest with a layer of
> tissue, did she and the
> others think no one

The head was a marbled sphere of greyish mottled pink, shut eyes
feathery slits in the crumpled face, the nose wide and flattened
under the feeble pressure of the water, and the wet shreds of
paper clung to it; now a tender scarf, now a semi-opaque veil

> (didn't she care, did she
> think it was a bowel
> movement, from the
> wrong hole, did she
> hope it would slide
> down one hole into
> another...did she
> hurt, down there?)

teasing across the wrinkled skin.
(None of them had been walking funny, but God, it's so
small, probably not much of her was torn—)
He makes a move for the door:

> Get the dean, call the police, round
> up the girls, get the school nurse,
> then come the reporters, questioning
> at the police station, having to take
> time off work for the trial (think of
> the taxpayers footing the bill for the
> trial, think of you paying more
> taxes, Slim ole boy) the testimony,
> the lowered eyes of the girl, the eyes
> of hate from her family, the kids in
> the stands, then coming back, to
> work with *them* ("*Snitch*" sniggered
> behind me, in the halls), to look at
> them and wonder, "Were there
> others, were they flushed all the way
> down while I was gone, or while I
> *was* here? Were they stuffed in
> greasy printed bags from the
> hamburger joints, next to the cups
> from malted and the last
> catsup-soggy fry? In twist-tied white
> sacks from the dorms, casually tossed
> in the back Dumpster? Flung loose
> into the gully behind the sports

center building? Encased in pillow cases, to be thrown out of a dorm window into the river that winds behind the students' rooms? Where *were* all the others hidden?"

(you didn't hurt much, baby, she didn't hit you, cuss you, blame you for her not getting a good guy to marry, she didn't get loaded on beer then give you a malty teat to suck, she didn't keep you alive, so she could go on WIC and then eat up all the food herself, or collect welfare, or the food stamps…so she didn't treat you so bad, little wet baby, dead baby?)

Bowing his head, for a moment (did she or the others do so much for it, he wonders), then, with resigned yet firm steps he walks over to his wheeled cart, where the red-capped

(like the diaphragm she was too busy to use)

plunger is and sends the baby back home to watery familiar closeness and safety.

* * * *

Later, out in the hall, feeling through the Dumpsters, and the bags within them, the cheerleaders pass him by in a swirl of pleated blue and clean white and blue legs, saying hello, not hearing the dread sirens, chattering aimlessly behind him. (He almost forgets to say hello, so intent is he upon his search.)

Looking up, he inspects bare legs for a tight gait, remembering the tiny wave.

AFTERWORD

I actually wrote this before a spate of babies-left-in-toilets/outhouses/port-a-potty cases in the Midwest in the mid-1980's; when all these babies were left for dead or actually died, I felt sick about it, as if my poem had somehow caused what happened.

I doubt the ladies who dumped their newborns had read my poem... but I'll never know for sure, will I?

Nor will I stop feeling a trace of guilt over having written and published this. Something I thought was too creepy to be real ended up being replicated in real life...not pleasant.

MOTHRASAURUS

I.

They watch her.
(From under beds, tops of pillows, silky surfaces of china mugs,
they watch her)
Elongated necks, ridge of bone, walnut-small brains, backing
the
tiny eyes that flatly observe
        (coiling, buried, the old thoughts of green
        and steaming earth and air, now overlaid
        with dusty nap of rug, mists of Glade and
        Arm and Hammer)
the woman; watch her bend and crawl after them, grabbing and
placing them among their fellow watchers…
…on shelves and in the toy-boxes of her running young.

II.

She cannot escape them.
(Puzzles on the floor, flash-cards in the children's hands, resting
under lunch plates and silverware, hiding in oval soap)
Day-glo colors, plush fur skin, pencil-sharpener mouths,
"Three-horned face" logo on her children's shirts
        (they inundate their letters to Santa, their
        rubbery bodies line the bathtub floor, and
        still they come, invading cereal box covers)
all dinosaurs; see the children follow their outlines in cut-
paper stencils, color them in with Brontosaurus yellow markers…
…while the Stegosaurus and Protoceratops eye the Mother.

III.

Ankylosaurus, Allosaurus
       (once, the living rooms and dinettes were their jungles,
their places of green leaves and water for sucking, swallowing)
      Tyrannosaurus, Triceratops
       (yesterday, they pounded the earth with their large steps,
and the air around them was clear-pure and green-smelling)
      Pterosaurus, Pterodactyl
       (not so very long ago, they ruled, a minute ago in the
cosmic
    clock of hours…and for the old, a minute is short)

IV.

Partyware, Placemats
       (only a year ago the children clamored for vegetable
name
    dolls and remote-control cars they saw dance and spin on the idiot
box)
      Tee-shirts, Tape measures
       (then came the first of them, innocent enough, *some-
thing to*
    teach them, she thought, *something of the past that* interests *them*)
      Corkboards, Coloring books
       (until the day came when the children's every other
word ended
    in "saurus" and they played brutal dinosaur games, as they roared)

V.

Their time is returning.
(In every home of every child, they sit, becoming part of the fiber
of their existence, filtering into consciousness)
    They attend the meals, bob about in the bathwater, support
pieces
    of birthday cake, come to life with the joining of jigsaw fragments
       (today immobile, too strange to move yet,
       yet with repeated familiarity comes freedom,
       acceptance…from the running young)
    bearing their imprint, with the remembering of their past comes
new life, new chances for dominance…
…in the world of the cornered woman.

VI.

She has realized their plan.
(The Old Ones will return, or so Lovecraft hinted, speaking of things
big, huge and malevolent, things that *wait*)
    their names twist and writhe, Protoceratops and Dimetrodon, yet
flow smoothly off the tongues of the young
                (the children worship them, pay lip service
                with each opening of the cereal box, each turn
                of the dinosaur skeleton's key...and she's
                seen their eyes shift)
    dinosaur slaves; the children clamor for the ancients, ignore
the new and living to immerse themselves in the bony dead...
...who watch the woman with baleful flat-paint eyes.

VII.

December the eighth started out as a normal day
    (fix breakfast, pack lunches in
    Brontosaurus bags, cover little
            Triceratops tee-shirts with coats,
            mufflers)
    until the mother found the puddle of wetness on the
children's sheets...the pool of moistness, green and scummy
    with the live Trilobite crawling on the wet polyester—
            ("terrible lizard," that's what the
            children said the word "dinosaur"
            meant)
—next to the single shed scale.

AFTERWORD

One morning, I saw one of those little Tylenol-shaped dun-colored
bugs crawling on a sheet on my mother's bed, and this poem just popped
into my head, of a piece. Plus dinosaurs were just huge for kids at the
time, including the dreaded B*a*r*n*e*y. Gee, am I ever glad I never
had kids!!

SOME MAY WONDER

look so peaceful when they're dead...
...too bad, didn't think of it sooner—

Five coffins,
> (*tiny sprays, ribbons gold-lettered "BABY" and those*
> *sweet little cards, name and dates embossed in gold*)
> sometimes one a year; if she's lucky.
> Mother cries another tear; some may wonder...

She would neither confirm nor deny,
only mutter, "They look so peaceful when they die."

Five little funerals,
> (*the florists, they send out such* cute *little*
> *bud vases, don't they look pretty on the sill?*)
> the papers continue to hint; they *know*, but *don't*.
> Darting eyes hidden by sunglasses tint; *did* she?

She would not look the officer in the eye,
only stutter, "Bu-but they're just so *peaceful* when they die..."

In memory of Lorlei and Heather Sims

AFTERWORD

The Sims babies, Lorlei and Heather, were killed by their mother because they were girl babies, and her husband only wanted boys—the case can be easily Googled—I just hate to give their scumbag parents any more wordage in this collection. Suffice it to say, I cannot understand why they didn't pursue other options for those two beautiful little girls....

JUST HERSELF

First she was Joe and Helen's baby girl
Then she was their daughter, when they gave her in marriage
Next she was Donald's wife
Then, the mother of little Katie…
…and later, Kirk's mother-in-law
Proud grandmother of Ashley;
When Donald died, she became *his* widow,
As old age withered her, she whispered, "now, *now* to
Just be myself—"
Just before her heart gave out,
And she became the worm's next meal.

AFTERWORD

Ever since I was small, school-age, my mother constantly griped about me getting more "attention" than she did when she was a child, and her complaints have continued throughout the years. Back when I was in college (and lived at home, which my professors kept telling me was a huge mistake, since my mother was showing up at literally every event there, and not endearing herself to either the teachers or my fellow students), she was unofficially known as my mother, not—as she liked to point out constantly—as just *her*, without my name being linked with hers. Many years later, when depression made me seek out a therapist for a while, she suggested that my mother was jealous of me—although I cannot understand how anyone who professes to loathe someone can also be jealous of them. I don't know what else to say about this, aside from the fact that a person being linked to another person isn't the worst thing on earth, even though some folks may see it that way….

UNTITLED

1/24/89

Ted Bundy's defunct who used to drive a metallic brown Volkswagon
and used to kill girls onetwotenfifteentwenty-six
just like that
lord, he thought he was a clever, handsome man
and what I'd like to know is
how do you like your blue-eyed boy, Mr. Florida Electric?

(with apologies to e. e. cummings)

AFTERWORD

One of my favorite poets is e. e. Cummings, even as one of the people I loathed the most was Ted Bundy…and when I first read cummings'
poem about Buffalo Bill, I immediately came up with this pastiche
concerning Bundy. Just one of those things I felt compelled to write; I
didn't mean any offense to the victims, should anyone think I was being too flippant when mimicking cummings' original work. I was just
so glad that the State of Florida finally executed that self-aggrandizing
bastard….

WILLIAM GENESIS WILLIAMS

Later, God had this to say:

I threw out
the people
who used to live
In the Garden

the man who looked
a little
like pre-middle
age Me

plus the other
one I made out
of the extra rib
the man didn't need

(Forgive Me
I lost count when
I was putting
them in his chest)

AFTERWORD

Who doesn't like William Carlos Williams' "This Is Just to Say" (besides my mother, that is)? And I know I'm not the only writer to do a parody of it...the poem is just so simple, yet so perfect, that riffing on it is irresistible. I just thought it was such a neat reworking of the poet's original tale of plum-theft, I had to put it down on paper.

This is perhaps my favorite poem-parody....

THE WAR POEMS

THEY USED TO PUT THE GOLD STAR IN THE LIVING ROOM WINDOW

Tick-tock soldier battalions
Mainspring mayhem…
When all…run down
Will the robot assembly line mourn?

DEATH OF THE STAR
FIGHTER GUNNER

From my syntho-womb I drifted into hyperspace
And nestled in its bowels nursed by an air hose
Sixty light years from Earth torn from its distant dream
To awake to a silent explosion from the nightmare vessels
When I died they jettisoned me watching as each fragment froze.

based on "The Death of the Ball Turret Gunner"
by Randall Jarrett, 1945

RUMINATIONS ON THE PHOTO OF THE LAST U.S. G.I. KILLED IN WWII GERMANY, TAKEN BY ROBERT CAPA, AN EARLY CASUALTY OF THE INDO-CHINA WAR

Lifted, pulled back, the silver ball on a wire falls forward,
momentum-driven, to hit the next silver—

—circle and scroll pattern on the balcony before him, and the distant bare tree beyond, are the last thing he sees; then the endless sky of plaster above, as the soldier falls backwards, arms, legs splayed, as Capa leans forward, with a short, sharp *click-whirrr* of his camera

(*robbed of the deadly force of multiplicity, the final raindrop*
in a hurricane still rolls, wetly, slowly, a tear on the face
of the wind-ravaged land)

and suddenly the final death on the German front is private no more, remembered in image if not in name; an isolated, magnified raindrop in a torrent, before the skies clear and the ground dries, and the photographer moves on, toward the next distant cloudburst
(*innocent, the first splash of the deluge rolls, a tear of joy*
down a new mother's cheek, sliding down the curve of her face)

only this time, Capa is the one to take a step blindly forward, into the lifting burst of a tripped mine, to join the eternal—

—*circle, propelled by momentum, moves free of its fellows*
arcing skyward, propelled by force of past action.

WAR CAKE

Death used to move me.
      When it was small
and involved situations
I could fit into.
      Like death coming right
After the
      dead-to-be has just bought
Christmas gifts for the family
that s/he won't see them open.
      Or like a long
time ago, when I was a kid,
and I saw some Shirley Temple movie
      (doesn't matter which
one, all the plots were the same;
Shirley goes through hell, comes
shining through, sings a song, roll
credits)
in which her mother bought her
a birthday cake with an airplane on it
      only, as she was crossing
the street, a car
      (naturally immune to the
pathos of upcoming birthdays and cakes
with propeller-tipped airplanes on top)
      hit her.
She died, and the cake ended up as a
plane wreck of smeared crumbs, which
the camera focused on
      because this was, after all
A Shirley Temple film, and not a John Ford
epic.

But being a kid, I cried a
little for the lady,
    and a lot more for the cake.

II.

When I was older, the Vietnam non-war was
going on.
    The evening news usually started
out with a big chart showing how many of
    "them"
were killed in the name of peace,
    and how many of
    "our boys"
were *slaughtered* while performing
necessary acts of defoliation.
I tried to picture all those
    dead G.I.'s laying on the
ground they'd killed with napalm
and Agent Orange,
tried to picture how all that G.I.
    blood was fertilizing the fields.
I *knew* I was supposed to
    cry in my mashed
potatoes.
    but being killed in the act of
poisoning land that didn't know squat
about Commies or democracy,
    land that just knew the touch of
the plow or the rain, or in the act of
killing the people of the country for their
own sake
    and for their own good
didn't make me feel sad,
    if it was supposed to do that.
All I could do
    was cry about
the lady and the shattered cake.

III.

The war of my grown-up years

was a sound-byte wrapped in
ribbons of yellow plastic
tied to light poles with rope or wire
        or pieces of that curly
Christmas ribbon that comes on a huge
cardboard tube.
        No bodies, no blood,
not even the smear of birthday cake frosting
on oil-sheened sand.
        And in the void between the
bombing and the body-bags,
I couldn't help but wonder:
        Just what flavor
was little Shirley's cake?

AFTERWORDS FOR
THE WAR POEMS

"They Used to Put the Gold Star in the Living Room Window":

This poem was written to accompany an illustration I did for an issue of the late Janet Fox's wonderful little market guide *Scavenger's Newsletter*, which also featured artwork, poems and short-short stories from her subscribers; the picture was a collage of found art which I clipped together and photocopied, showing a soldier figure made of pieces like a rolled up tape measure, machine parts and other assorted items. At the time, *"Scav"* (as Janet and her readers dubbed it) was a long, thin folded mailing, although later on, the publication was shaped like a small, squat magazine with a center fold, so my illo was sharply rectangular. The poem itself was printed on the flip side of the folded newsletter, near the subscriber's address. Taken together, the poem and illo were a bit more striking than the poem printed by itself; the poem was later reprinted in Issue 29 of *Eldritch Tales*.

"Death of the Star Fighter Gunner"

Randall Jarrell's poem "The Death of the Ball Turret Gunner" has always been one of my favorite poems; I just felt the need to update and re-imagine it for a future time of war....

"Ruminations on the Photo of the Last U.S. G.I. Killed in WWII Germany, Taken by Robert Capa, an Early Casualty of the Indo-China War"

I saw the photo in question on some PBS special about Capa, and was struck by the starkness and ironic ornateness of the background, with that circle and scroll patterned balcony railing, and the fine lacy filigree of the bare trees in the distance, contrasting with the inelegantly splayed dead soldier in the foreground. Then, when I heard of the circumstances of Capa's death, I just had to write this, if only to attempt to make some sense out of the senselessness of war in general.

This poem was published in one of those poetry anthologies which used to be advertised in the backs of Sunday supplement magazines, the kind which published virtually all the stuff sent to them, and offered the lucky writer the chance to buy a copy of the finished antho for a rather huge fee…the only reason I sent it in was because at the time, I was working for Writer's Digest School (one of those mail-in courses), and a few of my students had seen those ads for the poetry anthos, and wanted to know if 1) they'd consider even new writers, and 2) if they actually had to buy the book in order to be published in it. I didn't know myself, so I sent in a poem as a test case, to see what would happen. It was accepted, and I didn't have to buy the book it would be published in, so I could tell my students what was what with the publishers. A couple of them did submit poems, and were accepted, but they also bought the books, because they wanted to, not because they were required to do so. I don't even know for sure what the title of the book this poem was published in *was*; all I wrote down in my little book of published material was "Best Poems" so aside from it being published in 1994 or so, I don't know anything else about this work's original publication. I didn't buy the book, needless to say….

"War Cake"

This one's a strange work; it was eventually published in a small press 'zine which only lasted a few issues before folding, but I still like it for its starkness and cultural reference tie-ins.

I was one of those kids who was basically raised in front of the TV, thanks to my mother not wanting me to be outside in the apartment house courtyard, least I get kidnapped or worse by one of the admittedly sleazy fellow denizens of the apartment house complex (first in Inglewood, then in Hawthorne, both outlying areas of Los Angeles proper; the two apartment houses we lived in were virtually interchangeable). I was raised under very limited financial and social circumstances, in that my entire universe was my mother, her mother, and our television set, in the years prior to my going off to school, and even during that time, too, since I wasn't allowed to go anywhere alone before or after school, or during all of my summer vacations.

The TV was my only real friend, even if it sometimes showed me things which I found disturbing, like that Shirley Temple film with the mother and the birthday cake getting hit by a car (I have no idea what the name of the film was; now I can't stomach any of little Shirley's films, so I have no intention of catching them on DVD today!), or the footage from the Vietnam (non)War.

As an adult, I found the first Gulf War puzzling and disturbing in that it seemed like a night-vision version of Pong, all flying white bombs over a greenish sky/landscape. I didn't realize just how awful the war really had been until I saw the movie *Three Kings*, and even then, realized that the film only touched on the highlights of that hidden-but-horrible war. The lack of TV coverage worked against the soldiers, and worked against the veterans of that war, in that it made what they went through somewhat less real, less visceral than the actual reality of their day-to-day situation.

As gory as they may be, at least the videos taken by our soldiers give the current (and seemingly unending) Iraq and Afghan Wars a sense of reality, of horrible immediacy which, perhaps, is necessary for people *not* fighting the war to realize just how awful that war—or any war, anywhere—is.

And yes, I do think that viewers should see all the flag-draped caskets coming home—if not to understand the consequences of war, then to, at the very least, honor those people lying within said caskets.

Their deaths—whether or not one agrees with the validity or necessity of this or any other war—need acknowledgment.

HODGE PODGE

THE OTHER EASIER WAY

The heifer delicately munched the bouquet of clover flowers LouAnne offered it, until Mr. Clapp shouted, "*Miss* Bennet, would you be so *kind* as to join the rest of the class?"

Trailing the clover bouquet behind her like a pep rally pom-pom, LouAnne sighed (*mainly* for Steve Van Pool's benefit; but also because Ag 102 was a *pain*) as she rejoined her classmates, who stood next to the opened barn door.

With a moist swish of her manure-clotted tail, the roan heifer followed the dangling blossoms in LouAnne's hand.

The top of Mr. Clapp's grey-fringed bald head was almost as red as the barn behind him. When LouAnne positioned herself near the rest of the Ag 102 students, Mr. Clapp mouthed, I'll see *you* back at the school. LouAnne rested her head on Steve's shoulder and shrugged a cheerleader's shrug, shoulders up then down, in Go, Team *Go!* rhythm.

Mr. Clapp's head turned magenta.

Inside the barn, Mr. Ventura (the farmer who'd invited the class to witness the demonstration of high-tech cow insemination) held up a silvery doo-dad shaped like a large elongated antihistamine capsule. Pushing his John Deere cap off his freckled forehead, Ventura explained:

"See, kids, I put this in the cow—it contains a tiny radio transmitter and—"

"Does it get in WBIZ?" Steve Van Pool asked.

LouAnne giggled, and a white streak capped the magenta of Mr. Clapp's bald dome, as the heifer continued to chomp on LouAnne's clover pom-pom.

"Nah, son, them little dials keep falling off."

Ventura had had Steve's big brother, Brian out to his farm two years ago, and in the meantime, Ventura'd found out that WBIZ *was* a radio station after all. (Rock and *roll*, but it *did* take all kinds…)

Placing the transmitter next to the cow's exposed vulva, he continued, "After I insert this, I monitor the radio transmissions every twenty minutes. What I'm looking for is the frequency of electrical charges—" he indicated the dial-mounted box near the stall with a manure-stained thumb "—which increases when the cow is actually pregnant—"

"Whatsamatter, they don't make dipstick tests in giant economy size?"

Ventura sighed; Brian Van Pool hadn't been as mouthy or just plain dumb.

"Mr. Van Pool, after class we will talk." Mr. Clapp's smooth scalp now resembled the hide of a Red Polled bull.

"—after which I take a blood test, just to make sure the insemination took—"

"—know an easier way to do it." Ventura waited for Steve's punchline; he hadn't forgotten it from the time when Brian told the joke.

"—let the bull in!"

"*Steven*, I am *warning* you—"

But the rest of the class still acted as if they'd never heard the joke before. That part *always* surprised Farmer Ventura.

"Actually, the advantage of artificial insemination is that we can check very quickly whether or not the implantation has taken—"

"You mean sometimes the insemination *doesn't* take?" asked a short boy in a worn FFA jacket. Ventura could've kissed the kid.

"Nope, you'd think it would, but sometimes it don't, just like with… uhm, people—"

"Hey, I'm a 'people' and it'd *never* work on *me*—"

"*Steven, shut up!*"

LouAnne giggled, again.

Nonplussed, Ventura persisted, "When an insemination doesn't work, for whatever reason, we have to wait and try again when the cow is fresh—"

"Hey, what do you get if the insemination don't work, but the cow still gets—"

"*I-am*-WARNING-*you-Steven*—"

"—*Holy* Cow!—"

"*Eeeyouch!*"

Everyone turned to watch LouAnne jump up and down (Rah! Rah!) as she sucked her thumb.

The heifer, having discovered that cheerleader thumbs were much less tasty than clover heads, wandered off.

"*That is it*! LouAnne, Steven, *both* of you! My office! *After* school!"

Bending down, Mr. Clapp scooped up the last of the fallen clover and threw it so hard and so fast it landed in the middle of the pond behind him.

Ventura tried to finish the demonstration, but LouAnne kept boo-booing while the boys chanted, "Bull in, let the bull in!"

As Mr. Clapp screamed "Eff's, all of you! *Hear*? Big, fat, Eff's!" and Steve mooed in reply, the heifer clopped away from the noise, shaking her fly-encircled head.

Seeing the remains of the clover bobbing on the quiet waters of the pond, she trotted over to investigate, as Steve protested, "But what if the cow *was* pre—"

And far below, small fish circled and darted, oblivious to the calf feeding directly above them, the water just *barely* rippling under her damp hooves.

AFTERWORD

Yup, this is a "Holy Cow" story. Nothing more, nothing less, but it was one of those feels-good-to-get-it-down stories, and for that, I have a soft spot for it. In some ways, it parallels Fredric Brown's "J.C." short-short; I do know I read Brown's story before writing this.

The mouthy kid named Steve (whose older brother Brian was equally smart-alecky) was based on a kid (and his older brother) in my high school class—he was probably one of the most street-smart kids around, and far more astute and observant than most kids his age, although he did have a wicked side.

He came up with a fourth hand position for rock-scissors-paper, the pencil, which could write on paper...and utilized the middle finger of one's hand, as well as an origami/bad ethnic joke mash-up called "Polish toilet paper" which was the sort of thing Archie Bunker would've *loved*.

And once, when one of those traveling science-type exhibits-in-a-trailer stopped by the school, with some dioramas about sewer and waste management, and water reclamation, he got into a snarky argument about how "well" the local sewer plant kept the smell down—he told the woman running the exhibit that his neighborhood (which was close to the plant) smelled so bad come summer that if a house happened to go up for sale, the Realtors could only show the house in the winter, when the smell wasn't so terrible.

Plus he kept calling the sewage treatment plant "the seewie" which drove the poor woman crazy.

As prickly as this guy could be, he and I actually worked together on the high school paper (along with another guy); as part of the paper-writing-class, everyone was supposed to come up with a sports feature, a news article, plus a for-fun feature, all of which were later read by the entire class, and judged blindly (as in the teacher cut off the names after grading them), then selected for inclusion in that week's paper.

And since I had virtually no interest in sports whatsoever, doing those articles sucked for me, but my two writing partners helped me out by supplying me with stats for all the games which they attended. I never had a sports article make it into the paper, but at least I was able to get grades for what I did write.

Ironically, I never have co-written anything with women; even then, in high school, I was able to work better with the guys when it came to writing....

[*Editor's note:* Mary Wickizer Burgess and Ms. Morlan have since completed *Grave Waters*, a mystery novel, which certainly counts as a collaboration!]

THE MOGUL

Not so terribly long ago, in an Eastern metropolis, a mighty mogul ruled many blocks of that soot-stained, tall-walled urban nightmare which millions of much, much poorer people called home. But this man's home was high up in the tallest of the many tall buildings he owned, so high in fact that he never had to venture from its heights to the grimy, newspaper-littered streets below.

This mogul's entire adult life had been spent in tall buildings very similar to the one he lived in. From those barely-remembered days when he, too, toiled (or so it was rumored, for no one alive in the shadowy megalopolis could actually remember the mogul's early years—so ingrained was his powerful *façade* in the minds of the masses) in the mazes of fabric-walled cubicles in front of green-glowing monitors, to his current reign as the most powerful mogul in all of the country, this mogul's entire existence had been devoted to two omnipotent gods—Money and Power.

Once he'd amassed enough of the former, he instantly achieved the latter.

But the mogul's gods were most needy, most hungry for sacrifice in their mighty Names—and so the mogul's life was soon consumed by the quest for more and more Money, in order to fuel his grip on Power.

And so while the many factories (most located in Third World countries whose labor force would've been leaving teeth under their pillows for the Tooth Fairy, if they'd had either pillows or a belief in that dental deity) owned by the mogul churned out products which were coveted and bought by millions of people, thus bringing piles and piles of Money into the banks which were also owned by the mogul (or one of his many dummy corporations), that money didn't really mean anything, if people didn't know that the mogul had it.

So he had to buy into as many other moguls' businesses as he could, which meant hiring people to do the buying of stocks in the mogul's name (which took but a small cut of the mogul's money, since he paid his people only barely enough to live on, plus buy the items his many companies sold), then hiring more people to manage his new business interests, so that he'd have armies of underlings to boss around and write nasty memos to, and spy on via the e-mail messages they sent to each other in their cloth-walled cubicles—which did much to fuel his need for Power, but in turn was a drain on his (albeit) vast fortune.

So the mogul fired off even more nasty letters to the employees who ran his factories, telling them that if production didn't go up *while* manufacturing costs went down, he'd shut down that particular plant and sell the building outright to some Third World dictator, who would turn the place into a training camp for his private militia.

(That's the Third World dictator's private militia. The mogul did yearn to hire and train his own militia, too, but the laws of his country weren't *quite* loop-hole-filled enough to allow him to do *that*.)

Speaking of his own country, and of the city which the mogul all-but-owned-outright (save for a few rent-controlled apartment buildings on the lower West Side), though, the multitudes of hunched-over, bleary-eyed, overtime-deprived workers who toiled for him in his many office buildings lived lives of glare-screened, cubicle-enclosed desperation. There were no health plans or IRA's in any of their futures—only the prospect of five fear-filled days a week spent under the yoke of their mogul-master, with two tension-filled days to first get over his oppression, then anticipate it again come Sunday night.

Should they chafe under those bonds of servitude, they could look forward to the dreaded Letter in their File, or the equally daunting prospect of no Letter of Recommendation should they dare to leave one of the mogul's companies.

And none dared post a *resumé* on the Web, or seek out job prospects on the same, lest the mogul be E-Watching.

No one dared push-pin clipped-out comic strips to their cubicle walls. Coffee breaks were spent in huddled silence near the water coolers with empty bottles affixed to their tops. Office parties were as feared-yet-required as root canal work, since no one dared have so much fun that they might invoke the jealous wrath of the mogul or his closest minions, even as everyone was required to pretend to enjoy themselves. Contents of waste paper baskets were checked daily to make sure no memos from the mogul were defaced or covered with scribbles that somehow mocked the mogul's power.

And so it was that all of his workers silently prayed for a day of delivery from the mogul's unyielding oppression.

With each timid push of their mice upon their mouse-pads, with each frustrated tap of their computer keys, with every furiously-crumpled paper cup tossed into the mogul's many trashcans, his workers silently implored the gods of Fairness and Equal Opportunity to liberate them from the crushing rule of the mogul.

And so it came to pass that on one typically bleak, overcast-but-windless, autumn morning, a young man from a Temp agency came to the biggest of all the mogul's many buildings—the very one, in fact, in which the mogul lived—and walked into the Accounting Department.

This young man was slight of build, not very tall, and quite average of feature—but his blue-grey eyes grew round and dark with pity when he looked about him at the cubicle-trapped workers, and he shook his head of dishwater-blond hair in disbelief when he saw how no one there dared to laugh, or exchange gossip, or use their computers for anything but the assigned tasks before them.

Having worked all over the city, in those few buildings *not* owned or run by the mogul, the temp realized that these workers toiled under a most dreadful boss—for just the day before, he'd worked in a building alive with laughter, rumors and e-mailed messages on everyone's monitor, and the heart of this young, most average-seeming man went out to those stifled souls trapped in their maze of nubby fabric walls and chrome-backed chairs.

The temp waited until his break time to act.

Bypassing the clump of eyes-lowered workers gathered furtively around the brown-stained coffee machine, he instead walked down the industrial-carpeted hallway, between the rows of cubicles, and chrome-backed chairs, and monitors whose screen-savers all extolled the virtues of the mogul and all of the mogul's holdings, and did not stop until he reached the elevator doors.

Confidently pushing the topmost button, he waited serenely as the elevator slid down to his floor, and then—amid the gasps and the whispered asides coming from the direction of the coffee machines—he stepped into the elevator, and spoke the number of the floor upon which the mogul lived.

Rarely did anyone dare to venture into the domain of the mogul (the mogul had long ago fired the people who'd once guarded his top-floor sphere of action), since all of his workers knew better than to bother him.

And so the temp found himself in an empty hallway, which led to but one door, and that door was both massive and intentionally imposing, with the name of the mogul written in huge gold-leaf letters upon a slab of thickest oak.

No one who worked for the mogul had ever dared to merely step up to that door and simply open it, but—having been hired as a three-day replacement for a worker who'd had the gall to get hit by a bus owned by one of the mogul's dummy corporations—the temp considered himself an employee of his temp agency, and not a minion of the mogul himself. So up to the mighty oaken door he stepped in his black oxfords, and with one slightly carpal-tunnel-afflicted hand he turned the brass knob and let himself into the mogul's office.

The mogul was so dumbfounded by the unexpected appearance of the temp, he merely dropped the two phones he was doing his best to speak into at once and sat, dry-lipped mouth hanging slightly open, wattled chins piling up against each other over his too-tight collar, his eyes narrowing behind cheap-framed trifocals, while the temp stood directly in front of him (albeit across a five-foot wide and ten-foot long book-matched burl-walnut desk) and said, in his slightly nasal voice:

"You call this a business? I've temped for every office and every corporation in this city, and in this state, and never have I seen such a bunch of brow-beaten permanent workers like you have down there. I've seen better CEO's and corporation presidents than you—*I* could be a better boss than you are. You can fire me if you want; my work record is excellent, and my temp agency would never let me go…but I'll bet that there's about a thousand workers down there in your offices that would rather have someone like me for a boss than you, no matter how many companies and factories and people you own. I've seen veal pens where the creatures were treated better than the way you treat your workers—and the cubicles were bigger.

"So here's what I'm proposing: If I can be more powerful than you are, I get your company. I get all of what you are and what you own. I have nothing to lose, so I can afford to battle you. Can you afford to take *me* on?"

The mogul swallowed hard at this (even though it was impossible for the temp to see it, thanks to the mogul's many pancake-stacked chins), for he knew the power of a temp, many of whom knew all that was to be known of the ways of running a company, not to mention how to play Blackjack and games of skill on virtually any personal computer program.

And he knew that Temp Agencies were a power unto themselves, so he replaced the two phones in their receivers, and thought the matter over for a few minutes, thus exercising some of his Power (without having to spend Money on it, apart from the pittance he was paying this temp in the first place). Then he leaned back in his huge well-padded oxblood leather office chair, laced his fingers behind his head of sprayed-and-dyed straw-like hair extensions and weaves, and said:

"I've bought and sold a hundred men just like you. Hired and fired, blackballed and screwed outright. I could care less what my workers think of me—they're just a lot of anxious pasty faces clustered around the trays of cheese and crackers at the annual Christmas party. All living in fear of the Pink Slip—all living in fear of temps like you coming in and doing a better job than they ever will, and getting double the pay for it.

"I've bought out whole companies with margin stocks. Entire Third World nations worship me and live off my pocket change. But...I do enjoy the occasional stand-off. Not that you have any chance of winning—what I don't own or control isn't worth having—"

(Not that any mogul wouldn't have liked to have dominated the Temp market that day; he made a mental note to look into doing so as soon as possible, once this chino-slacked and oxford-shirt-wearing drone was out of his office.)

"—so you might as well trot back down to whatever office you crawled out of, and go back to work. There's no way you could best me."

"But you'd enjoy the fight, wouldn't you? Or has living up here made you soft? Or...complacent?"

The temp's voice was grave, yet just slightly taunting.

If there was one thing the mogul could not resist, it was a dare. That was how he came to be owner of one of those chains of fitness centers down South—even though the most physical exercise he ever got was pushing down buttons on his intercom and sliding a mouse around a pad of rubber—after another, lesser mogul bet him that the elder mogul couldn't run them any cheaper than the lesser mogul could.

Once the older mogul eliminated free shower water, profits doubled.

"Oooookay," the mogul drawled, his voice mock-friendly even as his tiny eyes glared at the temp. "I'll take you up on your little...shall I call it a wager? Power struggle? Potential buy-out? With nothing down?" he added as the temp merely smiled at him.

"Listen up, kiddo—these are my terms. My power comes from always being *here*, where my workers know I'm able to watch them, or spy on them, or tap into their computers should they be stupid enough to leave personal e-mails in their hard drives. Every time my building's shadow falls on the city, people know I Am Here.

"What I want *you* to do is *not* be here...I want to see if you can go someplace where I can't find you, call you, view you, or signal *or* summon you in any way. If I can't trace you or track you down within the next three days that I owe you according to my contract with your temp agency, then...all of *this*—" the mogul spread his Italian-silk-suit-covered arms wide, indicating not only his dark-paneled office, but everything beyond the massive ceiling-to-floor plate glass window behind his desk "—will be yours. Every stock, every building, every claim to the very soul of my workers.

"But...should I be able to find you, in any way, not only will you forfeit whatever pay you have coming to you for these three days, I'll personally make sure that your name and your likeness and your danged DNA is known by every potential employer in this whole country—along with my personal recommendation that nobody ever hire you again for any job more complicated than pushing a wet mop over a painted concrete factory floor. Not only won't you ever temp again, you'll never even *see* another office worker in your life.

"Deal?"

The temp's voice was firm, and his blue-grey eyes were level with the small hooded ones of the mogul, as he replied:

"Deal...but if you *cannot* find me, call me, see me, signal *or* 'summon' me—you absolutely can*not* trace me or track me down within the next seventy-two hours—you're finished here—and everywhere else your empire extends. You must leave this tower suite, and get out of this city...and never come back....

"*Deal?*"

The temp offered his hand to the mogul, the tips of his extended fingers barely reaching the halfway mark of the desktop. The mogul reached out his right hand, but only made a quick, glancing contact with the hand of the younger, braver man before interfacing his fingers in front of his expansive chest and belly.

"Deal," he agreed, then added, his voice a well-practiced purr from all the other deals he'd made during his many decades as a mogul:

"Now get the hell out of my office...and don't let me see you again, ooo*kay?*"

All the temp did was smile, then make a quick turn on one slightly scuffed black shoe sole, and walk out of the mogul's office and into the empty, somewhat lonely hallway beyond.

* * * *

Once the elevator brought the temp back down to the floor where he'd been assigned to work, he hurried without a word to anyone back to his temporary small stall-like cubicle, picked up his briefcase and clicked off the computer on his desk. Then he walked past the mogul's drones, who dared to stop gazing into their green-tinged monitors and craned their necks to watch his passing as he quitted the floor, taking the stairway down.

In the privacy of the austere drab painted stairwell, he took his cell phone out of his briefcase and called a travel agency in the next almost-as-big city. Next he called a taxi company, this time within the metropolis.

By the time he was on the ground floor and quite out of breath from all the stairs, a taxi was waiting for him…on the next block over from the mogul's building.

Using his debit card, he paid for a coach-class ticket to a state many miles from the mogul's private playground. As did everyone else boarding, he had to show his driver's license to verify his identity, but there were so, so many people boarding so many planes, he doubted that anyone really noticed him. After all, temps tend to be invisible in the office food chain, and this temp found it very hard to shake that mindset.

Once he arrived in the new state, which not only boasted the nation's most historical monuments (including a greasy-feeling old bell with a huge crack up one side) but also many, many rural places, he rented a car and drove through the countryside, coming to rest at last near a barn owned by some good people whose religion forbade them the use of virtually all the electronic necessities both the mogul and the fleeing temp considered essential for their jobs and their comfort.

But the temp did not mind the lack of a light when he parked his car behind some trees near the barn and crept inside the huge wooden structure as night fell across the rural countryside.

He felt secure in the knowledge that the mogul's sphere of influence did not extend to those people who were more pious and Godly than the mogul could ever profess to be—there was nothing the mogul could possibly want or have use for out here, among the simple folk, and so the temp curled up in a bed of straw, awaiting the dawn, and the chance to withdraw even deeper into the hinterlands….

* * * *

As the first wan wash of palest sooty ivory crept over the megalopolis, the mogul slid sideways out of his vast waterbed (for his back was bad from all the weight he carried on his pampered frame, and standing upright was a very gradual task each morning), then padded barefoot to his office—which lay just beyond his bedroom.

Eagerly rubbing his palms against each other with a disturbingly reptilian *scree*, he switched on his laptop computer (displacing the screen saver which sang the silent praises of his vast empire) and punched in:

ACCESS ALL CALLS MADE FROM THIS BUILDING YESTERDAY.

The computer asked:

INCLUDING CELLULAR?

Smiling so broadly that his jowls quivered in anticipation on either side of his greasy face, he tapped YES—ALL LINES, ALL CELL PHONES WITHIN BUILDING BETWEEN 10;35 AM AND 11:40 AM.

(The latter time was when the security cameras indicated that the temp had, indeed, left the building.)

And, because the mogul owned at least a one-quarter share in all of the long-distance companies serving the city and the state, within the time it took him to microwave a soft-boiled egg in his tiny kitchenette (which folded out from a spot behind the wet bar), the screen pages began scrolling information about call after call, listing numbers dialed, and the names of those people who'd been foolish enough to use cell phones in the hope of eluding the prying ear of the mogul.

Today the mogul was in a semi-charitable mood; he generously ignored (for the time being; he did save the file for future reference) the names of his own employees which appeared on the screen…for he was far more intent on one name.

* * * *

Once he had the numbers the temp called, it was so easy to cross-reference all the other data that the computer had everything the mogul wanted to see before the man finished buttoning the top button of his too-tight starched collar (buying a bigger size would've meant actually admitting he was, indeed, rather fat).

By the time he'd tied his tie, the computer had linked up with the satellite tracking system used by the car rental company the temp had gone to in that nearby semi-rural state…and just about the time when the majority of his office workers were going on their first coffee break, heading toward their accustomed spots by the coffee machine and the water coolers, they were startled to hear the sound of the mogul's private jet roaring in for a roof-top landing over the building-wide intercom system—not startled because the mogul's private haven had a large landing strip on the roof (and yes, the building was indeed that large), but because he was usually too cheap to turn on the intercom system.

He did shut the system off just before the plane's door flipped down; the wager he had with the temp was a private matter.

For his part, the temp was still somewhat dazed and half-asleep when the flight attendants who worked on the mogul's plane dragged him out of an empty stall in the huge plain barn and shoved him aboard with straw still clinging to his blondish-tan hair and rumpled oxford shirt.

But he was quite awake once, back in the office, the mogul began to tilt back and forth in his glove-leather chair, a very broad smile all but splitting his face in two.

"My, my, my," he chortled. "Thought you could outwit me out among the plain folk…very clever, but—"

"But the three days aren't over yet," the temp replied, as he brushed straw out of his hair and smoothed his wrinkled trouser legs—then crisply turned around and walked out of the office whose dark-stained walls gleamed reddish-gold in the rising sunlight.

* * * *

This time the temp walked a little slower through the building that housed the mogul. His high forehead was furrowed with thought as he finally exited the building out a back entrance, close to where the janitor's closets were located.

He hailed no taxi cabs, nor did he use his debit card or his credit card, or even those traveler's checks he'd squirreled away in his flat wallet— for at the bottom of his trouser pocket (along with some bits of straw from the farmer's barn) there were several subway tokens.

Walking a bit more quickly, he hurried to the nearest subway entrance, then took the stairs two at a time (which was difficult, for he was short of limb) until he reached the turnstiles.

Thumbing in a token, he hurried to the platform, and got onto the first car that stopped. He sat slumped in one of the uncomfortable metal chairs near the back of the car, and rode and rode until the subway moved no more, and it was time for him to get off.

His legs were cramped from sitting curled in that chair, and his neck was stiff from staring up at the same row of advertising inserts above the opposite bank of seats (most of which were for products either made by or for the mogul).

But once it was time to leave the subway station, he climbed out from the graffiti-scribbled viscera of the great city and into a neighborhood he did not know.

Here no one recognized his face, or had ever heard his name.

But here was a busy Cineplex, with over a dozen screens showing as many different first- and second-run movies, plus a silent film for the artsy-smartsy crowd. The glassy *façade* of the building was filled with hundreds of milling bodies behind the protective floor-to-ceiling window, and soon the temp mingled among them, letting the momentum of the tightest knot of people draw him to a random ticket-taker. Using cash, and some change, he paid for a ticket to a movie he wasn't interested in, and let the surging crowd guide him into the darkened narrow screening room.

He bought no popcorn, he purchased no soda. He did sit near the back of the sharply canted screening room, where he slid down in his seat until he was almost sitting on the floor itself, but that was only because the front rows of seats were empty or nearly so, and he could have been too easily seen.

And after one movie ended, he left with that crowd, then drifted like a dandelion seed to the next biggest crowd of people, and allowed them to move him to a nearby shopping mall, a high-rise thing built in an office building, with many stores on many more floors, all ringing a central atrium which rose all the way up to the high-domed ceiling.

Then he went from store to store, never buying, always looking, and when the crowd around him broke up store by store, he found new masses of people to tag along with, making sure he walked in the center of each new phalanx of humanity.

The last group he slid into carried him down the many escalators and out the doors again, so he found himself heading back to the cinema—this time with an artsy-smartsy bunch of grad students who bought tickets to the lone silent film showing at the Cineplex.

It was very late when the temp sat down in that most narrow and claustrophobic of screen rooms, sandwiched in among the candidates for Masters' and PhD degrees, and the room was close-smelling and warm from too many bodies and too many barrels of popcorn, and so the temp dozed off. No one noticed him sleeping there, and so none of the people who came in with him noticed when he didn't leave the room with them after the next-to-last screening of the film.

As a matter of fact, the room was empty as the projectionist ran the film again anyhow, because he was union and paid to do so, and therefore would run it whether or not anyone was watching the thing.

But, being silent, and lacking a sound-track because the projection man *did* decide not to turn on the sound because he hated the movie's inane piano score after listening to it six times that day alone, the movie didn't disturb the slumber of the exhausted temp....

* * * *

The mogul was already up and partially dressed before the first narrow ribbon of daylight shone between the tiny empty spaces in the cityscape's forest of tall buildings.

All during the preceding day, starting the minute the temp walked out of his office, in fact, the mogul had been preparing for this day's search.

The plushy carpet under his flat feet was covered with undulating lengths of power cords and power strips, all feeding sizzling nourishment to the banks of computers, CD-ROMs, monitors and printers he'd had his lackeys haul into his office on metal and wooden carts with round rolling casters.

Several modem lines fed additional juice to his computers, linking them with many other computers all over the metropolis…including those computers that ran the hidden surveillance cameras in the subway system (a must once the population soared so high that not enough police could be hired to patrol the subways any more), in all the major movie complexes, and shopping malls, and upscale department stores all over the city and the surrounding boroughs.

The entire island upon which the city was sprawled was hooked up with cameras in any location where money (or people who either had lots of it or might want more of it) exchanged hands on a large-scale basis.

And deep within its spray-paint-splashed bowels, there were even cameras on the subway trains themselves, artfully hidden behind every other rectangular cardboard advertisement slid into the holder above the seats.

All the mogul had to do was access the ID photo of the temp from the younger man's driver's license, which was on file with the DMV, click SEARCH with his trusty mouse, and prepare his morning cup of coffee while his ISP googled the millions of grainy, jerking images taken in every branch of the subway lines, in every Cineplex on the island, and in every major retail outlet as far as the eye could see—if said eye was located within the penthouse the mogul occupied.

There was a shallow pool of unsipped coffee in the bottom of the mogul's favorite mug by the time the computers had completed their task; with a few more swipes of his mouse across the well-worn rubber pad, the mogul bid the computers to create a file showing by-the-half-hour highlights of the temp's journey.

From the second he entered the subway entrance, to the second time he entered the Cineplex, to the second time the silent film was run in his presence, everything was there before the mogul…albeit in choppy bursts of skipped-frame black-and-white motion, punctuated by odd lapses and gaps in the temp's movements. But the worried expression of the temp was unmistakable, even in profile or three-quarter view….

* * * *

The temp awoke to the sound of film going through the projector, *sans* any other noise save for that of the film sock rushing over the sprockets, an annoying ratchetty-clacking clatter that made him jump in place, before moving his aching neck (from having slept in a strange position in the narrow, barely-padded chair) toward the screen…where he saw the following words within a border of dollar-and-cents symbols:

YOU DIDN'T THINK I COULD FIND YOU, EH?

S¢S¢S¢S¢S¢S¢S¢S¢S¢S¢S¢S¢S¢S¢S¢S¢S¢S
¢S¢S¢S¢S¢S¢S¢S¢S¢S¢S¢S¢S

And, because he was a man of his word, the temp stiffly got up out of his seat and began the slow, agonizing walk up the aisle and out of the screening room…and even though there was no reason for him to do so, he chose not to take a cab or to rent a car for his trip back to the Mogul.

For he needed the extra time to think, and think hard, as he made his way back via the subway to the tall, tall edifice ruled by the waiting mogul….

* * * *

"You know, son, I'm actually beginning to enjoy this," the mogul chortled without preamble as the temp stepped into his office.

The temp said nothing as he stared at the jowly, squinty-eyed mogul, even as the power-filled man continued:

"Two times you've tried, and two times you haven't made good on your part of the bargain. Although I do think there's a spare mop in janitorial I can lend you—until you're able to scrape up enough bus fare for a one-way ticket out of this city. I hear that the burger places on the mainland always need some help swabbing out the restrooms—or perhaps you can work your way up to putting the tiny packets of catsup and mustard into those little bins under the counters.

"Seems to me that if you squeeze enough of the catsup into hot water, you'll get *something* like soup—"

"You still owe me one day," the temp cut in softly, his voice barely audible over the hum of the still-plugged-in banks of computers and monitors.

"What's left of it, that is," the mogul shot back, with an expansive wave at the cityscape beyond his huge picture window—and since the sun was already at its zenith, there was only half a day remaining for the temp to begin his flight from the mogul's sphere of influence, his limits of power, and his omnipotence.

"It's still a day," the temp replied, before quitting the humming confines of the office.

* * * *

Not caring if the mogul's people saw him, the temp walked out of the building's front doors, in full view of all entering or leaving the building. He stood in the middle of the broad, clean sidewalk in front of the towering edifice, considering his next move.

Raising one shirt-sleeve-covered thin arm, he hailed a taxi and told the driver (who spoke but little English, but whose warning signs spoke of the dangers of smoking and leaving litter in the cab's back seat) to take him to the center of the megalopolis' busiest retail section, a place of huge ever-changing light displays, massive billboards with blank staring faces looming above him, and traffic which surged back and forth in endless spurts and sudden stops, accompanied by the blat of car horns and the sputtering sooty exhalations of car exhaust.

He had to pay for the cab with a debit card, because he had no more money, and had he used an ATM it would capture his name and likeness for the mogul's pleasure. But that mattered little to the temp; he now knew that there was no place in the mogul's domain where he could hide himself, and no way to escape the confines of the metropolis without detection. Everything was linked to everything else, be it by camera or by credit card slip or by photo ID and the nation-wide requirement that all public travel be documented prior to anyone boarding any sort or form of public transportation.

And he certainly couldn't walk off the island...any more than the thousands upon thousands of anguished workers who toiled under the mogul's watchful squinting eye could escape his oppression. Not when things like letters of reference were a necessity for securing a new job elsewhere, and not when the mogul had a plump, manicured finger in every job pie in the cosmopolis—all of the mogul's slaving workers were just as stymied and as trapped as the temp found himself to be.

And even though those people would still have jobs come the next morning, while he'd be reduced to almost less than nothing, they'd be no better off than he, for theirs would remain lives of trembling apprehension, clouded by the constant worry about job security, downsizing, budget cuts, no-smoking clauses, and random drug testing.

Not to mention the burden of needing to buy the mogul a suitable gift each Christmas and Bosses' Day, despite his having no need of anything more of a material sort.

(For to him, more than the thought counted—he thrived on being feared *and* venerated.)

As the temp stood in the middle of the noisy, busy square within the city, he began to cry—for himself, and for all the people bent low under the mogul's pension-plan bondage, and his increasingly wide-spread acquisitions...each of which took yet another small bite out of the pay-checks of his minions.

There was no escape at all, be it figurative or literal. The mogul saw all, the mogul knew all, the mogul owned all.

And as dusk settled on the square of milling people and honking cars, and the surrounding lights grew all the brighter and all the more beautiful, the temp raised up his arms and cried out to no one and to everyone:

"I give up—the man is *every*where. There isn't a thing he doesn't touch, or see, or own—there's nowhere I can hide, no place where I can escape him. Here, here's everything I own, you might as well have it!"

He finished, and with a flourish he emptied out his wallet in the middle of the street, in the middle of traffic, as the people and the cars whizzed past him, immune to his presence because the city was already filled with people who raged and cursed in public.

Once he was free of his credit cards and his other bar-coded and photo-and-thumb-print-emblazoned personal cards, the temp began walking into the ever-increasing crowds in the square, until he was swallowed up in the darkness and the bustle, just another broke, homeless person in a city teeming with the abandoned, the cast-off, the cast-adrift from society.

And as he walked, he came across more of his new kind, slumped against alleys, lying in gutters, all nameless, all virtually faceless, and all of them well-removed from the interest and the concern of any of their better-off fellows in the city.

None of them were wanted; none of them were missed.

And still deeper into the dank narrow places of the city the young man walked, hands in empty pockets, head drooping low, and eyes half-shut....

* * * *

The mogul bounced eagerly in his oxblood-padded chair as his computers dredged up the details of the temp's journey once he quitted the mogul's impressively-overbearing tower.

Records from all the taxi companies yielded a cab number and a driver's name, and a statement from the temp's debit card. The destination of the car was duly noted, as were some complaints to the police precinct (never followed up, though, thanks to the manpower shortages) from a few tourists about a crying young man who was shouting about 'giving up' to no one at all, and who dumped out the contents of his pockets in the middle of the square (again, the littering complaint wasn't followed up on either, after being called into the station), and then stalked off into the night....

"Well?" the mogul thundered at the monitor screen when no more information scrolled across its pixelated surface.

But there was nothing more to report—the last recorded instance of the temp's existence was the pocket-dumping incident in that busy, busy square. And that had been logged in only because the person who saw it felt sorry for the young man, who was obviously distraught, and possibly suicidal.

(Just as the person who'd phoned in the complaint was obviously hoping to emerge a hero should the possible suicide be publicly prevented.)

"*Well?*"

No other precinct had recorded any other calls about slight young men doing anything out of the ordinary in a teeming city full of angry, frustrated people. None of the morgues reported any early-thirty-something office-worker types among their John Does. And no one had been picked up for attempting to hitchhike along public highways. The shore patrol saw no one swimming in unauthorized public waters.

"WELL?"

No landlords had filed complaints about squatters, no vagrants were reported in front of expensive jewelry stores or high-rise apartment buildings. Even the nightly opening of the homeless shelters brought no reports of any young men resembling the temp, according to their head-county tallies.

The mogul's jowls began to quiver, as his face grew mottled-red. He stood up so quickly his huge padded leather chair flipped backwards and cracked the inside pane of the double-pane glass in his picture window. With a sideways swipe of his arms, first to the left, then to the right, he cleared his massive desktop of all his phones and laptops, sending them to the plush carpet in a clatter and a rattle of plastic and curly cords.

"I am still the most powerful man in this city—in this state, in this whole damned country!" he bellowed, the sound of his voice a terrible thing to hear in the echoing office.

"No one hides from me—nothing escapes my attention!"

And for the first time in many years, he left his lonely floor of supreme power, and made his way through his vast building (past startled workers who had lived in fear of the day when the mogul would enter their humble domain, lest he take away whatever tiny pleasures, whatever minuscule comforts—like coffee in the machines, or paper in the toilet stalls—still grudgingly remaining to them), floor by floor, thundering his growing rage in a pulsing of stacked chins, and a crinkling of the fatty pouches above and below his enraged eyes.

By the time he reached the street outside his tower, a limousine waited for him, equipped with the finest of phones, lap tops and satellite television systems available—getting into it, he snarled at the driver:

"Just drive this thing—*everywhere!*"

* * * *

Hour after hour the driver drove; crisscrossing the city's grid-like streets, then venturing out beyond the city proper, into the nether regions the mogul had only seen on his wide-screen HDTV back in his penthouse bedroom, out past the malls, and the airports, and the housing developments—then the car rolled back into the city, as darkness began to fall around the fuming, starving mogul (for he'd neglected to eat, so great was his rage, so huge was his growing fear).

Just as the long, long car rounded a corner that brought it into the middle of the square where the temp had vanished into the night, the mogul screamed at the driver, "Let me out of this blasted submarine! I need air! I need to *breathe!*"

Obligingly, both because he feared the mogul and because he hated the sight of the man in his rear view mirror, the driver opened the automatic doors, waited until the mogul had wiggled out of the car (he was just a bit wider than the door frame)—then relocked the doors and sped off into the incandescent and neon-sparkling night.

"Where in the hell ARE yooouuu?" the mogul bawled, throwing his hands up in the air and glancing all about him, past the people and the cars and the blazing lights of the advertisements, toward the darkened alleys beyond the square of life and light.

Running with a jiggle and a heave of his belt-cinched belly, the mogul didn't notice when someone picked his pocket, nor did he feel it when another person snatched his $50,000 watch off his plump wrist, for he was too busy darting his head back and forth, eyes open wide, ready to take in the faces of the street people around him.

But the temp was not among them.

Yet the mogul still trudged on, down one alley, then another, until his fat feet ached in his expensive loafers and his sagging gut hungered for nourishment...but no one he spoke to (reluctantly, hesitantly) had seen the temp.

Only with the first coming of silvery-ivory light along the horizon (or what he could see of the horizon from this street-level vantage point) did the mogul stop by a cracked concrete stoop, and lean against the greasy, crumbling bricks of a soot-caked wall, head drooping low against his heaving chest.

All around him were the sounds of the city, coming to life after an uneasy, restless slumber…but suddenly there was a more familiar sound, that of a certain pair of footsteps, coming down the sidewalk toward him. The sound of hard oxford shoe soles was unmistakable to a businessman like him—

And when he looked up, to see the temp—a bit more rumpled, a lot more gaunt, and just a little more confident than he'd last seemed in the mogul's presence—all the young blond-haired man said was, "It's the fourth day. You don't own anything anymore. You don't own anyone, anywhere, anymore."

And because…despite his greed, and his lust for Money and its sibling Power…the mogul was a man of *his* words, he merely nodded his head of disheveled hair extensions and blubbery jowls, and trotted off on sore feet into an alley way, never to be seen by the people in his former city again.

When the people in the mogul's tower heard from the limo driver what had happened, how he'd vanished into the heart of the city, they rejoiced, and awaited the coming of the temp who'd freed them all.

But…the temp never came…although it was rumored that he'd used his ATM card to somehow access the mogul's private account and withdraw more than enough money to live upon comfortably for many, many years (since he was well-versed—as are all temps—in the ways of PIN numbers and the manipulation of software programs).

However, the rumors remained only rumors, and even though the temp was never seen in the city again, his deed did not go unremembered by the people he'd freed.

After they'd assumed control of the mogul's vast holdings and turned the bulk of his assets into an employee-owned, employee-run conglomerate, they made sure that even the lowliest of temps had access to the parent company's pension plan, and health insurance packages, and whatever other benefit might be available to them for however long they worked at the company, should they take the company up on its offer to hire on as a full-time employee—

—albeit at slightly lower pay rates than they'd earned as temps.

Mogul or no mogul, the company did have to think about the all-mighty bottom line….

Based on the Russian fairy tale "The Sorcerer" as retold by Teje Etchemendy, in Tales of Old Russia, *Rand McNally & Company, 1964, as well as the films of Terry Gilliam and Joel and Ethan Coen.*

AFTERWORD

Let me make something clear—the title character of this story is *not* Donald Trump, or even a fictionalized version of him. I know it might seem that way, but I was thinking of a generic, all-encompassing version of a Powerful Man, as opposed to the non-powerful cog-in-the-wheel type of person. (Personally, I find The Donald somewhat amusing/entertaining, in a good way. And he is a smart businessman—he managed to avoid the whole Bernie Madoff mess, which is definitely a sign of astute business acumen....)

I originally wrote this for an anthology of updated/modernized fairy tales, using an old Russian tale called "The Sorcerer" as my template, but the editors didn't like my story, so I began shopping it around elsewhere, until it made it into what was *Space & Time*'s 100th issue—and since *S&T* was one of the first magazines I started subbing stories to, back in the mid-1980's, I was extremely happy and proud to have had a story in the centennial issue.

The Russian version of this had the unnamed young man who challenged the powerful Sorcerer vanish by asking the All-Mighty for help, but, being a non-believer myself, I wanted to go a different route—as in the young man taking himself off the grid. Didn't work for the first editors who saw it, but eventually it worked for someone....

WITH COCKLES AND MUSSELS, ALIVE, ALIVE-O

We was on the way from Florida to Georgia, from "oranges to peaches, with the 'maters up the road," like Daddy likes to say when he ain't in a bad mood, and he's looking forward to picking the tomatoes up in South Carolina, which I guess is like someone who ain't a picker saying that there *is* that light up yonder in that tunnel—only, Daddy wasn't in no looking-forward kinda mood that night, while he was driving me and Mama and Cherrie down that highway in the dark, 'cause driving in daytime is miserable without no air conditioner in the car.

'Course, the 'conditioner never did work when the car was new to us—not new-new, just new-bought-by-Daddy—so's that wasn't what was making Daddy mean.

It was Cherrie. *Again*.

Oh, not actually Cherrie, on 'count she's his favorite, like I'm Mama's, but what Cherrie was *singing*, over and over in that little bitty voice of hers, real thin and pure and unsteady-sweet, like all little kids Cherrie's age got.

Not real loud, least not as loud as the old warbly eight-track in the player on the dashboard—the one that come with the car, both the player and the tape from the little frayed shoe box full of them that was sitting in the footwell on the passenger side up front, 'cause the guy who sold us the car said he was switching over to cassettes—

—but 'parently Daddy could hear Cherrie anyway, even with his bust eardrum on one side, and that singer in The Doors sorta shouting out that "L.A. Woman" song over and over 'cause the tape deck always plays one of the sides of the tape twice through before clicking on to the next side, blaring in Daddy's good ear.

Since he was driving, Daddy couldn't reach behind him real good to bop Cherrie a good one, so's he yelled above he music:

"Shaddup, Cherrie, Daddy don't wanna *hear* it no more," while Mama's just looking out the window as Florida sorta rolled on into Georgia, without it being sight-plain, like when one colored state turns to another color on a map.

Only, I don't know if Mama knows how that is on maps, or on a globe. She can't read too good, so I don't think that's what she was thinking on as she was looking out that window whiles Daddy's yelling.

But I could see a little reflection of her face, in one of the mirrors mounted outside the open door window, and she didn't look too happy, but she wasn't saying nothing to Daddy about him blowing up at Cherrie. It never worked before, not even when *I* was Cherrie's age, and I used to sing.

Can't remember if I ever sang *that* song; I guess it's sorta like forgetting what-all your mouth and tongue and teeth can all do if they're working together to do something other than eat, so your whole lower face can't even entertain the notion of talking if it don't know after a long time.

And ain't got no way to remember it without a brain of its very own.

But…yet, the way Cherrie sings the last bit of the song, the way she goes up real high and *pining*, like she's wanting something so real, *real* bad, but ain't never gonna get it no *way* no *how*, no *time*, but still wants it all the same—I dunno; it just makes me feel like that—

—which don't make no sense on 'count of it just being this dumb nursery rhyme, something she learned in some picker camp from some other fruit tramp's kid or wife, or *some*where, a fancy-talk song that really don't have *nothing* to do with us pickers at *all*—

Cherrie just blinked a little when Daddy hollered at her, and hugged her plastic block against her chest, digging it into the soft skin ' tween her armpit and chest, and rubbing the block with her tiny fingers, and her mouth shut in this wet little line while the piano player on the tape was doing this tinkly bit, all bouncy.

Then the singer came back on with his strong, sorta chuffy voice, like he's having a real good time but is sorta winded, too. Sorta like how Daddy and some of the other picker men sound when they're playing cards in front of the campfire, passing the bottles of beer and slapping the cards on the rickety folding table one of them's pulled out of the back of his station wagon, or out of the trunk of his car.

Once, I was watching them all play—Mama, too—and they was all happy and joking and card-slapping away, and I was halfway up the side of this big old tree, steadying myself with my bare feet, while the night breeze blowed out my little nightgown behind me, and Daddy looked around at me, shifting on the upside-down herbicide bucket he was using for a stool, and he goes:

"Wind's gonna catch you up, blow you far 'way," and everyone 'round the table laughs at that 'fore picking up their cards and bottles again—

—and just by listening to that tape in the machine, the tape that was starting to get warbly and let little bits of sounds from the other sides of the tape leak through somehow, so you'd get the main song plus all little snatches of the rest of the songs, too, listening to that tinkly piano—or maybe it was an organ; sometimes it sounded like one, too—and that singer repeating and repeating "L.A. Womaaaan" in a sorta plaintive, needing-*some*thing voice—

—it was like I was back there balancing on the bottom trunk of that big tree, the wind blowing through my nightie, bringing the smell of beer and the beans cooking on the fire into my nose again, and I think I was only four or five then—if it was beans they was picking during the *day* of that night, then I was already five, on 'count of that being the time of year, North Carolina way, where we always are after my birthday during peach time in Georgia—

—anyway, that's how the music I was hearing made me feel, happy, yet not happy-*now*, but can't-be-this-happy-*again* happy.

Like—and not like—the way Cherrie's song makes me feel inside, like wanting for there to *be* the happy time to remember later on. Like Cherrie *needed* what she's singing about, even if she can't understand half of what she's saying 'cause the words are too big for a three-year-old.

I don't know how she *remembers* them, let 'lone sings them.

But she does, and did, not too long after the guy on the tape gave up singing 'bout (but not *wanting*) his L.A. Womaaaaan, and the tape hissed and crackled with bits of almost-song.

And before the next song started, Cherrie started up again, real soft, real thin and high and fine:

> *In London fair city/ Where the girls is so pretty*
> *There lives a fair maiden/ Named Molly Malone*
> *She walks her wheelbarrow/ Thru streets broad an' narrow*
> *Singin' 'Cockles and Mussels! Alive, Alive-o—*

—Only, she don't sing it straight out like it looks written down, but like words is jumping up and down and real high and heart-rending like this:

-o—

'Cock   Mus   Alive
les and   sels! Alive,
in'
Sing

Something like that, anyhow. I can't sing it onto the paper.

But this time, Daddy pulls the tape outta the machine, tosses it into the box with the rest of the tapes close by Mama's feet, and keeping one hand on the wheel, he leans over and smacks Cherrie on the side of the head, not hard enough to make her head jerk none, but hard enough to muss up her hair so's it's bunched up funny under her duck barrette.

"You *quit* it now, hear? Daddy can't concentrate," he adds, like that's why he done it in the first place—but I know it ain't the reason, on 'count of Mama not getting her dander up when one of her young'uns got hit for doing nothing *real* bad, like kicking on the back of the seats up ahead, or fighting.

That's when I knowed Mama was unhappy on 'count of Cherrie's singing, too.

All she done was toss us a thin blanket, the one made up of two baby diapers sewed long side to long side, and say, "Get you girls some sleep," 'fore turning around and rooting in the box of old tapes.

She didn't find none she hadn't heard twice through already since leaving the orange grove at sundown, when Daddy collected his pay and Mama finished packing up the car.

All's we got to pack is clothes, a few blankets, sheets, some dishes, and Daddy's packs of cards. And Cherrie's blocks, and my notebook and pencil. We'd picked up what was stored under that picnic table we was camping out under, threw it in the trunk, and we was ready to leave once Daddy got his and Mama's money.

(Which was sorta mine, too, since I picked almost a third of what they did, but kids my age—eleven—ain't supposed to be working in the fields or the groves, or wherever what it is that we're picking is sprouting or hanging or just sitting waiting to be harvested, so I didn't get none of the money.)

I was tired out from picking oranges (and keeping an eye on Cherrie, too), so I tucked the blanket around Cherrie, and then pillowed my head on her hip, and fell asleep, with her little, thin voice going up and up on the "*Cock*-les" part of the song, over and over, until I 'bout cried myself to sleep with the wanting and not *having* of it all.

* * * *

Come morning, we was at the peach camp, this time a line of shacks, each a big room with no curtains, no locking doors, and no bathroom or 'lectricity, or water, or—with cardboard walls that wasn't too soggy near the bottoms, and some old pictures hung on the exposed joists and struts inside the shack.

Pretty good place to stay, considering. 'Least there was a bed in the middle of the room, and a wood-burning stove. Daddy said the rent was "fairly fair," which is 'bout as good as it gets. Sometimes them growers rent us tents with little holes in 'em, or (like what happened to us once in South Carolina when I was six), an old pigsty with cots lined up in it.

Only thing I didn't like none was how the camp was so close to an outlying street in the town nearby, and how town folks' kids sometimes walk past, looking. Always *look*ing, like they do no matter where we go or where they happen to be.

Only, they won't look at us up *close*. Cross to the other side of the street, or road, or whatever they's walking on that they don't want to share with us any closer than an arm's length, sometimes turning their heads just enough that they don't think we can see 'em looking down their noses at us.

Mama and me, we was taking what we owns into the shack, when the first of 'em, one of them town kids, shouts:

"Filthy *pick*ers! Nose-pickers, butt-pickers—"

And I wanted to drop what I was carrying and take off after them, but Mama just shakes her head *no*, and goes, "You knows what Daddy says, Peaches. Only words—"

"*Sick* words," I say back, turning my head to stare and stick my tongue out in them kids' direction, but they was already gone, hiding, laughing at us from behind a screen of trees. Mama just steered Cherrie into the shack, and lifted her onto the big bed, then sat down next to her, patting the mattress for me to sit, too. I wouldn't.

"Peaches," Mama started, her tongue working and working around what teeth she's got left up front (all her back ones is gone, like all of Daddy's but the two big ones on top like she was trying to shift 'em all down into a single, full-looking row, and her eyes is watering a little, "You knows better than to start trouble with them—"

"*They* was yelling at us, not the other—"

"*Peaches*."

Only, this time not happy at *all*, and Daddy heard her and came in slapping the dirt off his jeans, making little clouds puff off his hips and thighs, going, "What *now*, Mattie!"

"Peaches again. Tauntin' the town kids—"

I bit my lips and crossed my arms and dug my toes into the packed dirt floor, I was so mad. I said—not looking at either of them, but at Cherrie, 'cause she wouldn't understand, and so her face wouldn't pucker up all bitter, like Mama's and Daddy's do—

"They was taunting *me*. And Mama, and Cherrie. Call us '*nose-pickers*,' like that's all we got the time to *do* all day, stand around with our fingers up our—"

Daddy looks at Mama, like he's asking, *She right?* with his eyes—only, Mama makes out like she don't see him by closing her eyes.

"And it was a bunch of them, five-six maybe, 'gainst us. And we wasn't saying *nothing* to them."

I kept on, getting all hot in the face and wet under the arms, and more frustrated inside, on 'count of this happening again and again no matter where we go, or whether we're settled for the month or the whole season, and whether we're living in some picker camp (don't never call 'em *migrant*, even to myself), trying to steer clear of the Haitians or the other dark-skinned folk from out of the country who'll work for the *real* cheap, plus drunks and whores who hang around there, or living in something real decent, like a trailer up on blocks or maybe even a room above a tavern or little store, like we sometimes do come cabbage, pear, and cherry time up in New York State (like we was when Cherrie was born)—

—no matter where we happens to be, or how much we keep to ourselves, and our own picker friends, town folk is always *after* us.

And what burns me is how they sure do like to eat what we broke our backs and butts for out in the field. Even Cherrie helps pick, even though it's maybe a bushel or a box of this or that for the whole day, on 'count we get paid by the bushel or box or whatever they're using to store what we've just picked. No matter who picks it in the family.

But set foot in the same store that's got what we pickers picked up on the shelves, all fancy and canned or frozen or put in them little packets that's fixed so that you just toss 'em from the cupboard into the microwave do-dad and then onto your plate, and none of them folks wants *anything* to do with them that's done the actual picking.

Like the food just leaps off the vine or tree or outta the ground and into a line of open and ready cans or boxes.

With no sweaty fingers touching them, getting dirt so deep under the nails you can't get it out no matter how hard you scrub 'em in the river or gas station washroom or wherever, so your hands never look *quite* clean no matter how clean they are, and so's the girl or guy behind the store counter won't let their fingers touch yours, just drop what change you got coming with money that was *worked* for (not state-given like them food-stampers I seen laughing and buying steaks and long plastic trays of shrimp and breaded veal cutlets whose food coupons them checkers take *gladly*), onto the counter, sometimes so hard and so fast the money rolls off the counter and onto the floor, so's you have to bend over and grub for it around people's feet, and all the while you just *know* they're snickering or whatnot above your bent-over bottom.

I could've told all that to Mama and Daddy, but they've been pickers since they was littler than Cherrie or me, and been picking way longer than both of us have lived put together into one age, so's they've heard it all, and seen it all, but yet they just don't unnerstand what it's *like* when them town folks dig at us.

Oh, I've heard 'em *say* how they're proud to be what they are, and how they can't live no tied-down life once the itchy foot sets in come spring, but it don't stop 'em from having that hurt in the eye when someone snubs one of 'em.

Yet…they won't fight back, won't tell them people to their *faces* what they're feeling, like there's just no chance any of 'em will maybe unnerstand that we're people first, then pickers, just like any of them is a banker or a checker or a housewife or a school kid or a truck driver or a *something* on top of being a person first off. 'Fore they had jobs or titles or anything. Like they got no hope of being unnerstood, like picker talk won't filter into non-picker ears.

Like other folks got them labeled "*Migrant*" or worse and won't let no other thing into their heads when it comes to thinking 'bout people like us.

So…I just stood there, looking from Cherrie's face to her parched sundress and back again, like whatever I wanted to say might be hidden somewhere on Cherrie herself, and Mama and Daddy can't say nothing I ain't heard already, when Cherrie pipes up with that song, just the last couple of lines, 'cause she don't know what else to do or say, and the silence is getting real thick—

> *cock*   *mus*
> *W'*   *les an'*   *sels*—

Mama looks all jumpy at that, and starts to tickle Cherrie, so's she'll fall backwards onto the saggy bed, and then Daddy starts to play with her, too, like playing is the most important thing in the world, more important than the picking we gotta start doing pretty soon, or getting the shack in some sorta order, for the weeks we're gonna be here.

Only…I see their eyes, 'fore they started playing with Cherrie, and I knowed that it was only 'cause the walls is thin and sound carries pretty fair in the hot stillness that they weren't hitting on her, and yelling instead.

* * * *

I learned to grit my teeth until they felt like there was no more white on them from all the gritting all the time we was picking peaches that summer 'cause every time the town kids would ride past on their bikes, or walk past on foot, it was the same old chant, "Nose-pickers, butt-pickers, pick me a bunch of—"

And I had to swallow hard over and over until my ears felt stuffy so's I couldn't hear what them kids *claimed* we picked. On 'count of Mama and Daddy and Cherrie working right near me, either on the ladder or on the ground, putting the fruit in the baskets real tight so it couldn't bruise too much once it was in the trucks.

I wanted to yell back to them kids, "We ain't no worse than you; you don't like what youse see, *you* make us look better, or turn your stupid heads"—only, I'd 've been bopped outside the head just like Cherrie was when she sang that song.

Out in the trees, Cherrie's voice had this way of carrying, and echoing in your head worse than that warbly eight-track machine, and since every peach picked and put in the basket was money to us, Daddy didn't have no time to go bopping Cherrie too often 'less she was within quick reach, so's he yelled a lot—only, sorta low, so's the town kids wouldn't hear us, or think he was yelling at them.

And Cherrie'd make that wet little line of her mouth for a while, 'fore she started humming or singing the song, and sometimes I'd sneak a peek at the other pickers around us, to see what they thought of Cherrie's singing, and the looks on their faces was like what I felt inside, and always when she came to that last line, and the "Alive, alive" part, like they was longing for something that wasn't gonna come and maybe even *shouldn't* come, but they wanted it anyhow.

Like that singer on the "L. A. Woman" song—only, not even trying to pretend that they was having a good time with the wanting and the needing of...*whatever* it was.

* * * *

After peaches was over, we hit the road again, 'cause it was tomato and cucumber time to the east of us.

And the tapes sounded looser, more fluttery in the tape deck, and sometimes Mama took to reaching over to shush Cherrie, and I wondered why she and Daddy just didn't teach Cherrie another song, or why they didn't have her try to hum along with the tapes (the radio was bust on the car when Daddy bought it).

But once, at a rest stop, I actually asked Mama about it while she was washing Cherrie up in a ladies' room washbasin, using what little was left of that squirt soap in the dispenser on the wall and a wad of doubled paper towels, but all she said was, "Singin's for them that knows it"—which didn't make no sense at all.

So I asked a different way, and as she was drying Cherrie off with fresh towels, Mama said, "It's like pickin's for us who *live* it. We knows it, and it's good to us, 'cept when it rains out a crop, but that's the Lord's will, and none of our doin', so's we just have to make do a little more then. But singin' if you ain't lived the song...."

And she let her voice just peter off, like what else she might've had to say wasn't worth the saying, or the thinking of saying.

And it still didn't make no sense, 'cause I'd *heard* her and Daddy sing, and sing plenty loud and loose and free when they was downing a few poker-game beers, or sharing a bottle of something cheap and potent come the end of the picking season.

Only, I never heard them sing *that* song, Cherrie's song, 'least not *recently*—

—and it was Mama washing Cherrie the way she was, with Cherrie sitting in one empty washbasin, with her feet soaking in the next, water-filled basin, that got me to thinking, and remembering.

I was 'bout seven or so—had to be, since Cherrie was already born but not walking yet—and we was staying in this shack in New York State, one with power, and water, and even a real flush toilet like in a gas station or rest area (maybe on that last one).

It'd been kinda cool out, 'cause Mama had opened up the 'lectric oven and then turned it on, so the heat coil was lit up like a squiggle of neon lighting in a tavern window—only, it didn't say BEER or nothing—and I was sitting on an upended herbicide bucket, like the one Daddy'd sat on when I was two years younger, back when I was standing on the sloping trunk of that huge tree, watching him play cards.

And I had my bare feet sticking into the oven, not much further in than half the door, but it felt good, having warm feet, and Mama'd fixed me a cup of coffee with a little Quik tossed in it from an old can of it she'd found on the lone wooden shelf above the cracked and rusted enamel iron sink next to the stove, and put in a little baby formula, too, and I had on one of Daddy's old flannel shirts with the sleeves rolled up to make big cuffs over my sleeper.

And behind me, Mama was washing Cherrie in a big plastic pan that's supposed to hold wet cement, and while she was washing Cherrie, Mama was singing that "cockles and mussels" song, real soft, like a lullaby—only, Daddy heard her anyway from where he was resting on the sway-middled sofa in the next room, and yelled something like:

"Don't go givin' her none of them *ideas*," like a baby's got much of a mind for accepting ideas, let alone do more than spit up bubbles or poop her diapers.

If Mama sang the song to Cherrie again, it wasn't when I could hear it, but as soon as Cherrie could talk halfway plain, she was singing it.

Funny how I'd forgot that day, but Mama so seldom bathed either me or Cherrie in a sit-down way. Usually it was a birdbath, from a basin or a pail or whatnot, with no stepping in the water, same as Mama and Daddy washed.

As Mama finished drying Cherrie, and Daddy honked the horn outside the rest room, I didn't say nothing else about it, even as the last of the song echoed in my ears, but I wondered why even Mama hated the song now, when she'd taught it to Cherrie in the first place....

* * * *

Was close to beans time in North Carolina that we picked up again, loaded the car and left the tent we'd been living in, but on Highway 95 the car started overheating, real bad, and we had to park it real close to the bridge going over Lake Marion, so's we wouldn't stall out over the bridge itself.

While Daddy tinkered with the car engine, doing whatever it is that men seem born knowing 'bout cars, Mama and Cherrie and I stood outside the car, watching Daddy, and trying not to listen when people'd shout rude things out their car windows at us.

Like we had "picker" branded on us somehow.

We were real close to the lake, a sort of loose, laid back *L* shape, with a scenic trail close by. Nobody was on the trail, 'least not that time of afternoon-going-on-evening, and since it was so late, Mama took to yawning and finally told me to watch Cherrie while she sat down next to the car, on the side facing away from the highway. And the people.

Cherrie wanted to go near the lake, and since I was holding her hand, I figured it was O.K. to let her. Since Mama wasn't awake to yell or anything, I figgered Cherrie could maybe sit on the banks of the lake, dangle her feet in the water. Keep her quiet, keep her from singing that dang song, maybe.

As we walked closer to the lake, I got to thinking how it's be nice to put my feet in the water, too. Funny thing, we've traveled for miles and miles up and down the East Coast, yet always managed to stay pretty close inland. I don't know how to swim, not a stroke, can't even paddle in a bathtub. Never *been* in a tub, 'least not that I can remember.

But I figgered that as long as I held onto Cherrie near the water, she wouldn't fall in, and I wouldn't have to swim when I couldn't and fish her out.

From where we padded on down to the edge of the lake, it was sorta marshy, sorta squishy underfoot, but the wet felt good. And the sun was low enough in the sky to make the lake look like it was covered with golden scales, patches of color that rippled and flattened in the breeze.

Past the lake were trees, a wall of them, or so it seemed. The sun coming off the water made my eyes water, so I squinted and shielded them with my hands, like a visor, and I wasn't sure if I could make out people on the other side, but something smallish was moving, and I wondered, if they were people, if they could see me, if they could tell from that great distance of water if I was a picker or just a *person*, walking near the lake on the way to someplace clean and neat and mine forever, not just another shack or tent or flat of grass under a picnic table or bench.

And the more I looked, the more I wanted me to *be* that other person I wasn't quite sure the people across the lake could/couldn't see.

Not a picker wearing Daddy's old sleeveless T-shirt over an old pair of cutoffs Mama'd found at a launder-mat one day on the way from there to *there*, with embedded dirt under my nails, and a daddy whose car radio didn't work at all and the eight-track just barely did, but a *person* other people wouldn't be afraid to walk near, or touch even if it was to drop a penny's worth of change into my palm.

Not a fruit *tramp*, kneeling under the hot sun until my back and neck and shoulders screamed and knotted under my sunburned flesh, and I cried and cried, but Mama and Daddy couldn't stop picking long enough to come over and dry my face, and that was when I wasn't much bigger than Cherrie—

—covering my face with my hands, I suddenly felt cold inside.

I wasn't holding onto Cherrie anymore.

My knees almost buckled, until I heard her singing not too far from me, that little warbling, *keening* voice, singsonging:

-o—

	'cock	mus		Alive
Singin'	les an'	sels! Alive,		

And I let out my held-in breath loose and easy, until I figgered out *where* her voice was coming from, and dropped my hands from my eyes real quick, even though I *knew* there nothing I could *do*—not with her out in the water like that.

But....

Cherrie was out maybe five-ten feet from me—it was hard to tell 'cause the sun glinting on the water made it hard to tell how far away Cherrie was, on account of having nothing close by to compare her with for size.

But Cherrie didn't seem to care how far away she was. She was too busy petting something on the water, reaching down past her barely wet feet and *down*, into the water below her, babbling something about the "fishes," and laughing as they touched her fingertips.

And if I squinted my eyes just right, I could *see* them, all the fish darting close to the surface, bobbing up to see what Cherrie was doing there on the water, walking on *top* of them…with just the soles of her feet and maybe a quarter-inch more of them submerged, like she was walking on wet pillows or something, the water *giving* only a little as she went further and further *away* from me, just a little picker baby toddling on the lake, toward the distant, busy shore.

And with every step, the fish darted under her, more and more of them, nearly surfacing to see what the commotion was about, and their scales glinted in the sun, too, like glitter under the sparkling ripples of water; and I was about to wade into the water, to go after Cherrie before she went too far, or wouldn't want to some *back*, when I heard Mama behind and above me—

"Peaches, don't you dare."

It wasn't what I expected, not at all. No yelling about Cherrie, no screaming that she might drown. Just her not wanting *me* to dare—

Cherrie stopped walking, bending down to look at some fish, while Mama hurried over to stand maybe five feet or so behind me, no closer.

She stared at me, and me at her, and I was about to set foot on the water, to go after Cherrie, but all she said was, "You do it, and nothing'll be right; you'll see."

But I didn't see, 'least not what she was talking about, so I turned from her, and started to put my foot into or onto the water, when I remembered all them town kids making fun, laughing when they had no cause to, and for a second I imagined me showing all of them what I *could* do, what Cherrie was already doing, and wanting to rub their faces in it, in my difference for a change, because the change was good, it was special, it was different—

But as I rested my foot on the water, the first step on a shimmering golden path that led somewhere that wasn't where *I* was headed, and I saw Cherrie bobbing gently before me, not knowing that where she was was impossible, not knowing that fish weren't things to pet and walk *over*, like bunnies or kittens, I remembered what Cherrie wasn't old enough to know, wasn't old enough to read of—

No matter what I could or couldn't do once I started out across that lake, folks weren't gonna treat me any better than they did when they called me a "picker" or worse. They hadn't treated Him any better, had they? And He sure as heck wasn't a picker to start out with....

But yet...it *seemed* so easy, so natural, watching Cherrie...even though I knew enough to know that people have a way of not being kind, or understanding, even when it's something *simple* like a picker—

"Here, Cherrie. Time...to go home," I called to her, and she splashed toward me, arms reaching for me, eyes not on that soft yielding ground at all, until she was in my arms, and I stepped away from the lake and back onto the marshy ground, and Mama was looking at me, just looking sad-like, until she glanced away from me for a second, her longing eyes resting on that molten, strangely unyielding lake beyond.

And when she looked back at me, all she said was, "Daddy's got the car fixed."

And I followed her back to Daddy and the car, only looking over my shoulder at the barred path behind me, and the land I could have no part of on the opposite shore.

* * * *

Daddy had to drive for hours and hours to make up for the time we'd lost in South Carolina, and all that time I sat saying nothing in the back-seat, and Mama only looked at herself in the mirror outside her window, face not showing anything, but her eyes telling it all, with no need for words, the story plain, though, like she *was* telling it to me.

Don't know how, don't know why, but other *people* will *be* people, *and they ain't kind and they ain't right, but long as they're* them *and we're* us, *we can't take no more chances, can we?*

The story don't have no beginning, but it don't need one. And it don't have a reason a *why*, but if it did, I wouldn't want to know it.

And it don't make it clear if we're the only ones, or if all us pickers are, or if it's the reason why we pick close to the solid land, seldom venturing by the water where nothing can be harvested by hand, but in the long run, it don't make any difference.

Not to a *picker*.

And I don't know if Mama's song is part of the story, or something that just makes the longing for what can't be come too close to the surface, like wanting and needing when what you're pining for just can't *be*, 'least not among all them *others* out there.

And Daddy fishes a tape out of the box near Mama's feet, The Doors one again, that singer who I heard somewhere died a long time ago in a bathtub somewhere far over the sea, singing over and over about that woman of his, even though he ain't gonna get her now, and knew even then that he wasn't gonna get her or keep her long even if he did have her, but keeps belting out the song anyway, over and over until his dead voice is lost in a flutter of stretched-out tape, like it's O.K. and not O.K. 'bout him and his woman, 'cause he needs her and can't ever need her, all at once.

Like a memory of something that never happened. Like me stepping on that water, and feeling it cushion me, ready to support me for however far it might take to walk across that lake, toward the people who couldn't, wouldn't understand.

And, without Daddy having to tell me, I bop Cherrie a good one when she starts singing that song of hers again.

AFTERWORD

For the longest time, I had this notion that the refrain of this one old song I'd heard ages ago might make for a pretty good story title...trouble was, I had no story to place *under* the title. Then, I saw a photo essay in what I think was *Life* magazine (just prior to it ceasing publication) about a family of fruit pickers down south, and suddenly I had a story to place under that title.

Many of the scenes were inspired by that black-and-white series of pictures, including the little girl sitting with her feet near the open stove. These people were dirt poor, but beautiful; the children were uncannily good-looking.

Something about that photo essay triggered memories of the way my family was treated once we moved to Ladysmith (aka Hell on Earth); we were beyond dirt-poor, well below the official poverty level as stated by the IRS, but we didn't take any welfare, food stamps, or other charity, even though I was accused of not only belonging to a family which "moved here for the welfare" (according to the wife of the Realtor who'd sold my grandmother the unlivable wreck of a hovel [calling that monstrosity a "house" was a stretch], then set about destroying our reputations in town because my grandmother had dared to flirt with the woman's husband while he was showing her various houses during her visit here prior to my mother and I joining her from L.A.), but which was comprised of "three whores" who had no business moving here in the first place because we had no relatives already living here.

(During my first year of school I learned that people who came in without being related to current citizens of LadyShit were not only not welcome, but that they would *never* fit in...or be allowed to get a job, etc. As it was, it took my mother over a year to find work; she was literally laughed out of the first place she tried, and was rejected by business after business after that, until a motel owner originally from out of town took pity on her and gave her a job.)

Nowadays, what I endured is considered bullying, but then, it was simply thought to be normal behavior toward an "outsider"; I was not only ridiculed, taunted and physically attacked/threatened by my classmates, but many of my teachers joined in—one of them, a high school teacher who was slowly going nuts on the public dime for years, but couldn't be thrown out due to having tenure, was so vicious in her attacks that she escalated to physical violence my senior year (and also attacked a classmate of mine who accidentally broke her beloved white plaster bust of Shakespeare—the kid did man up and tried to apologize, but was beaten up anyhow), and eventually the school forced her to take early retirement at the age of 55.

And the irony was, despite all the verbal and physical abuse, as well as emotional abuse, I still managed to graduate seventh out of 112 students—and in college, I was fourth in my class of over 80+ students. But it didn't matter at all; I was passed over for both the National Honor Society in high school and Who's Who at the college level. (That I was learning-disabled [dyslexia] and neurologically impaired [Asperger's Syndrome] didn't make learning any easier, either.)

I suppose being in the top ten of my class in both high school and college isn't on a par with being able to walk on water, but considering the cesspool of a high school I attended, where a high percentage of my classmates didn't even graduate *per se*, but instead received "Certificates of Attendance" in their diploma folders, I think it is something of an accomplishment nonetheless....

PRETTY BIRDS

There was a baby girl lying on the back lawn.

Again.

Arna leaned into the window until the screen pressed against her right cheek, and tiny squares of powdered flesh were outlined in gray-black grid-work.

It was on its back, fat-creased arms and legs rhythmically flailing while the fingers and toes wiggled, and she—if the pink-check sundress could be believed to be an intentional choice—was looking up at the odd pigeons flying above her head.

The sky was overcast, so Arna knew that the baby wasn't staring up into the sun but still, those birds, those small-headed pigeons, might relieve themselves on the baby in mid-flight—

"She's out there again, Dehaan. I should call someone about her mother—"

Dehaan didn't look at Arna as he shoved his cell and his wallet into his pockets. All he said was what he always said when she saw the baby on the lawn:

"C'mon, we're going to be late. Lynet doesn't like it when we're late—"

"Yeah. Especially when she shows up like half a minute before the session is due to start."

Arna found herself saying the words she always said in reply, before taking a last look at the baby and the circling pigeons, there in the back-yard.

Her backyard. Hers and Dehaan's. The spot where this baby was lying, again.

She knew from the other times she'd seen the baby that Dehaan wouldn't come look at it (*her*), wouldn't consider calling the police to come check on this baby lying out there alone (*save for the birds*), wouldn't even admit that there was a small infant back there (*on the lawn*, our *lawn*).

Riding next to Dehaan in the silent car, leaning against her shoulder harness strap until it cut into her neck, Arna told herself that Dehaan's indifference was the Beltrans' fault.

Paloma's stories of the little baby boy sitting on her back deck, on her kitchen floor, on her husband Jonas' footstool in the den, they'd made Dehaan skeptical.

Just as they made everyone else in group think Paloma was more than slightly *off*...as if the stories the others there told, of dead infants lying under warming lamps in the birthing room, of the tiny pastel knit caps and fuzzy blankets supplied by the nurses for "the picture" of the stillborn infant, of searching for just the right container for the handful of cremains, as if those tales were somehow *on*, in a positive sense.

But as Arna listened to Paloma' tales, as translated by her husband (whose English was less than fluent), she'd found herself more than empathizing, especially since she and Paloma shared a bond within the group, a small subset of a Venn diagram of expectation, loss, and hoped-for acceptance.

Both of their babies had vanished within them.

One day, they were looking at the print-out from a normal ultrasound, that sugary miasma of what looked like a tiny body swirling in black-ness, like a lump of sugar starting to dissolve in a cup of hot black coffee, so that there was a main shape in the middle, surrounded by wing-like protrusions which leeched into the darkness beyond.

And then, after a day or so of unexplainable unease, coupled with a gradual lack of movement, of presence, from within, another ultrasound, only this time, the coffee had absorbed all the sugar.

No baby. Just a swelling void, which in turn became a flattened-out void.

Arna and Paloma had no snapshots of a permanently wrinkled, yet oddly flaccid little face under a pulled-low knit cap, no folded little blanket sealed in a zip-top plastic bag, no...nothing. Just that grainy ul-trasound image, and a distinct sense memory of having been full, then having emptied, with no definite in-between stage.

There, gone.

As they pulled up to the center, Arna saw the Beltrans' SUV parked next to the Hollebs' little hybrid-power two-door. Thinking of the Hol-lebs' (a couple new to the group Lynet counseled, who hadn't had much of anything to say in the last session) combined size and girth, Arna was seized with a clown-car image from her childhood, and began to muffle the giggle which welled within her.

Dehaan paused as he took off his shoulder harness, saying, "You up to this today? I could leave a message, tell Lynet you're not—"

"I'm fine."

Just as they quitted their car, Lynet pulled up in her burgundy four by four, exactly a minute before the group counseling session for the parents of "preborn departures" was set to begin.

* * * *

The group session room was located at the back of the mental health care clinic, not much bigger than the average family entertainment center, and made smaller by the inclusion of the card table which held (or would hold, once Lynet brought them in) paper plates covered with small shaped crackers, plastic-tough squares of sliced cheese, flat fillingless cookies, and personal-sized bottles of flavored waters.

There used to be a carafe of coffee, but no one ever drank it—just as no one picked up the bottles of water—so Arna guessed that Lynet had switched to the same brand of bottled water she herself drank, so she could recycle the leftovers more efficiently.

While Lynet set the plates of food (carried in a tote which reminded Arna of a diaper bag) and bottles of water out, the other couples stood around awkwardly, not really saying much of anything, and not allowing their eyes to meet even if they did speak.

Arna saw that the Fugols were still carrying around that scrapbook of Fala's stillborn, which was big enough for the obligatory ultrasound image. The scrapbook jutted out from Fala's oversized purse, just shy of being diaper-bag sized. Arna knew that the scrapbook would be passed around at least once during group.

And Mrs. Vogel was carrying the plastic-bagged knit cap, with a couple of fine hairs still adhering to the band, in her sweater pocket. That, too, was usually passed from non-parent to almost-parent, as the Vogels took turns speaking.

Arna did find herself wondering if Paloma would tell another tale of the phantom boy-baby who would appear in her home.

Lynet never seemed comfortable with those twice-told stories (first in jumbled, hurried Spanish, then in slowly spoken English), the words coming in small clusters, like big round baby beads on a choke-proof string, perhaps because they were too mundane, too quotidian in their unadorned reality.

They were not the anxious fantasies of a childless mother, but the simple observances of a woman seeing a baby in her house, a baby which merely acted like a baby, and not some angelic or hyper-real version of infancy, courtesy of Hollywood CGI magic, or aging A-list actor voice-overs. Hadn't Paloma-via Jonas said that the baby even smelled, as if he'd filled his diaper?

And every time she'd seen this boy-baby, Paloma had found herself distracted by something (a phone ringing, the doorbell, a bird bouncing off the front window) for a fraction of a second, and in that minute slice of time, the baby would vanish. But she'd said something about the smell lingering, even after he was gone. And she had once patted the empty seat next to her, while emphatically sputtering and Jonas had mimicked her flat-palm-on-empty-vinyl motion while he translated:

"The seat, it stay warm, where he sit."

Once Lynet had finished putting out the plates of food no one would be eating later that evening, she sat down in the circle of couples (who all sat next to each other, with empty spaces between them, like breaks in the pattern of water-filled pillows on a teething ring), and said in that small, chirpy voice of hers, "Well people, shall we begin? Who would like to speak first?"

For the first few minutes, Arna found herself looking down at Lynet's sandal-covered feet, and bright carnation-pink toe-nails. It was better than seeing the slow droop of Lynet's mouth as she once again realized that despite all the weeks they'd all been coming to group, next to no progress had been made.

Arna wondered if she should mention the baby girl lying on her lawn, in case someone else in the group might want to make a call to child services for her, on the child's behalf, but the Hollebs began to speak at once.

"Our situation, it is somewhat—"

"We realize that you folks went through a lot, giving birth to—"

"Ok ok, talking is good, but talking both at once is confusing...how about if your wife...Sagirah, isn't it?...how about she speaks first?"

Sagirah lowered her eyes, casting dark wings of lashes across the tops of her broad cheekbones, before beginning again:

"I was saying, we, my husband and I, we realize that you women especially have been through a lot of pain, giving birth to...but we just want you to know that our situation is not quite the same as all of yours. We had the exams, the ultrasound, and everything was going well, but then, when I went in for the next ultrasound, the woman with the device, that slid over my belly, she went white, and called for someone to help her...she was gone.

"Our daughter. Just not there.

"All that was left was this dark void inside me. A cave, just empty space inside my body. She was over five months along, she had bones, and a heartbeat, and even hair, you could see it on the ultrasound, and suddenly...she was just *gone*.

"The doctors, they said she…reabsorbed into me, but there was so much of her, and she…so *quickly*. I had thought she was just being quiet. I thought she was giving me a break, from all the kicking—"

Arna and Dehaan's baby had been almost six months along, when she went wherever it was she went to, inside Arna.

One morning, she had been kicking and somersaulting inside her mother. Dehaan used to call it "bouncing on the walls," only Arna had thought of it more like the baby flying around in that watery space, with her pre-birth wing-arms grazing the sides of her temporary submerged cage.

That was why she had suggested the name Olitia, which meant "winged" in some language….Dehaan had agreed, especially since the baby could change it to something like Litia if she didn't like the sound of it once she was old enough….They'd called her that, while speaking to Arna's growing belly each night, patting her taut flesh, and murmuring the name against the skin, hoping the baby within could hear them.

But then came the morning when, after a dream of flocks of birds, small-headed pale birds, flying low over her head as she hung clothes out to dry in the backyard, their wings beating and flapping in time with the wind-whipped snap and flutter of the wooden-pin trapped sheets and pillowcases bobbing on the green plastic line before her, Arna had felt her belly, and all her hands could detect was warm skin, with only the subtle throb of her own breathing and distant heartbeat pulsing under her splayed fingers.

No kicking, and worse yet, no heavy sensation of something within her.

It had been a few weeks since her last ultrasound, but when she'd climbed up on that table, and found herself watching the ceiling rather than look as the technician slathered her jutting belly with the clear lubricant, because she knew that her protruding abdomen wouldn't jerk and shudder from within anymore as the tech slid the sensor-thingie across that gleaming mound of full-full-full flesh…and thus, she didn't see the look on the tech's face as she stared at an empty screen but she did hear the panic in the woman's voice as she called for help, for a witness….

There were tests, after that, and doctors shaking their heads, and finally, the referral to Lynet Mochini's therapy group.

After their first session there, after handling the scrapbooks and the plastic-shrouded knit hats and limp blankets, Arna had donated all of would-be Olitia's baby things to charity. Even the passed down things from her mother, and Dehaan's mother.

Which hadn't set well with either Dehaan or his family, but Arna considered all those waiting-but-unused items to be jinxed, tainted by the mystery of their vanished would-be occupant. They were not meant to be worn by her, so there was no use keeping them to hex another future child of hers and Dehaan's....

"—so that's why we're not coming back to group next time," Çapek Holleb was saying, after his wife's voice grew thick and clotted with unshed tears.

"Oh, I wish you'd wait until after your next visit to decide that," Lynet soothed, her small pinched face pulled into a *moué* that started at her lips and yanked her entire face into a beak-like protrusion.

After a beat of silence from the Hollebs, Paloma began saying something, a rush of lilting Spanish with no pauses between the words, and as soon as she did take a breath, Jonas repeated:

"The boy, she see him again. Walking, this time. Eating a cookie, and what not go in his mouth, it go on the floor. She try to keep watching him, talk to him, but she hear my car in the driveway, and...."

"But this time, she keep crumbs. Sweep them into bag—"

Poking his wife in the side, Jonas watched as Paloma rooted around in her jeans pocket for a small clear zip-top bag, the seal marked with a vivid stripe of green where the yellow and blue sides meshed together. Under the bright verdant seal was a moist clump of buttery-yellow crumbs, and a rounded piece of unchewed cookie like the petal-shaped outer surface of those Baby Bites cookies Arna tried not to look at in the store when she went shopping.

Holding the bag up so all could see it, Paloma began speaking, pointing at the bag with her free hand, while Jonas said, "You feel the crumbs, they still moist. From his mouth. We take to laboratory, they do tests on it. They say they contact us, with result. Test the spit on the crumbs. Prove it from baby—"

Arna could predict what Lynet would say before the woman finally opened her mouth—

"That's true, they can do tests on food for saliva, but Paloma, where did you *get* the cookie? Children, they eat things in the park, and drop them on the grass...."

Jonas quickly translated, and Paloma began shaking her head. Then, through Jonas:

"No, not on grass. Not in park. See, in the bag, thread from the rug. See, it is red—"

As Lynet explained that yes, she did believe that the carpet in the Beltran house *was* red, and that there was a fiber visible in the bag, but it still didn't prove that the cookie crumbs were on the carpet...

...and around that time, Arna stopped listening altogether, and spent the rest of the evening looking at people's shoes, at their purses and bags resting on the floor beside them, all the while wondering how she could place an anonymous call to the police, child protective services, someone, to report that person who kept leaving that baby on her lawn.

* * * *

The baby was gone from the back lawn when they returned home after group.

Dehaan made a point of shutting the sliding window once Arna had peered outside at their darkening lawn, and pulling the drapes over the closed glass, while Arna pretended not to notice him.

As she went into the kitchen, looking for something to toss into the microwave, Dehaan said, "I think I'm going to spring for that air conditioning. There's no reason not to…."

Before, when Olitia still fluttered and swooped within her, there had been a reason not to install A/C—that money was earmarked for their daughter's college fund.

Arna wondered if Dehaan had made his decision based on her own unfitness for carrying a baby to term, or if this was a quick fix to prevent her from needing to look out the dining room window, to even open the drapes themselves anymore—

"What Paloma was saying…I think Lynet was wrong. At least, I think she should've waited for the results of those tests to come back—"

"What results? All those two needed to do was kiss, swap spit, and expel it in a bag with some crumbs. They're in denial, only now they're manufacturing proof of—"

"Of something that might actually be real?"

"Don't start in on that again—"

"On what?"

"That whole baby thing…seeing them. I mean, I know I can't fully empathize with you on this, there's no way I can know what you went through, but…just don't start this. You got the idea from Paloma, and next thing you know, that Holleb woman will start seeing them too."

"I know one thing—they're not the only ones who won't be there at group next time. I mean, we don't belong there, not really. It's not like we have a baby hat, or pictures to—"

"There's the ultrasound—"

"Of what, exactly? The more you look at it, the more it could be any damn thing. There's hardly a face, let alone—"

"Her ears, they stuck out. Like mine. There's that—"

"So do a lot of other kid's ears. She's gone, and that's it. No amount of sitting around talking to other people is going to change it, either. Make something for yourself. I'm going to do some work in my office."

Once he'd gone into his home office (which was going to be Olitia's room, *before*) and shut the door, Arna pushed aside the drapes and peered out the back window one last time, even though the yard was empty, as empty as the house for sale next door…

And no birds flew anywhere above the grass.

"A/C would be good," she mumbled to herself, as she thought, *The baby wasn't eating, not yet, not on her own, so she wouldn't leave any crumbs, but maybe…just maybe….*

* * * *

Without the group meetings to look forward to every other week, time seemed to pass more quickly, the days, weeks, months merged into a repetitive whole (eat-drive-work-drive-eat-maybe-have-sex-sleep-eat-drive).

And once Dehaan made good on his promise to have the A/C installed, not only did Arna have less of an excuse to periodically peer out the dining room window, and scan the lawn for stray babies, but once Dehaan bought those shrubs from the nursery on the other side of town, the view from that window was quickly obscured by something quick-growing and thick-leaved (she never did bother to read the plastic tag still affixed to the shrub's stem), which turned the yard and sky beyond into a choppy, incomplete mosaic of bright green and blue beyond the darker green of the shrub.

No way to look for babies.

And with the money they didn't spend on Litia's food, clothes and medical bills, Dehaan found enough to hire someone to mow the lawn for him, so that Arna had no reason to look out that way, or even walk around there.

Once a "For Sale" sign went up in front of their house as well as the one which was still empty next door, all of Arna's time was spent packing, and cleaning, and getting things ready for Dehaan's move (job related—at least that wasn't one of his excuses, his cover-ups designed to make her stop fixating on that lawn baby).

So she almost forgot about the baby…until she went shopping for the last time in their favorite grocery store, for food they could eat during the drive to their new town, and Dehaan's new job.

Moving her cart down the aisle with the beef jerky and other preserved meats in skin-tight wrappers, she saw Paloma pushing a cart toward her from the opposite end of the long aisle. There was no way to avoid her, and since Jonas wasn't around, no way to understand her—

"Hello, Arna! Been so long time, no? You ok?"

Wondering just how good the woman's English really was, Arna smiled and said, "Dehaan and I are doing well—he has a new job, in—"

"You miss group, you no hear...the test, we get back. Baby real. Baby, he ours—"

Glad that Dehaan wasn't around, Arnba leaned over the handle of her cart and said, "You mean DNA tests? The spit, it matched yours and—"

"*Si, si*, it match. They say, come from *our* baby—"

Wondering what Lynet had had to say about *that*, Arna asked, "But do you still see him? The baby—"

"*Si*. He big now, running down hallway. I run, but no catch. But he real. No matter what Lynet say. He talk. To me. Call me Mama. It not strange to him, to be here, not be here. Jonas, he not see him, but he believe. Like Hollebs, they believe too—"

"They kept coming back to group?"

"*Si*. They curious, about test. Then, Sagirah, she see her daughter. With dark hair, like in ultrasound. Lynet, she not know what to do, but we no have picture, or knit things to show off, so me and Sagirah, we share what we see. I tell Sagirah, look for what falls from her, pick up whatever she find. People, they shed things all time, same for babies—"

And birds, Arna found herself thinking. *The birds, who always circled the baby on my lawn. They shit. They shed feathers—*

Still not able to mention the baby she'd seen, so many months before, Arna nodded and told Paloma she was happy for her, that she was still seeing her son, and handed the woman a piece of paper with her new address on it, just to keep in touch, later.

Smiling, Paloma shoved it into her opened purse in the top basket of the cart, and pushed her cart past Arna's, while Arna threw whatever jerky and meat treats she could find close by into her cart, wondering if she could make it home before Dehaan arrived home from work that afternoon....

* * * *

The person Dehaan hired to cut the grass had set the blade of the mower much too low—the grass was dried out to short brittle stubs above the easily visible ground. There was a great deal of bird dirt all over, thin watery splotches surrounding the tiny curled squiggle of dried matter in the middle. Most of the mess was concentrated near the spot where the baby had been resting on the grass, close to the neighboring yard, but still on her side of the property line. There was a vaguely baby-sized spot in the middle where no dirt at all was visible.

She did find a feather, a thin dun-colored thing, but she heard no birds cooing, nor did she see any sign of them in the trees which surrounded the yard. No trace of the baby, but yet there was no proof it hadn't been there, either.

Kicking herself because she hadn't gone outside to actually look at the baby when she'd seen it, Arna wondered what Paloma or Sagirah would do once they finally caught their babies. When they overcame whatever it was that was still holding them back from actually snatching the child up and holding it, tight, tighter, never to let it go.

Standing there on her burned grass, Arna unconsciously put her hands over her empty abdomen, and whispered aloud, "Olitia, I wouldn't have let go of you if you'd just stayed around long enough to come out."

As the wind picked up, reminding Arna of that dream she'd had, the night Olitia went away, either disappearing, or dissipating into her surrounding body, she found herself looking skyward, for those flocks of small-headed birds, until she felt the cool, damp softness on her exposed lower leg, followed by a gentle shove against her calf.

Looking down, she saw the baby, only the baby was walking now, a bit unsteadily, but upright and mobile nonetheless. Barely combed pale brown hair, the same shade as Dehaan's, framed a pinkish-tan wide face, and just like Arna, her ears stuck out past the hanging strands of her hair. Blue-gray eyes, like Arna's, like her own mother's and all her siblings' eyes. Typical baby nose, still too unformed to hint at what it would look like later on. Little mouth, pink-lipped and slightly wet, as if she'd been chewing something and had generated additional saliva.

She was wearing a yellow jumpsuit, short puffy sleeves and balloon pants down to her mid-thigh. Plastic sandals the color of dandelion flowers over bare feet. Her hands were moist, and slightly sticky, from whatever she'd been eating.

Gingerly reaching down one hand, Arna felt the top of the baby's head, hard and sun-warmed under the glossy hair, yet not too hard, the bones beneath the scalp still barely pliant if she pressed down too hard, which she didn't.

"And who are you?" she found herself cooing, in that small high voice adults invariably use when speaking to young children they didn't know, as if their ears were too fragile for normal adult tones.

The little girl looked up at Arna, her eyes narrowed, either from the sunlight hitting them, or from puzzlement. Then she smiled, as if to say, *I know what you're doing...you're fooling me*, before she leaned forward and rested her cheek against Arna's lower leg, and wrapped both small fat arms around her calf—

The sound of birds flying overhead, making a flapping, rushing noise, distracted her, made her look up. As she saw the last of them wing quickly against the noon sun, her leg suddenly felt very cold and naked in the summer heat, and she didn't need to look down to know what had happened, despite all the times she'd heard Paloma tell the same basic story, and no matter how many times she'd been warned what not to do.

And when Dehaan came home for his lunch break, to help her finish packing, she wished that the baby had been older, better able to understand big words like "moving" and "find me," but something Paloma had said to her in the store, about the boy baby being hers, gave Arna some comfort—if this little girl in yellow was Olitia, she would find Arna again. From wherever she came from, and kept going back to....

* * * *

The new house was a condo, in a long line of other condos all squashed together without a yard, and without any place that a baby might stand unattended within her sight. No one else in the complex had children, either—

Arna suspected that this was how Dehaan wanted it. He had picked out the condo, after all. She'd seen it before they moved in, but hadn't really thought about it all that much. Once she was there, the reality of her new surroundings hit hard, and all she could think of was the feel of those warm, sticky tiny hands on her bare leg, and the sweet pressure of that soft cheek against her skin.

Arna hoped that the other women, Paloma and Sagirah and whoever else might eventually join that group with their own baby sightings, were able to touch their babies.

One thing Paloma had said, about the baby only coming when she was around, made more and more sense—the mother's body had been the last place the baby had been before not being there anymore, so if it were to somehow come back, wouldn't the mother be the most obvious person it would come to?

Home turf, so to speak?

(She refused to believe that a baby, especially a baby so close to being at least a premie if it were to be plucked from her body, could just dissolve like that within her, reverting cell by cell into maternal ooze, no matter what the doctors and Lynet said about it.)

As she opened up box after box of belongings, and set about putting the contents all over the new condo, tucking things into whatever nooks and corners she could find, like hiding Easter eggs amid shrubbery, she remembered what her mother had said, when she'd phoned after hearing the news about Olitia on her answering machine after Dehaan made the call from the hospital waiting room—

"Arna, sweetest, when I was a little girl, I had an aunt who…lost a baby. That's what everyone said, 'Aunt Mary lost the baby' and all I could think was, 'Well, then why aren't all of you out *looking* for it?' The poor baby was lost, and no one was searching for...oh God, Arna, I'm sorry, I'm rambling—"

Perfect child-logic; you lose something, you go look for it.

Her mother never mentioned it again, so Arna never knew if her mother had actually voiced her suggestion, but that was a long time ago, when kids were expected to stay quiet.

Yet, it made a sort of sense, if you thought about it...and wasn't that what group was all about, anyhow? Finding, and holding on to whatever remained of the lost baby?

Tossing aside the now-empty box, Arna tried to remember which one of her cousins was later born to Aunt Mary...it had been at least forty, forty-five years since the woman "lost" that baby, but Arna wondered if perhaps one of Mary's later children had heard more about the matter, from their mother—

"—yeah, it's been a *long* time...thanks for that card you and your husband sent after, y'know, we both appreciated it...anyhow, I just got to wondering, what with what happened to me and all, did your mother ever tell you exactly what happened when she lost that baby a few years before you were born? I was just wondering if there was some sort of genetic, y'know—"

As her cousin (second, third cousin?) Callie spoke, Arna found herself staring out the window, at the lightly clouded sky beyond their second-story condo, wondering where the birds were.

"It was really strange," Callie said. "Ma was about five months along or so, heartbeat was fine, the baby was kicking, only back then, there was no ultrasound, so she never did know what it was—anyhow, she goes to sleep one night all right, and come morning, she starts freaking out, Dad claims, saying she was 'empty' and sure enough, the doctor couldn't find a heartbeat, and couldn't feel anything in there, either. She never expelled anything, just got flatter and flatter according to Dad. The doctor didn't know what to make of it, but told her to tell everyone they'd lost it. Mom never told me any of this, but Dad remembered—"

"How did she act later on? Did she ever talk about it?"

"No, and the only way I knew what happened was when someone in the family mentioned it, when I was about seven or so. But it explains why she did a lot of standing there, not talking, just sorta spacing out, every so often. Like she was listening for something—"

The birds, Arna thought, *maybe she was looking for the birds. Or listening for her baby's voice.*

Hanging up the phone a few minutes later, Arna tried to remember what Aunt Mary looked like, but by then the woman was old, and distant, and all she could recall with any clarity was the way the woman's eyes never quite focused on whomever she was talking to....

* * * *

Dehaan was away at work more often since his promotion and transfer, leaving Arna alone in the condo.

In the following years, she took up some hobbies, needlepoint, and egg-painting, using resist dye and wax work that took up huge chunks of time, before she bundled up the finished eggs and sold them at a craft store downtown.

She barely knew the other people in the condo, didn't want to after a few awkward exchanges which soured when they asked if she and Dehaan had any children. Either way she answered, her words would be lies, so she kept to herself.

Even though she bought pre-blown eggs for her work, she did like to go down to the small park a few blocks from the condo complex, to see if she could find any broken bird's eggs on the ground near the trees, or perhaps even an ejected whole egg. She loved the smallness, and the inherent contradictory fragility and strength of those tiny orbs, and always, as she looked, she'd keep an eye out for those oddly small-headed pigeons she'd seen circling around the lawn baby so many years ago.

The birds which somehow looked familiar, even as she couldn't quite place them, or even find them in the bird books she'd paged through in the bookstore near the craft shop.

Pausing to catch her breath as she walked home through the park one spring morning, Arna leaned against a maple trunk, and closed her eyes, until just the sun-lit blood in her eyelids filled her line of sight.

Then, a small voice:

"I found one...it's whole, too."

Opening her eyes suddenly, Arna's line of sight was still red-tinged, but she could make out the little girl standing before her quite clearly. The same stuck-out ears, only now they seemed to stick out all the more thanks to the girl wearing her shoulder-length hair in a lace-covered scrunchie. The hair was darker now, and slightly thicker, not baby hair. But the nose—it was Dehaan's, that much was apparent. And the mouth, something like hers, just as the eyes were hers, and her mother's, and—

The girl was holding a fallen egg in one slightly grimy palm, a tiny blue one with a smudge of dirt on one end. Looking past her hand, the egg cupped there, Arna saw that the child was wearing some sort of uniform, not a school one, but a club outfit, not Brownie or Camp Fire Girl, but...something dun-colored and two-piece, with a vest over that which had various embroidered badges and enameled pins affixed to it. And she had a beret-like hat on her head, which Arna had missed, because it was so close in color to the child's hair.

"It's beautiful. Not even cracked. What are you going to do with it?"

"Same thing I always do. But this is a *really* nice one. Not like the ones at home."

"Oh? And where is home?"

Arna hoped the child wouldn't become scared of her, run away—

"Here's home…sort of. I forget, you don't really *know*, do you? But I'm glad you didn't cut your hair. I always thought it looked better this way—"

Not caring if the girl was frightened or not, Arna knelt down and put both hands on the child's shoulders, feeling the coarseness of her vest and the underlying warmth of her lightly fleshed bones beneath the cotton blouse she wore, and as she looked into eyes that were oh so familiar to her, she asked:

"Who *are* you? What is your name?"

"You know my name. And you know who I am—"

"Don't get weird, please…just tell me your name, *please*—"

"Olitia Galvin. You knew that. Only now, in 'Birders, we all took new names, for the birds we like best, and mine is Pules now, for pigeon—"

"That can't be your name. You were never born…and I don't know who you are—"

"You don't like 'Pules'? Daddy doesn't like it either, he wanted me to pick something like Zitkala or Doli, only I didn't like the Zee one, 'cause it sounds like zits—"

"Stop speaking gibberish!"

"It's not 'gibberish' it's Indian—no, Native American names. Mine is Algonquin, and Zitkala is Dakota, and the other is Navajo—"

"I don't care! Why are you doing this to me? Where did you come from—"

"Here. Sort of. 'Almost here' is how most of us describe it."

"'Us'?"

She stared at the child, who looked back at her with the same bland fascination of someone examining a flipped-over beetle on the ground, its many legs flailing wildly, before it either righted itself or a bird swooped down and devoured it.

As she stared at the child, felt her warmth under her curling, digging fingertips, she noticed that the girl wasn't scared of her, not at all, despite her being a stranger who'd grabbed her in the park, and started shouting questions at her. There was no fear in her body, or in her eyes, only a gradual dawning of comprehension followed by a slight, sad smile on her lips.

"We're not supposed to do this, but all of us can do it without thinking about it. We just go back. To where we began. It just happens, 'specially when we're babies. No one yells at us then, 'cause we can't help it, but when we get older...our *there* moms get mad if we keep going back *here*. Like *you* used to.

"Only lately, you've been cool about it, and don't mind when I go off. 'Cause you know I'll come back. But it's been so long since I found you here, I forgot that you don't know. You don't understand, is how Daddy puts it. In *my* 'here' things are different. Everybody knows where the sudden babies come from, and they understand that sometimes, we go back, 'Cause we need to. 'Specially once we understand the sircum—sircum—circus—"

"Circumstances? Are you trying to say circumstances?" Arna whispered.

And with that, the child relaxed, and said, "*Yeah*. That *other* birds and bees stuff we learn about in science class. 'Sudden babies are special babies,' that's what Mr. Shale says. 'Cause we come from *here*, and end up in the other here, where I live.

"For a long time nobody knew where we came from, just that some mommies would wake up with the baby inside, and not know where it came from. Some of them went from skinny to fat like that. It wasn't until they made the last Mars landing that Dr. Cholena discovered the part about all the different *heres*, which she said were like cards in a stack that was miles and miles high, all touching, yet not realizing there was even a stack of them.

"Something like that. We saw it on TV in the Classroom last year. Dr. Cholena, she's Indian, not a 'Native American' she's not from India so I shouldn't call her that. But people used to call *them* Indians, too. But our 'Birders nest-mother always corrects us if we make the mis—"

"So...you came from *here*, in *here*—" she grabbed the child's free hand, and gently placed it on her abdomen.

Nodding, the girl said, "*Way* down inside there. Then, according to Dr. Cholena, the cards in the stack, they touched hard enough to lose all the space between them, and I went from your tummy to my mother's tummy. Which was the same tummy, only on a different card—"

The analogy was imprecise, but Arna could see why the mysterious Dr. Cholena had chosen it. It was simple enough that a child could understand it, without using words like parallel or universes—

"Why do you come?"

"Because when we find out why we're sudden, we figure out that we had to be something opposite *here*. Mr. Shale, he calls us 'lost' over *here*. I…'spose I just wanted to know if you were looking for me. 'Cause I was lost to you *here*…."

Such a simple concept, even a small child like Arna's mother could figure it out. Even if she couldn't voice it. Or act upon it.

"Ohhh…kay," she said slowly, then found herself asking, out of all the things she could have said, "I shouldn't cut my hair? Does it look that bad?"

Wrinkling Dehaan's nose, the girl said, "It makes your ears stick out more. Or look like they do. This is way better. Daddy says so, and he can't wait for you to grow it back."

"He can't?"

Arna smiled, and reluctantly let the child go, but before Olitia could move away, or do whatever it was that she just *did* to go from *here* to *here*, Arna asked, "Can you tell me something?"

"Uh-huh."

"Is there a little boy in your class, by the last name of Beltran? A little Mex—Hispanic boy?"

"Ohhh…Jonas-junior. He gets in a lot of trouble with his parents, 'cause he keeps coming *here*. *All* the time. He keeps bringing over his pet birds, and leaving them here, 'cause he thinks it's funny. And 'cause we have so many of them in our *here*—"

"What kind of birds?"

"The pigeons…our pigeons. I never see them when I'm here, unless some come over with me. But mine usually come back when I do.

"But Jay-jay, he leaves his *here*, on purpose. He says they're for his *here*-mom. She likes birds. And ours are neater than the ones *here*. Yours have too big of heads. His mom where I'm from, she can't make him stop, but his dad is cool with it. Says this *here* needs more birds anyhow. Like he knows, he's not a sudden, but he understands us sudden kids. Not like Daddy.

"But *you*, you're really good about it now. Not like when I was a baby and would just *go* while you were sunning yourself in our old back yard, before Daddy got promoted. You'd freak out, tell me later on that you were so afraid someone would call the police about a missing baby.

"But now, you're ok about me going, 'cause you know I'll come back soon. Like…I gotta go now. But I'll see you again…ok?"

Trying not to stare at her, trying not to show how hungry she really was for her own flesh and blood, Arna nodded her head, and said, "Go on, before…I miss you. I'll be waiting for you—"

In the distance, Arna heard the rumble of the big truck which brought the daily newspaper into downtown, and even though she knew she shouldn't, she couldn't help but glance at it…and in that nanosecond, Olitia was gone.

But on the ground where the child had stood was the perfect bird's egg, pale blue and still slightly smudged with dirt. Cupping it in one hand, she walked to the newsstand, and watched as the vendor cut open the bundle of paper, and tossed the string aside like so many long white worms onto the sidewalk. Giving him a couple of quarters with her free hand, she took one of the papers, and tucked it under her arm during the long, lonely walk back to the condo.

It wasn't until she'd arrived home, and set the small egg in a place of honor on her worktable, that she unfolded the paper, and read one of the sidebar headlines:

ONCE EXTINCT BIRD DISCOVERED IN STATE

—and under that was an article describing how live passenger pigeons, previously deemed extinct since the early 20th century, had been discovered, a find recently authenticated by renowned ornithologist Dr. Luyu Cholena.

There was a picture of her, along with that of a live passenger pigeon, which looked very much like a regular pigeon, only its head was smaller than normal, and it was a pretty bird, a most pretty bird indeed, for a young boy to bring as a present for his mother.…

AFTERWORD

When I was thirty-nine years old, my mother finally decided to tell me something concerning my gestation—between March of 1957 and August of 1957, she was carrying two babies.

Back then, ultrasounds were not an option when a woman was carrying, nor were any of the other modern-day options for discovering just what was going on inside an expectant mother, save for X-rays (yup, they exposed unborn babies to X-rays in those days), and even those weren't utilized until very late in the pregnancy.

All she was told was that the doctor heard two heartbeats in her womb up until August. Then there was only one heart beating. Considering that this happened midway through the pregnancy, that other baby was fairly well developed, had to have had all its limbs, a head, a body… all of which disappeared during the next five months she carried me (I was due to be born December 15, but didn't make an appearance until January 3rd of the following year).

Did the other occupant of her womb deteriorate bit by bit? Was I aware of having had company for a few months, then…nothing? Unless the unborn fetus somehow magically vanished, I was in the presence of a dead corpse for who knows how long, before it went away.

Something else my mother told me, from the time I was very small, actually, also stuck with me: One of her aunts had miscarried a baby when my mother was very young, and the only thing all the adults around her would say was "She lost the baby."

In her child's mind, my mother wondered why no one went *looking* for this lost baby….

I suppose some people might think that the subject matter here is indelicate, even offensive; quite a few editors passed on this before Dave Switzer of the now sadly defunct Canadian magazine/e-zine *Challenging Destiny* took it. Personally, this story shows what hope can do to a person in the face of sadness and loss; perhaps, in a maybe-just-maybe sort of way, those children who are "lost" eventually do find themselves in another place….If not another universe, then some place better.

As far as the passenger pigeons go, perhaps in another parallel universe, the people there weren't *stupid* enough to hunt them to extinction….

CATS IN FANTASY, CATS IN FACT

On January 20, 1840, a magazine called *Alexander's Messenger* (and don't even try looking for it in your Publisher's Clearing House sweepstakes envelope—it ain't gonna be there) published an article called "Instinct vs. Reason," written by Edgar Allan Poe. In it, Poe jested, "Black cats are all of them witches."[2]

Anyone who knows (or remembers) their American Literature will recall that in 1843 Poe published the seminal Black Cat Story, called (ironically enough), "The Black Cat." The images in it are memorable: The cat with the eye gouged out; the wife behind the bricked-in wall; the avenging cat with the gallows noose on its chest. Numerous horror films have borrowed elements from it; even Richard Wright's *Native Son* borrows the old theme of a cat which witnesses a murder (and who then "unmasks" the killer). But those who are somewhat unfamiliar with the real Poe (not Rufus the Doofus Griswold's posthumous DöpplePoe, who was a creature of Griswold's lurid, if pea-brained imagination) might misconstrue Poe's true feelings towards cats.

Poe—unlike his *Black Cat* protagonist—loved cats; in fact, he actually owned a black cat himself. (Among others at various times in his life; prior to his wife's death, one of their cats tried to keep her warm by sleeping on her chest.)

It was this long-ago writer/cat relationship which inspired me (in part) to utilize one of my own Real Black Cats[3] in my "first" novel, *The Amulet* (actually, the novel was written *after Dark Journey*—which started out as *Ewerton Death Trip*, then was dubbed *Dark Summer* by an individual I consider to be *my* personal Griswold, *then* was christened *Summer Shadow* by me, until the novel was bumped from an October publishing slot to a December release, which necessitated a "non-seasonal" title—my editor's assistant thought up the current title—but it *was* published first).

Bruiser the Cat-Character was based on Bruiser the Real Cat; unlike the character cat, Bruiser is *still* a Real Cat, however.

2 After living with several dozen cats (at once), six of them black, at least I think Edgar was joking!

3 Not counting the daubs of white on his chest and lower belly.

And he is aggressively, totally, indisputably A CAT. About the only truly positive trait that this twenty-pound slab of muscle and fur can lay claim to is that he never sprays (contrary to the popular Myth, neutered cats *can* and often *do* spray—on what*ever* their feline fancy desires!)

Oh, he's loyal...to the point of shoving his large neckless head between my hands and whatever "upstairs cat" I might be trying to pet (my cats are Separate but Equal; one crew lives in a three-room connected "suite," while the rest stay downstairs—personal politics and all; it can and sometimes *does* get ugly).

He steadfastly sleeps on my head at night; alternately chewing or kneading my hair, licking either his paws or the pillowcase (even *here* he alternates...I can tell by the sound; cat tongue on flannel goes *rasp, rasp, rasp*—cat tongue on cat goes *slurp*), growling at potential interlopers (both real and imagined), and resting his freshly-washed[4] paws protectively across my face.

Since I've had Bruiser (1988, although he wandered around my old house for at least two years before that, after some former next-street neighbors moved and left him behind). I've learned one Important Thing: it is *impossible* to lift a twenty-pound blob of cat off one's head while lying in a prone position. This is especially true if the mattress is old, sway-middled, and covered on all available flat surfaces with *other* cats; all of whom are pinning down the covers about me in an attempt to have me play Gulliver to their roles as the Lilliput extras.

That's why my character-cat Bruiser was an obedient, thoughtful creature who conveniently rested on the protagonist's *legs*, and watched for bad things through her bedroom window.

Character-Bruiser also pitched in during the novel's climax to Save His Person from Evil.

I have no idea if the real Bruiser would think of doing the same for me. I *do* know that he gets Mighty Ticked Off if supper is late, or if the nightly *entreé* isn't to his liking (a certain store brand of dry cat food is on His Bruisership's "don't-you-dare-feed-me-that-again-or-I'll-jump-on-your-back-and-bite-off-your-scalp" list of things I shouldn't do). As long as I clean the "coal dust" (well, what do *you* call that brown gooey stuff in your cat's eyes?) out of his eyes every morning, tell him he's my "Ruuuba-Rum-Runner, my Brupie-poopie" (okay, so he's irresistible *despite* his flaws!), and pick him up at least once a day (remember, this cat weighs twenty pounds!), I'm His Person, The Goddess Who Brings The Food....

I suppose Poe had a similar loving relationship with *his* black cat. But I wonder if the thing slept on his head and licked the pillowcase—if

---

4   May be read "wet and slimy."...

so, it isn't too hard to figure out why Poe sat down one day and began to pen in that small, cramped hand of his, "For the most wild, yet most homely narrative which I am about to pen, I neither expect nor solicit belief...."

If your cat had a pillowcase fetish, Edgar, I'll believe anything you say....

AFTERWORD

On September 2, 2000, my cat Bruiser passed away; he'd just turned seventeen in August of that year—on the calendar I'd made a little notation next to the date of his death:

"The Best Damn Cat Ever"

I loved that cat; I had two of his littermates (Apollo, who lived to be eighteen, and Rocky, who passed at sixteen), plus some half-siblings from different litters (most of whom lived to be in their teens), as well as his mother-cat, Princess, who'd lived with some neighbors of ours in a converted trailer down the block (the same trailer which made an appearance in "From the Far Away Nearby," plus her owners were mentioned briefly in *The Amulet*) until they couldn't afford to feed her, and let us take her in, after she'd had twenty-five kittens in four litters within a couple of years. We ended up with seven of them. Princess was in her late teens when she passed. Bruiser's father was also part of another story of mine; he was the black street cat in "Hunger." I know this because I happened to see the conception of Bruiser's litter when looking out my living room window one day....

I wish I could say something as glib and as funny as the original little essay, but after losing so many, many cats over the years, it's just plain hard. But I'll say it again, I sure did love that cat....

THE WINTER OF THE *ALMOST* PERFECT CHRISTMAS TREES

(from the outlined-but-unwritten Ewerton novel *Homely in the Cradle*; this would have been the first chapter.)

"Homely in the Cradle/Handsome at the Table"

—Old Folk Saying

"Wednesday's Child Is Full of Woe"

—Nursery Rhyme

"God gave us memory that we might have roses in December."

—James M. Barrie

Long before thoughts of getting even big-time with that art-fart Vachel Scoville began to occupy nearly every waking second of Kealy Shipman's days, Kealy's thoughts—when not being directed out of reluctant necessity on some mundane task, like making sure he didn't get plowed down by some on-coming car while jay-walking across Ewert Avenue—used to drift to the early winter of 1968, when he was five, his sister Clichelle was an already improbably mature-looking nine, and his cousin Sloan was an equally immature-looking seven years of age.

That was the winter of the *almost* perfect Christmas trees, the ones his dad Claude Shipman cut down one bitterly cold December morning.

It was one of those frigid, yet almost airless mornings when it hurt to draw even the smallest breath, for the air went into your raw-tipped nose, and past your cracked lips like tiny shreds of cigarette-pack cellophane, that clear crinkly stuff that always stuck to the inner paper wrapper when Dad got his cigarettes wet (which happened a lot when he'd get too drunk at the Rusty Hinge Bar and forget to put the pack in his pants pockets and stuck them in his shirt pocket and then slopped beer all over his shirt-front, while Kealy and Clichelle took turns spinning belly-down on the bar's only working revolving bar stool and Momma just sat there at the table by the window with Dad glaring at her and Uncle Ernie, who'd bought Dad the beer in the first place), so that when Dad finally noticed that his pack of smokes was wet, again, he'd swear and sputter and yank the cellophane off the paper pack before gently peeling open the pack and setting the damp cigarettes in the oven on the top rack after Momma had finished baking something like another tuna-noodle casserole that Dad would burp up all night during the NBC Nightly News....

Even before he'd turned five years old, Kealy had discovered that if he held the piece of paper-backed cellophane up to the light of a bare bulb (this could be accomplished by shoving the cellophane under the lampshade, so that all you could see was the glaring brightness of the unshielded bulb), the combination of the crinkly-clear wrapper and the paper adhering to it resembled the stained glass in the windows of the Missouri Synod Lutheran Church, where he and his parents and his a-lot-older brothers Artur and Collin, plus Clichelle, of course, sometimes made an appearance.

Only on holidays, or for weddings or funerals, though.

After what happened to Dad in the war ("The Big One," he'd say over his drippy mug of Pabst, with the words verbally capitalized just like the way Huntley and Brinkley on TV spoke about The Vietnam War), what with his bad leg and bad back, Dad didn't put too much stock in church-going.

"After all," as he liked to say over and over through a haze of Camel smoke over the dirty dishes on the supper-table. "It didn't do none of us Joes no good havin' that there Chaplain—"

(Another of Dad's capitalized words, only this one he always mis-pronounced like the last name of that comedian with the derby and over-sized shoes.)

"—in the outfit, didn't stop no bullets, and it didn't make them gre-nades not go off like they was supposed to. Damn sonofabee was stand-ing butt-cheek to butt-cheek next to me when that g'damn Jerry shot me.

"*Twice*," Dad never failed to add, usually tapping his inch-long baby-finger of Camel cigarette ash onto one of Momma's saucers for emphasis.

"But tell the kiddies the *rest* of the story," Momma would say with-out realizing just how much like Paul Harvey on WERT's afternoon show she sounded like.

And Dad would snort Camel smoke through his nostrils, making the hairs in there wiggle like the hairs on the back of a caterpillar inching along a succulent twig, before grousing, "But-not-*one*-of-them-bullets-hit-the-Chaplain, *ok*? I still think it was 'cause the Jerry just didn't notice the essobee—"

All Momma would do was shake her head of tightly permed and hair-sprayed-in-place curls and give a soft, close-mouthed snort at Dad as she carried the last of the supper dishes into the kitchen.

But Momma snorting didn't make Dad any more receptive to church-going, regardless of how many times the Jerry missed the Chaplain that evening back in 1944. And, since Momma didn't have a driver's license, and Dad did, Momma could only go to church whenever Dad decided to do so, or if Dad got it into his head that he needed to hear the Word of God long enough to allow him to drift off to sleep in the pew for an hour or so.

(Oh, Momma could've gone to church with her sister Betty and Uncle Ernie, but thanks to Uncle Ernie's relative good luck in The Big One—nary so much as a scratch on the nose during his three years Over There, although Dad claimed that Ernie was so damned fat he wouldn't know he'd been hit until the wound scabbed over—Kealy and Clichelle's junk-dealer uncle had Gotten Religion, and joined the Catholic Church. And while Momma was a religious woman, she couldn't bring herself to go kissing a holy statue, or have some priest go looking at her exposed tongue while waiting for a Communion wafer.)

But come Christmas time, Kealy knew that he could look forward to at least one visit to church, where he could sit in one of the generations-of-behinds smooth-polished pews, and stare at the huge stained glass windows (one of them even had a camel worked out in chunks of black-banded colored glass, but it wasn't quite as detailed as the ones that sometimes stuck to the cellophane from Dad's pack), and imagine the people up in those windows saying things, just like the people in his comic books or the funnies in *The Milwaukee Journal* "Green Sheet" did, with the words hanging in front of their faces in those puffy black-bordered balloons.

And, thanks to the bitter coldness of the morning air on the day he and his sister and his cousin Sloan and Dad all piled in the front seat of Dad's '35 Ford pick-up (not to mention the fact that Sloan was allergic to cigarette smoke, so Dad had to leave the windows open on both sides, and poke his head halfway out the driver's side window so as not to fill the cab with smoke, which meant in turn that every time Dad exhaled, the truck did a little shiffle-shuffle on the snow-crusted blacktop road leading to Uncle Ed's tree farm in Lumbe), Kealy and everyone else in the truck had those puffy balloons of nearly pure white hanging in front of their mouths.

But, unlike the people in the funnies, nothing that they said was actu-ally written on those fast-dissolving balloons.

"Know what I think, Dad?" Kealy asked, as his father made the sharp right-hand turn which took them out of the outer fringes of the city of Ewerton, Wisconsin (Home of the Ewerton Rams, or, as some of the old farts who sat around the tables in the Rusty Hinge were wont to call them, the Ewerton Sheepfuckers), and into the eight-mile stretch of unincorporated woods and farmland which separated Ewerton from its baby-sister village of Lumbe.

Claude Shipman paused to blow a double-nostrils blast of smoke out the window, quickly jiggled the steering wheel to straighten out the truck then grunted a typically noncommittal "wha'?" before lifting his right hand from the wheel to bring his nearly-spent Camel to his cold-chapped lipped mouth.

Kealy waited until his father had taken a deep, noisy draw on the smoke before saying, "I think it'd be neat if people could write what they're sayin' on their breath when it's cold...like when you draw on a steamed mirror, or window—"

"Sounds to me like you been hanging around with Sloanie too much," Dad said flatly, before leaning out the window to let out more exhaled smoke.

Kealy (who was sitting closest to his dad in the middle of the seat) was tempted to sock Dad on the arm or in the ribs for that crack about Sloan, who was jammed up against the passenger-side door, but before Kealy's body had a chance to obey his mind, he glanced past Clichelle at Sloan, and noticed that his older (but no bigger than he was) cousin had *his* head poked out the open window, so Kealy figured that maybe, if he was lucky, Sloan hadn't heard what Dad said.

At least Kealy hoped so.

It had been his idea to bring Sloan along to help cut trees at Uncle Ed's tree farm. Otherwise, Kealy would've only had his sister along, and she was less fun to be around than Dad was, only essential, since she couldn't steer the truck and keep both feet on the pedals.

And Sloan wouldn't have even been sleeping over at his Uncle Claude and Aunt Rochelle's house if his folks didn't have to bug-bomb the house on account of Sloan's big sister Hildie's dog Spunky getting all those fleas from the time when Uncle Ed Shipman brought over his coon hounds before Thanksgiving.

(Kealy's aunt and uncle didn't say as much, but Kealy guessed that Sloan was probably allergic to bug bombs, too.)

But, Sloan happened to be in the house the night before when Uncle Ed called Dad and barked so loud over the phone he almost could've stuck his head out his kitchen window and shouted at Claude's house if all those strands of pine hadn't of been in the way:

"When you gonna get yore butt over here an' chop down them trees I been askin' you to chop down already? Should'da been cut down 'fore Thanksgibbing, you dumcluck."

And, because Uncle Ed had been even less lucky than his brother Claude when it came to the subject of The Big One, bullets and things exploding too close to his right ear, Dad bellowed into the receiver, "Whats you want me to do, chop 'em down by moonlight? I'll chop 'em when I chop 'em down, no sooner, no—"

"Well it's *already* 'later,' bean-brain, so either you cut 'em down or I'm gonna douse 'em with kerosene and be quit of 'em once and for all—"

"If they're bothering you so damn much, why don't *you* chop 'em down?"

Dad cradled the phone between his jaw and his shoulder, while coaxing another Camel out of his pack on the table.

At that point, Sloan got up from the table so fast he knocked the chair over behind him, ducked down to right it, then scurried into the kitchen to help his Aunt Rochelle wash the supper dishes, and, because he didn't want to be left alone with just Dad (who was more or less oblivious to everything but the amplified, tinny blare of Uncle Ed's voice and the problem of trying to strike a match-book match one-handed) and his *sister* in the dining room, Kealy followed Sloan into the kitchen, and missed out on all but a swinging-door-muffled version of the rest of the call.

By the time Kealy stepped into the kitchen, Sloan was already helping his Aunt Rochelle scrape the remains of tonight's casserole (something which tasted vaguely of venison, yet sorta fish-like too, smothered with lots of mushroom soup and limp bow-shaped egg noodles) into the 'slop box—a cut-in-half waxy-paper carton from chocolate milk— Momma kept out on the back porch, where it was cool enough not to attract those little flies that seemed to spring forth full-grown from any sort of standing food-garbage, when she wasn't busy filling it in anticipation of next spring's compost heap under the near-liquefied pile of raked-up fall leaves alongside the garage.

"I think this box is 'bout full," Sloan was telling Kealy's mother, while lifting the full-to-sloshing-over box up to her nose level for emphasis.

When Sloan did things like that—needing to show people things even as he was telling them about whatever it was he was talking about—Kealy wanted to kick the three-tiered kitchen step-stool out from under him, just because Sloan wasn't content to be smart, he had to go rubbing folks' noses in it so's they were forced to congratulate him, tell him what a *smart* little boy he was. Just like Sloan's mom Aunt Betty and his sisters Hildie and Sister Ernestine (who was not only Sloan's sister-sister, but a Nun-Sister, too; while the Shipman's still called her Ernestine, her nun-name was Sister Mary-Peter, on account of her Servite order all taking names that started with Mary and ended with some other Bible-name) did all the time.

But what probably annoyed Kealy most of all was that Sloan *was* smart, and cute to boot, what with his bright blue eyes and slightly wavy dark brown hair that Aunt Betty kept looking sort of mussed up and shaggy so's people wouldn't notice that Sloan wasn't any taller than his two-years-younger cousin Kealy.

Who may've been tall for five, but wasn't anywhere near as cute as his cousin. Or as smart…least not in any overt way.

"Why so it *is*…well, I guess you know what *that* means—somebody I know will have to help finish off that carton of chocolate milk in the fridge, won't he?"

(Through the now-shut kitchen door, Kealy could hear Dad snort, "'Dumb'? Someone who's dumb 'nough to try an' milk a bull's callin' *me* 'dumb'? Damn *right* I'm right Ed—")

"Only if Kealy and Clichelle can help," Sloan replied, with a sideways glance and gap-toothed smile at Kealy, who for his part was flustered for thinking such rotten things about his cousin even as Sloan offered to share the last of the chocolate milk without needing to.

Momma whipped her head around so fast and sharp some little bony thing in her neck popped loud enough to be plainly heard over Dad's shouting ("—and where am I supposed to put 'em once I cut 'em?") and the tinny strains of "Jingle Bell Rock" coming over Momma's little plastic kitchen radio.

"Oh Kealy, you're in here…I don't know if there *is* enough milk in the carton for all of you—and Sloan here has all those growing bones," she weakly rationalized, even as her eyes darted from her too-tall son to her bordering on short-short nephew, while Kealy just fidgeted in place, putting his hands in and out of his back pockets on his corduroy pants.

The sound of the rubbed corduroy was soon the loudest sound in the kitchen, drowning out Bobby Helm *and* Dad in the other room.

"I'm pretty full of supper, so I don't need that much milk," Sloan offered, with another broad smile that showed off the place where his upper front teeth used to be.

His own eyes slightly lowered, Kealy smiled weakly at his cousin, while continuing to make his corduroy pants wheeze and scratch behind him.

"Well…how 'bout I pour whatever there is into those little Flintstone jelly glasses? An inch at a time so everyone gets equal?"

By now, Kealy wanted to kick Momma, only she was standing there by the sink in her house slippers, not her pumps, so it would've been pretty hard to knock her off her feet just then.

Turning her back on her son and his cousin as she went to the glasses and cups cupboard to get the jelly glasses, Momma began to hum along with the song on the radio (which had switched to Gene Autry singing about "Rudolph the Red-Nosed Reindeer" by now), her muffled voice all off-key and off-sync with the melody.

And, after Sloan pointedly looked at Kealy again, this time not smiling except with his slightly crinkled eyes, he backed off the step-stool and said, "I better go get Clichelle," before running past Kealy and pushing open the swinging door just in time for Dad's "—right, all right Ed, come sun-up I'll be there to cut down your God-damn trees, so shaddup and get off the f'ing phone, all *right*? Damn right, all—hey, the essobee hung up on me!" to carry loud and clear into the kitchen and completely drown out the part about Santa asking Rudolph to help guide his sleigh even after every other reindeer was rotten to him.

Which suited Kealy just fine; he always hated that song.

Before the door swung shut behind Sloan, Kealy caught a glimpse of Clichelle, sitting a couple of chairs away from Dad at the table, with her arms loosely crossed in front of her and her head pillowed on her forearms, so's she could look directly at Dad while he talked and smoked and completely ignored her as he did so.

Once the door was completely shut, Momma placed the three half-cup-sized glasses on the Formica counter with a brittle clank, and mumbled, "It's just that you're growing *so* big…maybe you're getting too much milk," before hurrying to the fridge and getting out the carton of chocolate milk.

Kealy wanted to say something, but he was, after all, only five, and as articulate as he may've been for his age (and never mind his upbringing), words like "hypocrite," "coward," and "spineless wimp" were still beyond his intellectual grasp.

(Years later, when Kealy actually did say those things to his mother, plus a few others which applied more succinctly to the situation at hand, they just didn't feel as purging as they would've felt to him back there in that kitchen in 1968, with "Rudolph the Red-Nosed Reindeer" coming in all static-fuzzed and cheerful on the little Philco, and the waning light from the lone kitchen window obscured by that tattered old cardboard Santa face with the mica-flecked beard and hat-trim—and Momma openly turning her back to him while slowly pouring out that chocolate milk, one dutiful, careful inch at a time in each glass, until the pastel outlines of Fred and Barney and Dino were darkly filled in with the frothy milk. Easily enough milk in each glass for all three of them to get a good-sized five gulps a piece.)

Just as Gene Autry quit singing about Rudolph, and the announcer from WERT (Ewerton's local AM station, located out across the Dean River to the west of Kealy's home) came on with an advertisement for one of the town's three feed mills, Sloan and Clichelle came back through the swinging door, and—with words Kealy made sure he remembered *just* as Sloan said them that afternoon—Sloan glanced first at the three brimming glasses of milk on the counter, then up at his aunt, and said in that bright, almost bell-pure voice of his:

"I could've told you there'd be enough milk for all of us."

And, as slightly smart-assy as Sloan's words were, Momma didn't dare reprimand him—nor did she get a chance to, because Dad elbowed his way into the kitchen a few seconds after his daughter and nephew came in, cigarette in one hand and his almost-drained cup of coffee in the other, and said without preamble, "I gotta get up early tomorrow. Ed wants for me to cut down his trees."

"Can I go, Daddy?"

Clichelle was tugging on Dad's rolled-up plaid flannel sleeve, but he just flicked her fingers off with about as much energy and interest he'd afford to knocking the ash off the end of a cigarette, while Momma chided her:

"It's 'May I go?' and the answer is *no*. We're baking cookies tomor-row—"

"The hell you are, Rochelle. You got mending to do. I can see day-light through my socks, let alone my toes. Hell, all you do when you bake cookies is do it so early they're hard enough to roof a house with come Christmas Eve," Dad groused between puffs, while Sloan coughed discreetly behind one flattened hand as Dad exhaled.

"So *may* I go, Daddy? *Please*?! Clichelle added, as a little something he couldn't yet define died inside of Kealy upon hearing her say that.

This time, Dad grunted what sounded like an assent, which brought a smile that didn't make her any prettier to Clichelle's wide-cheeked (and chinned) face, while Momma just sniffed loudly and turned her attention to the scraped-clean dishes in the sink.

Since tomorrow morning was a Saturday, and Clichelle didn't have to be in school anyhow, what Dad said (or grunted) was gospel, so Momma didn't dare sass him back.

Kealy had figured out as much from just-about-babyhood, back when Artur and Collin used to have to fight whatever Momma said to be able to do what they wanted to do, and *that* was long before each of them hired-out as farm hands over at the farm that used to belong to that old sourpuss Palmer Nemmitz before he sold the land to a neighboring farmer, just so's they wouldn't have to listen to what Momma said any longer before doing whatever the heck they wanted to anyhow.

But usually, when it came to Clichelle, Momma's word was law, on account of her being the only girl and all (even if she wasn't as pretty as Momma hoped she'd be, or even as pretty as she was proclaimed to be when she was dubbed the "prettiest baby born in Ewerton Memorial" in 1959), and also on account of Mom's father being what the old farts at the Rusty Hinge dubbed with more than a little derision "a *girl*-maker" which made Momma an expert in girl-things by proxy, because Grandpa Shipman was a "boy-maker."

This was the first time Dad over-ruled Momma's say about what Clichelle was supposed to do come Saturday (or any day, for that matter); for her part, Momma didn't take it much better than she did Sloan's comment about the milk, but there was just nothing she could do about it…especially since Dad's socks *did* need mending, along with Kealy's and Clichelle's.

The air in the kitchen was brittle with the tinny, clangy sound of the stainless steel forks hitting the china plates in the kitchen sink, a noise that sliced through the static-obscured strains of Bing Crosby's "White Christmas" and the soft slurping sounds of the three children sipping their milk, until Dad simultaneously stubbed out his smoke on the chipped saucer reserved for that purpose on the small counter next to the stove and spat out:

"*Shit*. My damn axe is rusted all to hell. And if I wake Ed up to borrow his—"

"Papa's got a bunch of axes, all sharpened and everything," Sloan offered, between sips of his milk.

Leaning against the top of the double-oven stove, so that the small of his back was pressed against the front Calrod burner, Dad fished his pack of Camels out of his breast pocket as he said, "Yeah? Where's Ernie keep 'em?"

"In the shed at the far end of the Yard," Sloan replied, with an extra emphasis on the word "Yard," since the messy patch of scrap iron and semi-rusted car and farm machinery parts which comprised the Shipman back yard was also Ernie Shipman's livelihood.

"He keep it locked?" Dad asked around the cigarette he was attempting to light.

"Usually, but there's nothing in there anyone would really want to swipe," Sloan added as he drained his glass, then reached up to place it on the counter next to the rest of the dirty dishes Momma hadn't washed yet.

"Think he'd mind if I helped myself to one-two of 'em?"

"As long as you bring 'em back, I don't think so—"

"Maybe you can pick them up when you bring Sloan home tomorrow," Momma ventured, but Dad wasn't buying any of it.

Sucking in a quick mouthful of smoke, Dad forced it out through his nostrils as he snapped, "I'm not waking Ernie and Betty up before sun-up. He'd kick my ass clear to Lumbe."

"Couldn't we pick them up tonight, Daddy?" Clichelle asked before blowing air bubbles into the last of her milk, and making the brown liquid froth all the way up to her nose.

Dad paused a second, then said in a tone of voice which made it seem like he'd been the one to think of it in the first place, "Maybe I better take a run over the river to Ernie's place, see if I can get the shed open myself."

(Uncle Ernie and Aunt Betty and Hildie were staying at Aunt Betty's folks' place, but the Byrnes only had enough room for them, not for Sloan too, since Hildie didn't want to share a room with him.)

"Papa's got a Yale lock on it, I think," Sloan added, with a sidelong glance and wink at Kealy, who kept quiet while he finished his milk because Dad didn't like to let on that he knew that Kealy could pick open locks from the time he could crawl (like the time when he jiggled open the lock on the pick-up while Artur held him up level with the driver's side door, after Collin gave him one of Momma's hairpins from her dresser-top china dish—only after Kealy got the lock open, Artur and Collin didn't give him a ride like they'd promised to.)

"Key anywhere's handy...in case he forgets his?"

"If there is, he didn't tell me 'bout it," Sloan dutifully replied, before giving Kealy a short sharp jab with his left elbow.

Kealy almost dropped his Fred and Barney glass on the floor before he said, "You might not need a key, Daddy...lock might be undone—"

"Oh," Dad said flatly through a haze of smoke, then, while pointedly crossing one leg in front of the other, as Momma tinkle-crashed her way through the dishes, added, "You wanna ride in the truck with me whiles I go see if the shed is locked?"

Momma's shoulders stiffened under her housedress, but she let the dishes in the sink do the crashing and the clanging for her while Kealy hurried, glass of milk still in hand, to the row of curved brass hooks attached to a long slab of varnished pine alongside the door to the porch, where his plaid wool jacket hung next to Dad's bigger, dirtier jacket.

Kealy couldn't quite reach his own jacket, so he got down Dad's, while Dad sauntered over, casually flicking ashes on Momma's clean linoleum, and lifted Kealy's jacket off its hook, and cousin Sloan was so seemingly astonished by what was going on that he forgot to cough....

* * * *

True to Cousin Sloan's word, the ramshackle shed in the back of Uncle Ernie's junkyard *was* locked, but after Dad gave Kealy a short piece of wire he'd had stashed in the glove compartment of the Ford, Kealy managed to jiggle the lock open in about a minute (just long enough for his bare fingers to start stinging from the early evening chill in the air), while Dad stood off to one side pretending to look over the randomly stacked piles of might-be, might-not-be sorted junk festooning Shipman's Junkyard and Scrap Metal Mart, but really watching his youngest son jimmie open the Yale lock like a three-time-loser thief in a pawn-shop.

(Once Dad had asked Kealy how he did what he did with locks and other small bits of stubbornly stuck-together machinery, but since Kealy didn't know himself, trying to articulate the innate was beyond him. But the fact that Dad had asked did make him feel good inside.)

"It's open, Daddy," Kealy whispered, mindful of the neighbors who lived on the north side of Uncle Ernie's house.

While the Shipman place was built back in the twenties, and spent almost forty years as the only house on this side of the river, lately a lot of cookie-cutter single-story houses had been built in Lego-tight rows to the north and east of Uncle Ernie's place—the Woodlawn Development, it was called, and every house was chock full of dutiful young couples who'd think nothing of calling the cops out late just to investigate a suspicious noise.

Even if that noise came from the nephew of one of the beat cops who'd married Momma and Aunt Betty's youngest sister Aunt Rhonda; if a call came through the dispatch, someone would have to check it out.

"Good boy," Dad whispered through a mouthful of smoke, before tip-toeing into the shed, then turning on his flashlight so he could see what he was grabbing without having to possibly feel out an axe the hard (and sharp) way.

The shed itself was so poorly and sloppily constructed that Kealy could see thin strings of golden light through the shed walls; praying silently that no one else might see them, Kealy turned his gaze upward, toward the inverted dark bowl of the night sky, where the few stars that were visible through the misty-pale scud of clouds twinkled like flecks of mica in those rocks he and Clichelle sometimes picked up from next to the railroad tracks on the way home from the IGA.

Silently mouthing the words, Kealy began the "Star light, star bright" rhyme, only when it came to the part about the wish he'd wish that night, Kealy found himself stymied.

He'd lived through enough Christmases to know that wishing for something didn't mean diddley-toot come Christmas morning, and he'd broken enough wish-bones and blown out enough birthday cake candles to know that wishes were as plentiful and as tangible as raindrops falling into a barrel (not to mention just as substantial)...

But yet, he'd kept his eyes on the first star he'd noticed, and said the rhyme all the way through, so if there *was* a wish that might be granted, it was time to put up or shut up, like the old coots at the Rusty Hinge used to tell each other.

Silently, he added, I wish that all the trees Dad cuts tomorrow will sell...

...just before Dad backed out of the shed, with a couple of axe handles forming a stiff set of tails behind his rear and, then turned to Kealy and said, "Let's go, kiddo," before snapping the Yale lock back on the jutting ring of the padlock, and hurrying Kealy back to the waiting truck.

They drove the first couple of blocks away from the Shipman house with the headlights off, then, as they crossed the bridge, Dad turned them on, so that the illuminated road before them seemed to be covered with glittering snow-snakes which writhed and undulated in the breeze which had picked up in intensity since they'd left the junkyard.

And as Dad headed for their house on Wilkinson Avenue, driving slow past the paper mill because Uncle Bib Stanley had warned his sisters-in-law and their husbands that that spot was a speed-trap, Kealy snuggled up next to him, and rested his stocking-capped head in the crook of Dad's right arm, so that his head bobbed up and down as Dad worked the clutch, but at least Dad didn't shake off Kealy's head, like he'd done with Clichelle's hand earlier in the evening....

* * * *

They almost didn't make it out to Lumbe before sun-up that Saturday, because Momma tried to insist that Sloan should stay at home with her, "Just in case his folks come to pick him up early."

But Kealy piped up, "If he can't go I'm not gonna" before even Dad had a chance to tell Momma off.

So all three of the children piled into the front seat of the pick-up, and the four Shipmans were heading south down Linden Avenue, then west on Mill Road with its sharp "S" curve where the cops like to hide and wait for speeders, then across the bridge and through the Woodlawn Development (although not past Sloan's house).

Then it was strictly blacktop roads from then on, as they rattled and chuffed past the rust-mottled trailers in the trailer court on the outskirts of town, while the cold air whizzed past the truck windows, and swirled about in the cab before getting sucked out again.

And the sky above them and beyond the scraggly spruces, pines and tamaracks which lined the sides of the narrow two-lane road was a pearly-sickly whitish-peach color which only began to show hints of washed-out blue when the blazing cold ball of the sun began to peek through the strands of trees they'd just passed, so that the first glinting rays which were visible through the trees shone right into Dad's rearview mirror.

Which meant that between taking a puff, sticking his head out the window to exhale, then righting the steering wheel, he had to fiddle with the mirror so the sun wouldn't blind him when he glanced at it.

And rising sun or not, it was still cold enough to make great near-opaque billows of steam come out of a person's mouth when they exhaled or spoke, which was why Kealy had said what he had said about writing things on those condensation clouds in the first place.

And a few seconds after Dad made that crack about Sloan, Sloan pulled his head into the truck cab long enough to mumble past his wind-chapped lips, "I think we're getting close to Uncle Ed's farm."

He stuck his head back out the window before Clichelle asked Dad, "Can I help you chop one down...*please*?"

Dad had just pulled his head back into the cab in time to hear her plea, but all he did as he took another draw on his smoke was go, "Mebbe... mebbe not," in a tone of voice which actually suggested the latter option.

And Kealy cringed when Clichelle reached her hand past him, in an effort to tug on Dad's sleeve.

Thankfully, Dad poked his head out the window again, so he didn't even see Clichelle's fingers wiggling in a grasping motion just an inch short of his coat, while Sloan began to bounce up and down on the cracked leather seat of the cab, shouting, "We're here, we're here...see the sign?"

The sign Sloan was referring to was a home-made affair, fashioned from a five-foot-by-three-foot slab of scrap plywood barely coated with a coat of might've-been-white paint that showed each cross-wise grain of processed wood on the sign's surface, which was nailed to two two-by-two uprights, one of which wasn't quite *right*, even as it was just barely standing *up*.

And written in downward-slanting black letters—in a mix of capitals and lower-case ones which paid no heed to the rules of typical punctuation—was the following inscription:

ShIPMaNS' TrEE FarM—U-CUT 'EM, I-SELL 'EM—ChEap!!

"I guess 'U' ain't shown up to cut 'em," Dad said to none of the children in particular, as he turned off the ignition and shooed the three cousins out of the truck.

Sloan—in a motion which belied the notion held by his mother and his aunts that he was somehow more delicate than most seven-year-olds—jumped down and off the truck in an arms-waving dive that took him clear past the running board—and knee-deep into a drift of snow next to the usually gravel-covered shoulder of the road.

Behind him, Clichelle cautiously used the running board to slow her descent, so that she stood upon the road itself when she quitted the truck.

As Dad's hand steadily pushed him out of the cab, Kealy was torn—step down like a girl, or jump and maybe land ass-down in the snow like his cousin (who was slowly extricating himself leg by snow-encrusted leg from the drift he'd landed in)?

He was the same size as Sloan, so he sure as heck wouldn't get sucked in over his head in the snow, so Kealy took his chances and jumped—and landed face-first on the snow-coated gravel, which, when actually landed-on, felt a lot more like boulders.

"You god-damn *dumb* shithead of a brat," Dad was chuffing through a fog of cigarette smoke and steaming breath as he scooted on his prat across the seat and out through the passenger side door.

But Kealy didn't wait for Dad or the other two kids to pick him up, even though his face was stinging like it'd been stung by a swarm of bees, and his eyes were watering so much everything was a wiggling, pale sunlight-illuminated blur before him, with only a faint hint of snow-flecked green in the distance; in a jerking motion which felt like a push-up only more painful.

He got to his knees, then his feet, before Dad had a chance to come up behind him and swat him a good 'un on his rear-end.

"I'm ok, I'm ok," Kealy kept mumbling, even though he didn't feel ok; but nothing hurt-hurt *bad*, like when he'd sprained his ankle last summer, or Artur had slapped him a good 'un across the face for snitching about him and Collin taking Dad's truck for a joy-ride because they hadn't taken him along.

So after a few minutes, once his vision cleared and his face didn't sting quite as much, Kealy was able to believe that he actually *was* ok.

"You better be," Dad snarled, before going around to the back of the truck and picking up Ernie's axes, plus several coils of rope which he intended to bundle up the trees with.

As he passed the children on the way to the rough sun-greyed wooden fence which kept people out of the tree farm (this time, however, Dad did have a key for the gun-metal grey iron padlock affixed to the gate), Dad handed each of them a couple of coils of hemp rope, but kept the axes in his own hands…

…which meant that in order to tap the ashes off his smoke, he had to shake his head hard and fast to one side, so that they drifted onto the front of his coat, to join the other long dark ash-smears which covered the filthy black-and-red plaid fabric.

Kealy wondered which one of them would get to fish the key out of Dad's pocket and open the padlock, but as it turned out, none of them got to; Dad rested one axe along his shinbone while using his free hand to undo the lock.

"Uncle Claude, which trees are we to cut?"

It amazed Kealy how Sloan spoke better than even his own kindergarten teacher.

Dad snorted in annoyance before saying, "Ones in the back of the lot, these are too small," which they were, being only one to three feet high.

As the three of them hurried into the lot itself, before Dad reached over the gate to re-lock the lock behind them, Clichelle said, "These trees look like the little one Charlie Brown picked in that special on CBS… you think they'll have it on again?"

"If Dolly Madison'll sponsor it, they will," Sloan said, before following his uncle deep into the strong-scented rows of young trees, while his cousins just shared a rare glance of genuine amazement at Sloan's off-hand, but succinct comment, before hefting the heavy coils of rope and following him in a single file, with Kealy bringing up the rear of the line.

As the four of them trudged through the trees, occasionally moving slow thanks to drifts of surprisingly dense-packed snow, the sun rose ever higher in the sky, until, when they reached the spot Uncle Ed had described to Dad over the phone, the sun was almost its normal pale-pale piss yellow in the sky.

But the sky itself remained an almost colorless shade of milky blue, which was occasionally obscured by the steam rising from all their mouths and noses.

And the air still felt like cellophane in Kealy's mouth and lungs (his nose was running so much he couldn't draw in a breath through his nostrils if he'd of wanted to), only he didn't have much time to reflect on *that*, because Dad was going:

"No *wonder* nobody cut these down sooner," over and over again, as he turned his head from side to side, surveying the scraggly rows of five- and six-foot high spruces and pines around him.

And Kealy's heart sank a little more with each repetition of the phrase, until by the time Dad shut up Kealy felt like his heart was sharing space in his scrotum with his balls, for wishing-on-that-star or not, *nobody* in their right mind would want to buy Uncle Ed's ready-to-harvest batch of trees.

Even Charlie Brown wouldn't have nibbled.

"These trees *are* ugly," Sloan whispered to Clichelle, who could only nod dumbly in agreement while cold-wind-tears dribbled out of the corners of her hazel-colored eyes, and the fitful yet sharp breeze coaxed her bangs out from under that plushy-fabric hat she was wearing (the one that made Artur call her "Marshmallow Head" the first time he saw her wearing it), so that they undulated in stringy brownish-blonde ripples across her forehead, much like the snow-snakes Kealy had seen on the headlight-lit road last night.

"Damn things must've been exposed to some sorta blight," Dad was saying more to himself than to the children, as he went up to this tree and that tree, circling around them, then coming back to the spot where the others stood, coiled ropes weighing heavy on their bent arms.

Shifting his coils of rope from his right arm to his left, Sloan began, "No, I don't think so, Uncle Claude…blight would mean brown needles, and that's not what's—"

"Oh shut the fuck up," Dad said with no hint of rancor, just flat out resignation, in his voice.

Sloan hugged the coils of rope against his wide-wale corduroy jacket with the sheepskin lining and shut the fuck up, just like he'd been told to, even though he was quite right.

Brown needles weren't the problem…but a general scarcity of needles, let alone the branches they were affixed to, was.

The double row of harvest-ready trees were remarkable for the amount of daylight you could see through each tier of branches; it seemed to Kealy that none of the branches which formed each horizontal row on each tree wanted to come within touching distance of the next row up, but yet, if there *were* enough branches on each tree, they might've looked just fine. Maybe even better than fine—

"Dad…it's too bad we couldn't take the branches off some of the trees and put 'em onto the others, in between the other branches already on the trees," Clichelle began to say, almost as if she could read her little brother's exact thoughts.

Only Kealy hadn't been thinking so much in *words*; rather, he'd been mentally merging one tree with another by scrunching up his eyes.

But it didn't matter whether he or Clichelle actually expressed the notion, for Dad did a fast 180° in the snow, so that it swirled up around his boot-tops like the peak of a Dairy Queen soft-swirl cone, and from the big smile on his face (wide enough to show the brown-stained molars toward the back of his mouth), both Kealy and Clichelle knew that for once, they'd come up with a way to please their father….

* * * *

Despite Sloan's claims that his own father let him carry heavy pieces of scrap metal *and* even allowed him to chop some kindling for the rust-patina'd Franklin stove Ernie kept in his shed for the times when he worked in there past dusk on cold days, Dad refused to let Sloan help chop down the trees.

Openly blowing smoke at his nephew, he said simply, "I don't wanna get the blame if you miss the mark and chop your fucking arm off."

(When Dad wasn't sitting around the house, like he usually did thanks to being disabled in The Big One, he said things like "Fuck" and "Shit on that noise" a lot.

Momma didn't like it, but the men at the Rusty Hinge never minded, nor did Kealy, Clichelle or Sloan.)

Sloan started to argue that they never so much as chopped stray chips off of whatever he was chopping, but Dad just told him to "Shut the fuck up and start tying those branches."

And since Dad had already chopped down six trees, none of which was less than four feet in diameter at the bottom, Sloan and his cousins had to sit down in the snow and wind the rope around the branches, so that they could be stacked in the back of the truck.

Later on, Kealy decided that that was the best part of the whole day; him and Clichelle and Sloan all sitting on packed mounds of snow, wrapping those branches, while the strong scent of the cut trunks filtered past even his runny-to-dripping nose, and the stray drops of sap ended up clinging to them all over, in yellow-clear globs that felt a little like that syrupy-runny ant poison Momma used to put on little torn-off squares of cardboard under the kitchen sink come summer, only tackier to the touch.

And after Dad had chopped down all twenty trees in the two rows, which didn't happen until well past noon thanks to Dad's bad back and gamey leg, Dad limped back to the truck, and got them the lunch Momma had had to stay up past her regular bedtime to fix for them.

And during the many times Kealy was to mull over the memory of the day they cut down the almost perfect trees in his mind, he gradually realized that even if he was to someday eat at the fanciest French restaurant, or wherever it was that fancy-folk ate, whatever he might order would never taste as good as those ham and Colby cheese sandwiches Momma made—especially with the flecks of cut-tree-trunk sap clinging to the Wonder Bread on the outsides.

After they'd bundled all the trees, then went one by one into the surrounding over-grown trees which Uncle Ed hadn't harvested for a good two-three years to take a pee before getting ready to leave, Dad asked Sloan:

"Your dad have a power-drill I can borrow?"

"Borrow outright, pick up for yourself? If you have to ask, he'll wanna know why you're asking," Sloan replied.

And Kealy wasn't sure if it was because Dad was too damned tired to cuff Sloan a good 'un across the mouth for sassing back, or if Dad knew all too well what a big mouth his older brother really did have, but at any rate, all Dad did was wrinkle up his lips like he'd sucked on something sour before asking:

"Think they'll be back in the house yet?"

"Not as long as Papa can eat another free meal at Grandma and Grandpa's house he won't be."

* * * *

On the way home, instead of driving straight through the Woodlawn Development down Spruce Avenue, Dad cut down Maple Street for three blocks, until he reached the Shipman house on the outskirts of Ash Avenue, which faced the cemetery about a mile down the road.

And Dad lifted Kealy out of the truck, and carried him under one arm to his brother's junk-yard, then carried him back to the truck once he'd opened the lock and Dad grabbed Ernie's power-drill, just so Kealy wouldn't fall face-first out of the truck right onto the sidewalk, and maybe break something for real this time.

But when they arrived home around four-thirty, Dad was in no hurry to go inside and eat supper; instead, he rolled the truck into the driveway behind the house with the lights off, so's Momma wouldn't see them arrive, then whispered for the kids to help him haul the trees into the opened garage.

Once they'd dragged and half-carried the trees in, Dad switched on a trouble-lamp (putting on the lights would've meant illuminating the windows enough that Momma might notice) over his workbench, selected a couple of coping saws, handed one each to Clichelle and Sloan, than plugged in the power drill and set to work drilling pilot holes in the trunks of ten trees (five each of pine and spruce).

While the two older kids hacked the branches off the other ten trees (again, five each of pine and spruce), with Clichelle handling the bigger branches even Sloan couldn't saw through (although he sawed through just about all of the ones on his trees, which finally made Kealy realize that his cousin's stories about all the work his Papa made him do in the junk-yard *were* true) after his coping saw blade came loose from its mounting, and all the while the others were working, it was Kealy's job to sort the branches, first by species, and then by size, in readiness for Dad's last step in the tree-perfecting process.

After dipping the ends of the cut branches in some carpenter's glue he'd squeezed out of the tube onto an old pie tin, Dad shoved them into the holes he'd drilled in the trunks, so that by the time six-thirty rolled around, and the garage was thick with the mingled scents of sap, Camels and old used car oil stored in glass cider jugs, an aroma so cloying Kealy's eyes watered, even as his cousin Sloan was so engrossed in his labors that he'd forgotten to cough for over an hour, there were ten perfect Christmas trees lined up along Dad's workbench.

"Daddy, they're beautiful," Clichelle whispered through lips dotted with tree sap and mustached with stray pine needles, and this time Dad didn't say anything mean like he usually did when Clichelle said something gushy (once Kealy heard Dad mutter "Damn no-neck brat" under his breath when Clichelle said something Dad really disliked).

Instead he reached out and put one sap-and-glue encrusted hand on her shoulder and grunted, "Uh-huh," which was as close as he ever *did* come to paying Clichelle a compliment.

"If you don't want to sell them from your place, Papa would let you sell them at the junk—" Sloan began, before Dad cut in:

"For a cut of the asking price, I 'spose?"

"I suppose you could put a sign on the front lawn and stack them on the front porch," Sloan replied.

Dad just smiled and said, "You might make an honest man if someone doesn't kill you before you reach ten years old," then shook his fist in Sloan's face just to show him who might be willing to do the killing before that time.

"Well kids, let's get 'em tied up again and loaded—"

"On the truck?" Clichelle began...

...and in the weird half-light of the trouble lamp, Kealy could make out his father mouthing the words *No-neck bitch* before he said, "Yeah, on the *truck*, so's we can get back *in* it and drive up to the garage like we hadn't been here already."

Which is exactly what they did.

Dad even honked the horn as they approached the garage with the headlights on, after he'd backed the car into the alley with them off.

And they had to unload the trees they'd just loaded, prior to stacking them like springy cordwood in the garage before trooping into the house to eat supper.

Dad had hid the ten denuded trunks behind a tarp along one side of the garage; a couple of years later, Dad remembered putting them there, and gave them to his brother for use in the stove in the junkyard shed, where—according to Sloan—they split like wildcats when tossed in the flames.

Kealy was sure that *that* particular casserole was cut-up chicken with egg noodles and peas in it, although he wasn't sure if the soup base in it was cream of mushroom or cream of celery.

Cream of *something*.

Sloan's parents came to pick him up after supper, so he wasn't able to chicken shit inspect while Kealy drew the sign for the Christmas trees on the back of a piece of white shirt-cardboard Momma had saved.

Years later (over twenty-five of them to be inexact), Kealy could still see that sign just by closing his eyes.

It was just as beautiful as the trees themselves, all decorated in the corners with feathery-limbed trees in two shades of green crayon, with the trunks colored in a mixture of grey and brown, because even at that age, Kealy realized that tree trunks weren't *really* all brown.

And he did the lettering (following Clichelle's carefully printed example) in a mixture of red, bright green and blue letters, all capitals (unlike Uncle Ed) which read:

CHRISTMAS TREES '4' SALE
PINE & SPRUCE – $2.50 EA.

And come morning, after Dad set the sign on the front lawn after nailing it to a scrap of two-by-two, and they'd set up the trees in bundles resting against the porch railing, *after* untying them so as to better show off their lush fullness, all the trees were bought up by the time the last of the churches let out come 1:00 p.m.

...and the first of them started to come back to the Claude Shipman house within a day or so after that, accompanied by an assortment of complaints, curses and what the Watergate folks a few years down the road would call "expletive deleteds":

"God-damn Christmas lights pulled out a whole row of branches, what the heck's going on?"

"What the fuck you pullin' faking out trees like this?"

"Very funny, Claude, but that's what there's a Better Business Bureau for, to take care of cheats like—"

"My wife's best ornament weighed down one branch, and pretty soon all of 'em's fallin' out of the trunk—"

And, the most frequently voiced question of all:

"Whose bright (stupid, jack-ass, fucking, *et al.*) idea *was* this, anyhow/"

To the other complaints and questions, but most especially in the case of the latter one, Claude Shipman had but one answer—and it was that simple yet awful answer that made the memory of the *almost* perfect Christmas trees stick for so long, and so painfully, in Kealy Shipman's mind...

...until that memory all but consumed him (until, at least, that whole Vachel Scoville business started in 1977, a full nine years after the winter of the faked-out trees);

"That no-neck brat Clichelle is who."

And that was why, long before he decided that he simply *had* to get even big-time with that writer who did his sister such wrong, in such a permanent way, long, *long* before either he or his sister or his smart-ass cousin Sloan (who got Clichelle hooked on Scoville's books before they'd even met), Kealy Shipman knew that he would never be able to forgive his father for what he'd done to his sister.

Or let him get away with it.

No matter how long it took, and no matter what he had to do to really stick it to the old man, the way he'd stuck those sawed-off tree branches into the trunks of those ugly trees from Uncle Ed's tree farm, before the old fuck let his daughter take the blame for his own greed.

And until the whole Vachel Scoville mess happened, and Clichelle went and...*did* what she did, getting even with his father was all Kealy Shipman could hope to do in life.

But, that was before he learned how to widen his emotional horizons....

AFTERWORD

This isn't a work I really like to talk about much; while I had originally planned on turning my novella "When the Bad Thing Comes" into a third novel about my fictional (but based on the town where I live) Wisconsin small town, Ewerton, a few years later, toward the end of the 1990's, I was goaded by a former pen pal into trying my hand at another Ewerton book, this one more mainstream in nature, dealing with a young man's attempt to revenge the suicide of his older sister, which was spurred by some vicious criticism from a writer/critic named Vachel Scoville (who was based on someone who'd been vicious to me, but that's a story no one is ever gonna hear!)

Around the time I wrote one sample chapter and an outline, I was looking for a new agent, and since I've never been the most bankable writer, I had few people interested in me, but one agent sent my query on to another new agent, a woman who asked to see some of my work...I sent her a couple of pieces, including the novel which would've been *Homely in the Cradle*, and she was so repulsed by the chapter-plus-outline that she reneged on her offer to represent me, and told me that it (*Homely*) was the most horrible thing she'd ever seen, and that I was terrible for writing it.

So...after that rejection of both the book and me, I stopped working on this completely. I figured that I couldn't deal with any more scathing, intensely personal rejections like that. That's why there's a major gap in Ewerton stories between the late 1980's to the beginning of this current century. The nineties were not good years for me, and the absolute rejection of this work signified my inability to write any more Ewerton stories for a long time.

My mother's father's family actually did sell some augmented Christmas trees down in Chicago many decades ago; as far as I know, the branches they inserted in the trees did stay in, though.

Clichelle is based on me (no surprise there), and her brother and young cousin also represent different aspects of my personality. Kealy was going to be revealed to have mild autism—something which I actually do have, but didn't know so for sure at the time.

Years later I found out that I have Asperger's Syndrome...and for a brief time I considered going back to this book to rework/update it, but virtually every book publisher demands that the book be available in an electronic format, which I can't produce, so that ended that, alas. But I do feel that a few passages in this lone chapter of a truly lost book might be worth looking at, and of specific interest for those readers who have read either my novels or my collection of Ewerton short fiction, *Ewerton Death Trip*.

Other than that, I really can't say much more about this—if I do, it just brings back that agent's revulsion over me and my work, and I really can't deal with it, even to this day....

ABOUT THE AUTHOR

A. R. MORLAN is best known as a horror and fantasy writer. She published her first piece, a quiz, in *The Twilight Zone Magazine* in 1983, and her first story, the novelette "Four Days Before the Snow" (the first tale set in her fictional Wisconsin town of Ewerton) in 1985 in *Night Cry*. Since then she has penned many more short stories, quizzes, novelettes, and novellas in more than 100 different magazines, anthologies, and webzines, as well as erotica written under two different pennames (one male and one female). Most recently, she has focused primarily on science fiction, culminating in an appearance in the thirtieth anniversary issue of *Isaac Asimov's Science Fiction Magazine* in 2007. She shares her home in the upper Midwest with many cats.